THE TRAVELER

WITHIN & WITHOUT TIME - BOOK II

D. I. HENNESSEY

arkHarbor press
www.arkharbor.press

This is a work of fiction. Names, characters, businesses, places, events and incidents are either the products of the author's imagination or used in a fictitious manner. Any resemblance to actual persons, living or dead, or actual events is purely coincidental.

WITHIN & WITHOUT TIME: THE TRAVELER © 2021, by D. I. Hennessey. You have been granted the nonexclusive, nontransferable right to access and read the text of this book. Unless otherwise stated, biblical quotations are based on the American Standard Version of the Bible, 1885 by the English Revision Companies. At least one Scripture reference is taken from THE MESSAGE. ©1993, 1994, 1995, 1996, 2000, 2001, 2002. Used by permission of Nav-Press Publishing Group.

Edition 2021

ISBN 978-0-9991221-4-3 (Paperback Edition)

ISBN 978-0-9991221-7-4 (Hardcover Edition)

Version 006142022

Dedicated with love
To Laura, my wife, partner and companion through 43 years of life,
who still does her best to tolerate me.

CONTENTS

"The farmer waits patiently for the precious fruit, until it receives the early and the latter rain. Likewise, be patient and establish your hearts, for the coming of the Lord is at hand.

— JAMES 5:7-8

CHOZEQ

Hebrew **kho'-zek**, qzx

Noun Masculine: strength, power, powerful one

1

RETURN

Awakening with a start, I found myself staring at a dark ceiling and carefully tried to get my bearings. My whereabouts gradually dawned on me as I recognized the hospital room. A dim glow of predawn sunlight was barely visible through the closed blinds but gave enough light to see mom asleep nearby in a reclined chair.

My head was swirling with memories of the past 48 hours. The point-blank shotgun blast that landed me here was certainly memorable. Mixed with that memory are recollections of old Mr. Van Clief's walk to the altar, along with flashbacks of the night my grandfather died in New York. More incredibly, I remember seeing Gramps, with Great-grandpa and dad, standing together at the cross as Mr. V. was saved! It was all so real; it's hard to tell which events happened last night and which ones were long ago — or from outside of time altogether.

I was distracted by these thoughts as I pulled the sheets aside and climbed out of bed. It was only after standing that it occurred to me there was no pain in my chest — every trace of my gunshot wound was completely gone! The memory of Chozeq's healing touch rushed to mind making me recall how his flaming sword touched my chest — just before I blacked out. Of all the confusing memories swirling in my head, it struck me as amazing that that was the one that was actually real and not a vision!

I was still lost in thought as I emerged from the bathroom to find mom awake with a frantic look on her face. She looked deeply relieved when she saw me.

"Where were you?" she exclaimed in concern, "why are you out of bed? I thought... I thought something happened to you!"

"Something did happen, remember?" I joked, pointing to the bandages around my chest.

"That's not what I meant...," she started to explain, looking annoyed.

"I know what you meant, mom; sorry for kidding around. I'm fine now."

"Yeah, I know you think you're fine, young man," she began to lecture, "but you have to take it easy...."

"Mom..." I interrupted seriously, "...I mean, I'm really fine." I swung my arms and thumped my chest loudly to prove the point.

She looked at me with a dawning realization, hardly daring to believe it. "How?" she asked in a nearly breathless voice.

"I think you know... It happened last night — while you were at the tent meeting."

Tears immediately began to well up in her eyes as she studied my face, then she wrapped her arms around me and shook with small sobs of joy. She was wiping her tear-streaked cheeks as she finally backed away.

"Mom, I know you prayed for me — I can't help feeling like your prayers saved me."

She placed a hand on the side of my face; I could sense the thoughts that were streaming through her mind and reflecting in her face as she relived those moments in the tent beside me just after I was shot.

"It's you who saved me," she answered mysteriously. "There have been so many amazing answers to prayer... I can hardly believe all that's happening. I wish you could have been at last night's service. I wish you could have seen it...."

I listened quietly, already pretty sure that I knew what she was about to describe. She looked at me with a broad smile as she continued.

"Mr. Van Clief was there...he gave his heart to the Lord!"

Even knowing what she was about to say, hearing her say it brought a thrill to my soul. "Praise God!" I couldn't help exclaiming as the memory of it flooded my mind as well. "It's unbelievable, everything that's happening."

"Oh, it is!" mom agreed, "it was so packed last night...people overflowed the tent and filled the whole field! There were so many being healed; it was like a scene right out of the New Testament!"

I just nodded, remembering how I'd witnessed the incredible scene in my vision. The thrill on mom's face was priceless.

She became quiet and looked at me intently, lowering her voice....

"What really happened to you Sunday night?" She choked back a swell of emotion as the memory of those events filled her mind. "I was holding your wrist...you had no pulse," she confided as she fought back more tears. "When you gasped for air, I felt something strange — it was like an electric shock, except I felt it flowing through my soul instead of my body. He sent you back to me...I know that He sent you back!"

I wasn't sure what to say. How could I explain what happened when I wasn't even sure myself? I didn't dare reveal Chozeq's involvement; that would only lead to more questions that I couldn't answer.

"To be honest," I answered carefully, "I thought I was gone too."

She studied my face as she seemed to be reliving those terrible events. "When you woke up, there was such a fire in your eyes — it was like an angel was staring up at us!

"And I knew right then — before you even said a word — I knew you were going to be okay."

Mom leaned forward and put her hands on my cheeks, surprising me with a kiss on my forehead. She messed up my combed hair and then wrapped her arms around me, hanging onto me as if for dear life.

"AN EPIDEMIC OF MIRACLES..." those words caught my ear as I overheard one of the X-Ray Techs talking to his coworker when I arrived for my scan. He continued in an astonished voice, not noticing me in the doorway.

"This morning, we had two kids walk in with their parents who insisted that they'd been severely disabled, but their X-Rays showed nothing — they were perfectly normal kids. The crazy thing was that their records showed they had severe muscular dystrophy! How crazy is that?"

"I know what you mean," his friend agreed. "We've already had five radiation treatments canceled today in Oncology. The doctors aren't even trying to explain it — they can't!"

"Some wild things are happening, that's for sure," the first added, "Did you see the interview with that Wounded Warrior guy? How do you explain that?"

The two of them finally noticed me in the doorway, sitting in a wheelchair. The nurses insisted on making me use it even though I felt fine. I was out of the chair the minute they invited me in, and the Techs had me climb onto a padded table that soon began moving, sending me through the CT Scan machine. A few short buzzes later, and they told me I could climb out.

"Looks clean," the tech said to me. "What are they checking for?"

"Someone shot me in the chest with a sawed-off shotgun," I answered him with a smile.

"Yeah, right..." he started to respond with a grin.

Just then, his friend nudged him in the arm holding my chart, and they both stared at it, doing a double-take. They rescanned my wristband and rechecked the chart as their faces turned white.

I smiled: "There's something pretty awesome going on at that tent behind Carmine's diner. You guys should definitely check it out."

THE DOCTORS WERE reluctant to release me so soon but finally gave me an all-clear after a group of them had conferred for a while. They all had nervous looks on their faces as they shook my hand.

Once mom and I were in the car, an idea hit me.

"Can we go to the tent?"

Mom looked at me, surprised. "Don't you want to go home first? You just got out of the hospital!"

Despite her surprise, though, she didn't argue with me. I got the impression that she was just as anxious as I was to tell everyone the news.

"Alright, I guess we can stop there on our way. But then you're going home to rest!"

We weren't surprised to find the tent nearly full of people, even though it was only mid-morning.

When Pastor Juan saw us walk in, he immediately ran to greet us. At first, he stood looking back and forth between mom and me, as if wondering how I could be recovered enough already to be walking around. I replied to his unspoken question by giving him a hug — squeezing as hard as I could. He laughed out loud and squeezed me back, but not too hard — he was obviously still unsure about my injuries.

I remembered how his arm had been broken when we visited the prison, looking at it as I took a step back....

"No cast?"

"Got it off already!" Pastor Juan (PJ) answered happily. "X-rays showed that it healed faster than expected."

I spread my arms, nodding my head in solidarity.

"Me too! I'm totally healed!"

"Praise God!" PJ exclaimed as he hugged me once again.

Our conversation was picked up over the Mic he was wearing, and a cheer of praise rumbled through the crowd. The musicians immediately kicked in with a chorus, and a group of people around the altar suddenly started spontaneously dancing. I've never seen that before in a church meeting!

Amid all the excitement, PJ nodded toward someone behind me, prompting me to turn around. Mr. Van Clief was looking at me with a broad smile on his face — his eyes were wet with tears. He just stared, shaking his head as if he couldn't believe what he saw. The look on his face reminded me of the expression he had in my vision last night — when he had hugged me at the foot of the cross.

I was expecting him to reach out his hand to shake, the way he always does, but this time he just wrapped his arms around me in a hug, beating me to it. Mom wiped a tear from her cheek as she stood behind him — she laughed and held her hand up to her nose as more tears escape down her cheeks.

As we finished hugging, I held up my hand to show him the ring I was wearing.

"I haven't lost it," I joked as we both looked at my great grandfather's school ring. It was tarnished and dull but looked like a million dollars, as far as we were both concerned.

He gripped my hand between both of his and patted it.

"It's where it belongs now," he said with a grateful tone of voice.

There was a commotion behind me, and I heard Pete's voice calling out. As I turned, he was running down the aisle toward us.

"JIMMY!" he shouted in astonished disbelief. "What are you doing here?"

Without thinking, I quickly lifted my teeshirt and proudly showed him my unscathed chest.

Mom slapped my hand. "Not in church!" She chided uncomfortably.

"Mom! I'm pretty sure God has seen my stomach before," I joked in self-defense. She just put a hand to her face and shook her head in embarrassment.

In reaction, Pete planted his hands on his head and did a complete 360 spin; his mind was blown. Then he looked at me with a gigantic smile and grabbed me in a bear hug, lifting my feet off the floor. Mom and PJ both called frantically for him to put me down, which he did with a quick apology.

I just stretched out my arms again and grinned from ear to ear to confirm to everyone that I was perfectly fine.

Moments later, PJ was back at the podium, officially announcing to everyone the news of my recovery. A loud ovation of applause quickly turned to waves of praises as the meeting ignited again in a renewed movement of the spirit. The music team launched into another chorus as the crowd erupted in song.

WE WERE LOST in the moment for a while when I felt Pete's hand on my shoulder, getting my attention. I saw him nod toward the back.

Anna was standing at the tent entrance with a hopeful look on her face, clearly out of breath from running here from home. She searched the crowd anxiously with her eyes, then spotted me with a wide grin and set off running down the aisle toward us.

She stopped just in front of me, catching her breath while her eyes jumped rapidly back and forth between my face and the front of my shirt. Before I could say anything, she rushed forward and wrapped her arms around me with an energetic squeeze.

"He healed you! OH, He healed you! We prayed so hard — I knew He would! I knew it!"

When she stepped back, her face was glowing with a huge smile and slight blush. She bounced up and down on her toes excitedly, holding her fingertips together in front of her lips in a praying gesture.

"This is so cool! God is so awesome!" she exclaimed as she clapped her hands.

Glancing down at a few empty seats nearby, she looked at me with a smile and motioned in invitation.…

I pretended to be ducking for cover as I ran from the isle to join her.

She looked back at me and laughed nervously, making me realize that my joke was not in the best of taste — the events from Sunday night were still too traumatic to be humorous for her. It surprised me that they didn't have the same effect on me, but I was honestly okay with the whole thing.

The music and singing were rapturous, making it sound like ten times as many people. Speaking of numbers, as I looked around, I could see that the tent was slowly filling with more people; lines were flowing in from the fields outside. Glancing at my watch, I confirmed that it was only the middle of the day.

To be honest, it wasn't even a meeting. People were just there singing and praying in unison... because they wanted to. Looking around at the seats full of people, I could see closed eyes and hands raised. People were praying for each other, some huddled close together and others worshiping alone, lost in their personal encounters with God.

PJ and Pastor Wilkes walked the perimeter, greeting new people as they arrived and praying for some who needed healing. There was a growing pile beside the altar of discarded crutches, braces, and wheelchairs that served as dramatic testimonies to the astonishing miracles that had happened here in the past 72 hours.

WHILE I WAS LOOKING AROUND, I happened to see a man standing just outside the tent, behind the front platform, staring back at me. His appearance was startling, but not in a frightening way. His eyes were deep blue and intense but revealed an immense degree of kindness. He was wearing a long jacket open in front that revealed a clean white shirt and neat trousers beneath. I couldn't help thinking that he looked out of place — like, a hundred and fifty years out of place. His outfit reminded me of something from the 1850s.

As I studied him, he nodded toward me and then waved, beckoning me to come nearer. I looked over at Anna beside me and nudged her.

"See that guy up there beside the platform? I think he's waving for me to come to see him. Have you ever seen him before?"

Anna looked at the platform and scanned all around it, then searched the open field behind it. There were dozens of people milling around outside.

"Which man? Where exactly?"

"Right there, next to the guitar amps." I was trying to avoid pointing at him, not sure if I wanted to acknowledge his waving.

"I still don't think I see him," she explained as she studied the area I described.

I glanced at her with a confused look, surprised that she couldn't see what I was talking about. The platform is not that far from where we were sitting in the 2nd row — the place where the man was standing was barely twenty feet away from us.

"He's right there...." I started to insist as I looked back toward him mere seconds later. But as I looked up, I was stopped short by what I saw.

"Hello Jimmy," the man said from the row directly in front of us. He was now sitting with his elbow over the seat, looking back at me.

I glanced quickly back to Anna, who was still searching the area around the platform and shaking her head politely. She seemed oblivious to the man sitting a few feet away.

THE STRANGER FOLLOWED my glance at Anna and then looked at me kindly, explaining...

"Your friend can't see or hear me. I'm afraid that only you can."

⌘

2

THE TRAVELER

I know a man in Christ... (whether in the body or out of the body, I know not;
God knows)...
~ 2 Corinthians 12:2

A chill ran up my spine as the realization dawned on me. This wasn't a vision — it was real. It was really happening, right there in the middle of all those people! I scanned the stranger's back for wings; he looked ordinary, aside from the way he was dressed.

"My name is Amos Van Clief. I believe you know my grandson, James. The man you've taken to callin' Uncle Jim."

My mouth hung open as I processed these words — I could feel my skin turning cold and clammy despite the summer heat. Quickly reading my face, he continued to explain before I could speak.

"I'm not a ghost, and I haven't come from Heaven. You're not the first to travel the whirlwind; the Bible is full o' folks like us — travelers. They're more commonly known as Prophets, I suppose. Well, God surely hasn't been asleep since those books were written. It stands to reason that his appointment of travelers hasn't stopped either. Though it's mighty rare company, I'll admit; there's seldom more than one in a generation. We're all given the same charge — to tell no one in our own time but to write what we see for a time to come.

"You've likely noticed that you're invisible when you're in your travels; the same is true for us all. Your bein' able to see and hear me now is God's doin'. It goes along with the gift. It's best if you just listen for now — the folks around here are likely to get the wrong idea if you start holdin' a conversation with a man who ain't there, the best they can tell."

His words sent a chill through me, bringing back all my old questioning about why God had chosen me, of all people. It occurred to me that the singing had ended, and Pastor Wilkes was leading everyone in prayer. Anna had squeezed her eyes closed along with the rest of the audience as they prayed earnestly. I used the opportunity to lean forward, closer to Amos.

He continued: "I'm real grateful for your family's faithful work in bringin' James into the fold. He'll be a wayward sheep, there's no doubt. Praises be to God's faithfulness!

"But that ain't the sole reason I'm here. Things are about to get mighty interestin' in the world."

WHILE HE'S STILL SPEAKING, the scene instantly changes around us, and I find myself seated on a set of steps. I recognize the setting immediately; it's the Van Clief's farmhouse. Amos is still in front of me, motioning for me to stand and follow him.

Looking up ahead, I can see the frame of a new barn being raised; it's a barn that I recognize. A scan of the surrounding horizon reveals only open land — farmland for as far as the eye can see in all directions. We walk together across the dusty yard toward the towering structure. I glance down, noticing that Amos' feet are leaving footprints, but mine are not.

"We're in your time... I'm the one traveling," I guess as I realize what's happening.

He just nods as he bids me follow him inside the half-finished barn. It's made of thick heavy timbers that have been meticulously assembled to form the building's rough skeleton. Wood planks cover a portion of the unfinished roof overhead. Amos leads me to a ladder at the center of the barn and begins to climb. I wait until he's halfway up and follow him, watching him step off the ladder onto beams that will support the barn's loft. He makes his way across, balancing on one of the thick beams until he reaches its end and points to the intersection of beams above him. He points to a place where the large central roof beam connects with a thick upright supporting the outer wall. I watch as he reaches for it and knocks on the wood... it sounds hollow. Then he presses his hand on a place where several beams are joined. To my surprise, the beam opens, revealing a secret compartment that has been hollowed out inside the thick wood.

Reaching then into the inside pocket of his jacket, he pulls out a leather-bound book and shows it to me.

"Herein is the record of my travels as God has revealed them. It's been made known to me that this record is not for my own time but for yours."

With that, he lifts the book and tucks it into the secret compartment, closing it to seal the book inside.

IN A DISORIENTING FLASH, I suddenly found myself back in the tent meeting. Amos was gone. I glanced at Anna sitting beside me to see her still bowed earnestly in prayer.

Another flash of light drew my attention to Chozeq as he stood beside the platform — he nodded his head at me in greeting, and I smiled back. Then he turned and looked toward the distant farm-house and barns, raising his hand to point at them with a guiding gesture. With that, he pressed his fist to his chest in a friendly salute, and then his enormous wings spread wide before disappearing in a flash of brilliant light.

I realized immediately what I needed to do.

ANNA LOOKED up at me in surprise when I touched her on the arm.

"I need to go... to... do something." It felt awkward giving as little explanation as possible. Still, I realized that I couldn't explain my reason for leaving even if I tried.

She shook her head at me in a sign that she didn't understand why I was leaving in such a hurry.

"I'll be back soon... as soon as I can."

The image of her surprised face stayed in my mind as I hurried back up the aisle with an unexplainable urgency in my spirit that grew stronger with each moment. I could barely contain it by the time I was outside and immediately bolted for the farmhouse in a flat-out sprint.

By the time I reached the old porch steps, I was gasping for breath and had to lean on my knees, gulping the air painfully. The mile-long sprint was only partly to blame; my heart would have been racing despite the run.

The sight of the place reminded me of my recent visit with Amos. The memory of how the old barn looked then, in its unfinished state, stood in stark contrast to the weathered old structure in front of me.

I tested the door doubtfully, expecting to find it locked, but was surprised to find it open. To be honest, I hadn't even considered what I would have done if it wasn't. Feeling uncomfortable about entering the barn uninvited, I looked around nervously to see if anyone was watching, then pushed the heavy barn door open a crack and slid inside. Shafts of sunlight penetrated through dusty windows and gaps in the old wood, giving the expansive space inside an ethereal feeling.

Quickly getting my bearings, I walked to the center and located the loft section where I'd seen Amos climb. It was directly above the stalls where the tent had been stored. The empty crates marked C.I.R.C.U.S. T.E.N.T. were still stacked inside.

Examining the rustic beams above the stall, I picked out the one he most likely walked on. It hardly surprised me that the details from my vision were so incredibly clear. It looked exactly as I recalled it, aside from the fact that the clean, fresh wood I'd seen then was dry and dingy now.

An old wooden ladder was mounted permanently against the loft nearer the back of the barn. I carefully tested the condition of each rung as I climbed it, finding it surprisingly sturdy — a testament to Mr. V's meticulous maintenance. The loft wrapped around the colossal barn like an enormous shelf. Its floor was covered with straw, and old hay bales sat scattered around — remnants of the days when horses and livestock filled the stalls below.

Making my way back to the area that Amos showed me, I easily spotted the barn's thick central roof beam and followed it down to the place where it is joined to its upright support. A knock on the wood confirmed the hollow sound of a hidden compartment inside, causing my heart to quicken further. I tried to remember how he opened it… he pressed his hand on a spot where several beams were joined. Although the wood is darkened and cracked, I was able to make out the lines of an old seam and began to press on it, feeling along its length. No amount of pressing seemed to have any effect. A small lip along one edge gave me an idea.

Stopping to look around for something to pry it with, my attention was drawn to a dim gleam of sunlight reflecting from the floor nearby. Whatever it was lay far back in the corner and was partially covered in straw. Dusting it off, I realized it was an old pocket knife — probably Civil War era. I remembered seeing one like it in a museum. Flipping it over, I was momentarily stunned by a set of initials embossed on the handle: 'A.V.C.'

"Amos Van Clief," I whispered to myself.

It was not a huge surprise to find something that belonged to Amos in the barn. Still, as I stared at it, I realized that I was holding physical proof that the vision I'd just seen was authentic. Amos called it Traveling — that actually explained so much about why my experiences with Chozeq have been so vivid! At least it meant that I wasn't crazy.

Another thought struck me as I stood staring at Amos' initials — this knife has remained waiting here unmoved for over 100 years! The blade was stiff but still workable as I carefully opened it. Its metal was dull and gray but still had enough of an edge to cut with. Lifting it to the beam, I found the lip I'd noticed earlier and tested it with the blade, gently prying the wood sections apart.

I could feel the compartment's cover lift slightly — just enough for the blade to slip inside. Running it down the length of the narrow opening, I soon felt it come in contact with some kind of catch. It moved when I pressed against it as if it was attached to a spring until the lid suddenly clicked open.

Despite my certainty that I'd find it, the actual sight of the open compartment sent a chill up my back. I stood staring at the old leather-bound notebook inside it — as if it was an artifact from outer space. After a few deep breaths and a quick prayer, I slowly worked up the courage to reach for it.

⌘

3

AMOS' JOURNAL

The old journal's thick leather cover felt dry but wasn't brittle; it was stiff like an old belt that had been stored for too long. The pages made a crackling sound as I gently opened them, but they were in decent condition, considering their age. The first page established the journal's ownership beyond any doubt. The penmanship was neat and well-practiced, spelling out the title page in tall letters.

I CAREFULLY TURNED the page and began to read...

The Personal Journal of

Amos Van Clief

April 9, 1870

When a man is spared from certain death, I expect he's spared for a reason. That's the only explanation I can come to for what has happened to me.

I've been struggling with that feeling ever since Fredericksburg, the day our Regiment was wiped out. We'd gotten ourselves pinned down in a bad spot, with Rebel artillery positioned above our heads. They fired on us for half the day with an unrelenting storm of hot lead and iron. All around where I set were the bodies of fine and brave friends who'd already left this life behind. I knew them... knew some of their widows and mothers too. It pained me to think how those women's hearts would be pierced through at the news of it.

I'd heard the whistle of bullets flying on past me, some so close that I didn't suppose they could've missed. But when the sunset and the guns finally fell quiet, there I was. Out of 100 men from our Regiment who started up that hill, only twelve of us walked off. All of us were thinking the same thing... God must've spared us for a reason.

It's been five years today since Lee's surrender, and I've carried that question in my heart ever since that day on the hill. Tonight I believe I know the answer.

It started like any other night. I'd quit working the fields at sundown and sat out beside the fire, just clearing my head. All at once, I wasn't there — what I mean to say is that I was all of a sudden somewhere else. It all happened in a flash.

One minute I was stoking the coals, and the next instant, I was standing in the center of the Nation's Capital. Leastwise, it was a form of the Capital. I recognized the Capital building and the President's Whitehouse, but the surrounding city was all changed — built up with buildings and teeming with people everywhere. Work on the Capital's dome had been completed, from the look of it. The roads were smooth and black as tar, and I was astonished at the sight of carriages that rode along without any horses!

A gust of cold wind stole my breath away, making me realize it was the winter season. I shook with a chill, but it wasn't altogether from the cold.

A great commotion made me turn, and I saw a multitude of people gathered, all facing toward the Capital. It had the appearance of a presidential inauguration, although there were no top hats or ladies in fancy clothes. It gave me the greatest surprise to hear an orator's voice calling out in loud echoes across the great field. The sound of it boomed as loud as the voice of God, or at least like the sound of an angel calling out over the four winds.

As I marveled at that, another sound came upon me. It was a loud and alarming noise, like the sound of a windmill in a hurricane. I looked up with a start to see the strangest sight I ever laid eyes on — it was some kind of machine as far as I could tell... a flying machine. The thing hovered above the crowd, thumping the air like a team of horses in full gallop.

Before I could make sense of the sight, I found myself moved again, just as suddenly as when I'd arrived. Seeing to my surprise that I was now standing up on the platform at the capital steps, where a large assembly of distinguished-looking men and women were seated. Looking out from the platform, I could see that same flying contraption hovering above the vast audience outside — it was way off in the distance where I'd been standing a moment earlier.

I turned awkwardly toward the man seated just behind where I stood and apologized for blocking his view, but also in discomfort over my sorry state of attire for such an occasion. The man, however, looked straight past me as if I weren't even there. As a matter of fact, I reckoned that he most certainly looked straight through me.

Well, that suited me just fine under the circumstances. I doubt that they'd have let me stay up there on the platform if they could see me, and I couldn't have explained how I'd gotten there any better than I could tell that man his name.

The more I studied the place, the more it didn't look like the Capital that I knew. The city looked better in some ways, and in some ways, it was worse. It looked finished and filled in, with proper tree-lined streets and organized rows of buildings. The capital building looked old, though, and the air smelled of something like burning oil.

I finally put all that aside and took notice of what was happening at the podium. There, a strange man was fixing to be sworn in as the President of the United States.

A middle-aged man was leading the swearing. I thought it odd that he didn't hold a Bible for the President to swear on; instead, it was some mounted sheet of paper. I figured from the man's comments that it was a copy of the Constitution. Seemed to me mighty presumptuous to be making such a pledge on a thing created by men rather than by the Creator.

Standing beside the new President was a woman I understood to be his wife. She was years younger than him and looked to be of a foreign origin with an exotic appearance. Being a foreigner wasn't anything to be noted in itself, except that she had a look that gave me pause. It was a covetous and cruel look, with the smirk of a malevolent soul gaining power that such a one probably oughtn't to have.

When the swearing-in was done, everyone on the platform took their seats, and the new President stepped to the podium. He didn't unfold any notes but instead looked to a few panes of glass that had his notes. The words moved as he read them, making me wonder at the power of such a man.

I can't recollect much of what he said. A great many of his references made little sense to me. But I did take note of a few things that struck me with worry and stuck with me.

One was how he kept mentioning the Separation of Church and State — that seemed to be his favorite phrase. Everyone with a fourth-grade education knows that's in the Bill of Rights, of course, and that it means to keep the government from interfering in religious liberties. But his way of spinning it made it sound like it had been intended to eliminate religious freedom altogether. He spoke of religion like it was a sickness that needed to be eradicated. I wondered at the kind of citizenry who would elect such a man to lead them.

He said he was making good on his promise to make churches pay taxes and require them to report their membership roles to the government.

The other thing that caught my attention was how he kept talking about a new day of world unity. Then he said his first act as President would be creating a new agency — the Unity Enforcement Agency. It would be headed by a new 'Secretary of Unity' with powers to, as he put it: 'enforce unity for the greater good.'

Then he announced that he would be appointing his wife to be the first to hold the post, with the promise that she would usher in a new age of cooperation throughout the world. The crowd exploded in cheering and enthusiastic applause at the news. I saw in the woman's face a look of pleased cunning as she basked in the crowd's approval. I'd seen such a look in men before — it was the look of a proud and treacherous soul.

Suddenly I felt a large hand grip my shoulder, and a voice thundered close beside me. I froze with fright at the sight of him — half-again larger than me. He was fearsome in appearance, a warrior with a sword as large as a plow shaft. The white of his robes nearly glowed, even in broad daylight. All of that made it clear to me that he was more than a man, but it was the fact that he could see me, along with the sight of his enormous cherub wings, that left no doubt what he was.

"Beware the unfaithfulness of Ahab and alert be to Jezebel's treachery," his voice boomed. "For when they shall say, Peace and safety; then sudden destruction cometh upon them."

While his words still echoed in my ears, I was shocked to find myself back beside the fire where I began. My heart was racing wildly, and I struggled to catch my breath. So ominous was the vision that my strength failed me, and I fell onto my knees on the ground.

"Lord, what's the meaning?"

The night air remained silent, offering no reply to my question, but into my mind came a scripture reference — just as clear as if it'd been spoken aloud.

...1 Thessalonians 5:3

I grabbed my lantern and ran to the house for the Bible, turning to the verse as quick as I could. The chill up my spine made me shudder as I read what it said:

'For when they shall say, Peace and safety; then sudden destruction cometh upon them, as travail upon a woman with child; and they shall not escape.'

I laid the Bible on the table and dropped into the chair beside it, wondering what this all meant. I was sure I wasn't dreaming. Despite the warm summer night, the extraordinary scene's biting winter cold still chilled my bones, and the memory of the angel's voice echoed in my head loud and clear.
Then a single word arose in my mind and kept slowly repeating over and over:

'Write...'

So I began to write.

MAKING MY WAY BACK, I was deep in thought, pondering the extraordinary discovery. Why would Amos have chosen to show the journal to *me*?

I was soon standing at the back of the tent, finding everyone urgently praying together. I could sense that the spiritual temperature in the open tent was rising as Pastor Wilkes' intercessory pleas grew more impassioned and anointed. Then my heart was finally drawn to the prayer that he was leading. For the first time, I tuned into what he was praying....

"Though the age may be dark and evil increase, we still know that You are the unassailable master of all. No power of hell can prevail against You or against Your work! We stand firm in the confidence that Your mighty hand has delivered and will deliver again!

"And so we commit this threat against Your work into Your own Almighty hands, certain that by it You will glorify Your name!"

THREAT? What threat was he talking about?

⌘

4

GENERATIONS

Anna's face lit up when she saw me finally making my way back to the seat beside her. She'd been saving it for nearly an hour despite the crowd that continued to gather all around her.

"I was beginning to think you wouldn't be back," she confessed. She glanced down at the book in my hands; "What's that?"

"An old journal... I found it," I offered without further explanation.

Her expression signaled that she didn't understand.

"I'll tell you later — I promise." I glanced to where mom was standing and pointed to her apologetically. "I just wanted to come back and tell you that I have to go... my mom's waiting."

Anna waved to mom with a smile; "I'm glad you're okay... I'm really glad."

The depth of her sincerity was plainly visible. I gave her hand a gentle squeeze and smiled back. "Thanks, me too. Thanks for praying... Thanks for everything."

· · ·

AS SOON AS we got in the car, mom had the same question that Anna had. "What's that you're holding?"

I considered my answer for a second and recalled what Amos said to me when he placed the book into its hiding place: "...*This record is not for my own time, but for yours.*" I felt an immediate sense that it wasn't a secret anymore... it was time to tell what the book says.

"It's an old diary by Amos Van Clief, Mr. V's grandfather."

"A diary?" she queried in surprise. "Did Mr. Van Clief give it to you?"

"Not exactly," I answered, suddenly realizing that I was going to have a harder time explaining than I thought. I looked at her uncertainly. "Would you believe me if I told you that Amos did?"

"Amos? You mean the grandfather? Is he still alive?"

"No, not exactly."

Mom's eyebrows raised as she studied my face in surprise. Her voice sounded worried as she began talking faster than usual. "Jimmy, what are you talking about — that's just too weird! Are you seeing... ghosts? How long has that been happening?"

I quickly realized that I should have spent more time planning how this would go. I could see myself digging a deeper hole with every reply that came to mind. I couldn't tell mom about my travels with Chozeq -- or why I was able to see Amos -- or that I traveled back in time.

I raised my hand, waving for her to stop her questions.

"He wasn't a ghost," I assured her. I struggled for an explanation, seizing on the first thing that came to mind.... "Remember the way Anna's mom had that vision the other night... and then you saw it too?"

Mom nodded her head slowly as she began to understand.

"Well, it was kind of like that. I saw him... Amos showed me where he hid this... I saw him show me."

From mom's expression, I could see that a chill was running up her back. She shook her head slightly and just stared back at me.

"Why...?" she managed to ask in a nearly breathless voice.

I looked down at the book and put my hand on top of it gently.

"He said it's prophetic.... It's about our time. He said that now it's time for us to know what it says."

"Do you think it's true?"

"Well — the book was right where he showed me. I'm pretty sure it was hidden there for over a hundred years."

"Mr. Van Clief's grandfather was a prophet?" Mom's voice sounded shocked.

"Mr. V. told me that his parents always went to church; they made him go when he was a kid."

Mom's eyes fell to the book, and she stared at it wide-eyed.

"What does it say?"

"I've only read the first entry — it was from 1870. It talked about an inauguration that I don't think has happened yet."

"That's over 150 years ago — how do you know the inauguration it describes didn't already happen? What makes you sure it's about the future at all?"

"It describes seeing a helicopter — he couldn't have made that up. And there were other things... they did the swearing-in with the constitution, not the Bible. The new President talks about revoking nonprofit status for churches and making them report their member-ship lists to the government. I'm pretty sure that hasn't happened yet."

Mom's face had suddenly turned white.

"What was the new President's name...?" she asked with trep-idation.

"It doesn't say."

"Jimmy, that's exactly what we prayed about this afternoon!" She explained, wondering how I missed it. "Senator Sheen just announced a bill to do exactly that!"

I stared back at her, realizing that must have been what everyone was praying about when Amos showed up.

"M-Maybe it's him... maybe he'll become President someday," I stammered.

"He could be -- he's running!" mom explains.

"Oh... wow."

Mom looked back at the book nervously, "Did you tell Mr. Van Clief what you found?"

That idea hadn't crossed my mind, I realized awkwardly.

"No, not yet," I admitted to her.

"Jimmy... you have to give it to him. It's written by his grandfather — it belongs to him."

"Yeah... you're right... I know."

I felt incredibly conflicted over the decision; what if Mr. V. just took it and didn't let anyone read it? I'm certain that Amos wanted... that God wants... for it to be shared as soon as possible.

"You feel like God revealed it to you for a reason," mom accepted perceptively. "If that's the case, then it'll all be fine. Doing the right thing is what's important."

I nodded in an admission that she was right and took a deep breath, releasing it with a sigh.

"Do you think it'd be okay if I read it some more before I return it?"

"If you don't, I will," she said with a mischievous smile.

"YOU MUST BE HUNGRY... I know I'm starving," she added.

She was right about that... the mention of food reminded me just how hungry I was. In our hurry to leave the hospital, we skipped breakfast and never got around to having lunch. I realized that it was after 2:00 PM already as the car stopped in front of Uncle Mike's sub shop.

The place was quiet when we walked in. Uncle Mike was busy sweeping the floor. He quickly dropped the broom against the counter and greeted us as we entered, looking at me nervously.

"Your mom called and said you were out of the hospital already — are you sure you're okay?"

I glanced over at mom with a smile and then lifted my teeshirt to show him. His face turned pale as he looked in disbelief at my healed chest. From what mom told me, I knew that he had been at the hospital on the night they brought me in — he met the ambulance there.

"Th-That's not even possible... you were.... Nobody survives that, let alone healing so fast. H-How?"

I heard myself answering before I'd even thought about it: "I'm pretty sure you know the answer to that question."

I'm not sure where that answer came from, but there was a look in Uncle Mike's eyes that hinted it may have triggered something. There was a moment of awkward silence while a range of emotions flooded his face.

Mom looked into his eyes with a comprehending expression and then glanced back and forth at both of us. She quietly excused herself to use the Ladies Room, pointing toward it unnecessarily, and then lowered her gaze to the floor as she walked away.

Uncle Mike dropped into a chair and ran both hands over his head. I grabbed a seat across from him.

"You're right, I guess I do," he confessed with an air of wonder. We sat for a minute in silence, then I heard him mutter to himself: "This is real… this is really happening…."

I could tell that he wasn't just referring to what happened to me. I took a stab at a guess...

"You mean the tent — everything happening there?"

He didn't answer right away but just stared out the window for a minute.

"You don't remember our dad — your Gramps Farro; he died before you were born."

I acknowledged his comment with a nod. Memories of last night's vision of seeing Grandpa Farro with Mr. V rushed through my mind. I kept them to myself.

"Dad always said that a time was coming when God would show Himself to the world in a way that no one could deny. He said it would be with all kind o' signs and wonders — unexplainable stuff, like the things that happened back in the New Testament times."

His voice trailed off as he thought silently for a second, then added… "He said it would be a sign of the end times… right before… you know… He comes back."

Uncle Mike hasn't been much of a churchgoer, but I knew that my grandparents were strong Christians; that's where mom got her faith. Over the years, she has shared a lot of stories about the two of them growing up in church back in Brooklyn. He was the big brother she looked up to as a kid.

Something happened with Uncle Mike, though. He drifted away from it during High School and stayed away, although he couldn't stay away from mom. He protected his little sister, even following her here to Center Springs after their parents died.

I picked up on his last comment and gently nudged the topic further... "That's right — PJ said the Bible calls it the Latter Rain when an incredible revival sweeps the whole world. I'm pretty sure that's what's happening... I really think this is it... this could be how it starts."

Uncle Mike looked at me with an uncomfortable expression; fearful would be a better word for it.

"Do you think He's coming back soon... I mean, like really soon?"

He asked the question like someone probing for some insider information on a stock deal. I answered the best I could....

"Nobody knows the hour, but Jesus gave us signs to look for."

I could see him shudder like a chill was running through him. After a moment or two of silence, I cleared my throat and carefully asked the question that had come to mind.

"Mom always talks about how you both grew up going to church. Why did you stop going?"

He didn't hesitate in answering... it was like he welcomed the discussion.

"I just kinda drifted away when I got t' high school. I guess life just got in the way — it happens like that, ya know?"

I nodded that I got it.

"Did Gramps give you a hard time about it?"

Uncle Mike sighed in resignation; there was a palpable sadness in his voice.

"I'm sure he would have if he'd had the chance. It was after he died — in my freshman year."

The realization hit me of how young he was when Gramps died — I hadn't made the connection before. I was about that same age when my own dad died. It gave me a new appreciation for the way Uncle

Mike had been able to relate to what I was going through myself at the time.

I just nodded my head in agreement with his last comment, looking down at the table briefly.

"I guess you didn't have somebody like the O'Malleys next door to keep you in line, the way I did."

Uncle Mike smiled at my suggestion, dismissing it at the same time.

"You didn't need them — you've got this faith business nailed… always have. Your Mom and Dad set you on the right track."

"Didn't Gramps do that for you guys too?"

"He tried. I was a tough convert. I've always been too stubborn for my own good."

I could relate to the stubbornness part — it must run in our family. Then I was reminded of the most stubborn man I know….

"Mr. V. got saved last night. Talk about stubborn — it took him 90 years!"

Uncle Mike looked up in surprise.

"Old man Van Clief? Wow, I guess we really are seeing signs and wonders!"

"Yup, I was there," mom interjected from just behind me. "He cried like a baby. It was so sweet!"

"I guess God really is patient," Uncle Mike joked.

"I just wouldn't count on having 90 years," mom added with a friendly jab. She smiled at her own wit and then looked back toward the empty counter.

"So, how does a customer get a little service around here? I'm starving!"

A FEW MINUTES LATER, we were working an assembly line in the kitchen, building the best set of ham, prosciutto, and provolone subs ever.

Mom handed me a twenty-dollar bill, and I walked to the register to ring it up, but Uncle Mike grabbed it out of my hand and handed it back to her.

"These are on the house," he insisted.

"In that case, make my drink a large iced tea - easy on the ice," she called to me with a smile.

I brought them their drinks and joined them in a booth by the window.

"So, what was Gramps like?" I asked as we started to eat. "Was he really strict?"

Mom looked at her brother with a sly smile. "You could say that — Mike was always in trouble."

Mike shrugged, "That's true."

Mom clarified, "I'm teasing. Dad was actually pretty easy on us."

"Easy on you, ya mean!" Uncle Mike objected.

"Well, maybe," mom admitted. "But he was still pretty easy going, all things considered."

"At least he didn't use a wooden paddle or anythin' like that," Mike joked. "But I think I spent the entire 8th grade grounded!"

"I thought you just liked being home having tea parties with me."

I raised my eyebrows — it was hard to picture Uncle Mike playing tea party.

"Here's a secret, Sis... I did like that." He shared a glance with her that made her smile, and she patted him on the arm.

"Mike was my protector — the schools in Brooklyn were pretty tough. Half the times he was in trouble were for fights he got in because of me."

"Thanks for the nice try — I got news for ya... there were plenty o' things I got in trouble for besides that."

I WAS ENJOYING the friendly banter. It wasn't often that I got to see mom and Uncle Mike together. He didn't get to stop over as much as he used to. After focusing on my sub for a few minutes, I interrupted the silence with a new thought, putting the pieces together.

"Gramps must have been pretty young... when he died, I mean."

Uncle Mike took a breath and let it out with a sigh. Mom looked over at him with a worried expression and answered for him....

"...He was only forty."

"It was so senseless!" Uncle Mike suddenly exclaimed with a surprising amount of emotion. "Gettin' hit crossin' the street... How does that happen?!"

I stared back at both of them; mom was looking down at the table awkwardly.

"Is that how he...? I never heard," I quietly admitted.

Mom put her hand on Mike to calm him. It was evident that it was still a painful memory, even after all these years.

"I'm sorry for bringing it up...." I said in apology.

"Don't be. You've got a right ta' know — he was your grandfather. God's the one I've got a problem with... Ever since that day...."

I was suddenly thinking about how Mr. V. and I were having an identical conversation just a few days ago.

The mood was tense as we all sat silently eating, afraid of getting Uncle Mike more riled up. Finally, I finished a sip from my drink and put the cup down, looking across the table at him. There was a surge of feeling welling up inside, and I felt like I had to let it out.

"I KNOW there's a lot I haven't learned yet about life... but I think I've seen what tragedies are like, and I know how painful they are."

Uncle Mike looked at me with a humble expression, and I could see the sadness in his eyes... "I know ya do, Jimmy... I know you definitely do...."

I kept talking, interrupting him...

"W-when dad died I-I couldn't understand it — I just kept reliving that night in the Emergency Room — when I was staring at the bed next to mine where he was lying with the sheet pulled over. And then when Kelly... when she...." I stopped and drew a breath, unable to finish the sentence.

"I was mad at God — I was really mad! Mom knows... she saw me.

"But something came from those times... I learned some really important things from them. The biggest was that when a tragedy happens, it doesn't mean that God's not there or that He doesn't care. I realized that He's closer then than ever! In fact, He cares so much more than we do — more than we even can. It's because He cares that

He makes hard choices because they're the right choices. Because they're needed for the really good things to be possible — the eternally important things."

I wasn't sure if my words were getting through to Uncle Mike or if they even made sense. I just knew that they seemed to pour out of me with so much feeling that it made my hair stand on end.

I realized that mom and Uncle Mike were staring back at me speechlessly. He had a stunned expression on his face, and mom had tears in her eyes. As I looked Uncle Mike in the eye, images of Hell's horrific inferno begin to flood my mind — I could feel myself tearing up.

"Uncle Mike — life is short. Leaving this short life without knowing Him is the greatest tragedy of all!"

THERE WAS SUDDENLY a tear in the corner of Uncle Mike's eye. He caught himself and quickly wiped it off on the sleeve of his teeshirt, then got up from his seat.

"I-I ah... I gotta get ready for the dinner crowd. It'll be startin' soon." He checked his watch... "I have to go get the rolls at Pintos."

When he raised his gaze, he looked me in the eye....

"Jimmy..., thanks. Knowin' what you've been through — it means a lot... just want ya ta know."

He turned toward the kitchen.

"Just lock up when you guys leave."

With that, he headed for the door.

I LEANED BACK and rubbed my eyes for a second, then dropped my hands into my lap, feeling like I'd lost all my strength.

"I'm worried about Uncle Mike."

Mom leaned forward with a look of deep concern, startled by my comment.

"What, Jimmy?! What about Mike... What have you seen?"

"It's not like that!" I assured her. "It's not like he's sick or anything."

I looked down at the table as I continued... "I'm worried about his... salvation."

Looking back at her, I wondered aloud: "What happened to him? Was it really Gramps' death? Is that why he stopped believing?"

Mom leaned back and flinched a little uncomfortably.

"Promise me you won't tell him I told you this?"

I quickly nodded in agreement — it wouldn't be the only secret I'd been asked to keep lately. I watched the painful memories filling her mind as she recalled them, etching themselves in her face.

"I WAS twelve when daddy died... it was on my birthday."

A sudden mist appeared in her eyes.

"Dad was upset that Mike wasn't home for my party. I remember the way he grabbed his coat and started for the door. He was saying: 'It's his sister, he should be here....'"

A single tear escaped and ran down her cheek — she wiped it off with her hand.

"I watched from the window of the apartment — Mike was out on the corner with a group of his friends. Susie Califano was there... he had kind of a crush on her then...." Her words trailed off quietly as if she was lost in thought.

"It happened so fast... When Mike saw dad coming, he just took off. He ran into the street, right into traffic. I could see dad raising his arms for him to stop — there was a taxi coming from the other direction, and Mike didn't see it. That's when dad rushed into the street, running straight for Mike. He had to dive to push him out of the way — his push knocked Mike to the curb just in the nick of time."

Mom's face was twisted with pain as she struggled to continue. She stared at the table, deep in thought.

"The cab tried to stop... but it happened too fast."

After a minute of stark silence, she looked up at me.

"Mike blames himself for daddy's death. He isn't angry at God; he's angry at himself. He can't forgive himself and doesn't feel like God should forgive him either."

She stopped and fought an agonized frown that was forcing itself onto her face, rubbing away a few more unwanted tears.

"I remember the way Mike kept repeating that he was sorry to mom and me — he was so devastated... the guilt ate at him. It was too much for any 14 year old to have to bear."

Mom closed her eyes and struggled for a minute to push back the overwhelming feelings of that day. Still struggling to control the rush of emotion, she avoided eye contact as she got up from her seat and silently began collecting the empty plates from the table.

⌘

5

YOU SAVED ME FIRST

fter we got home, mom and I couldn't resist opening Amos' journal. We sat together at the table as I read aloud....

Amos' Journal ~ April 19, 1870 ~

Things were seeming a bit ordinary the past week since my experience in Washington... assuming that it was, indeed, Washington, I can't be sure entirely. I was beginning to doubt that it ever happened, to be honest — until today.
I had just pulled my boots on and was barely out of the house when all in a flash, I was standing up in the north field looking out over an enormous crowd of people. There was a big top tent erected, but the crowd didn't fit inside it — it was much too great a multitude. There was merriment and rejoicing and the sound of music and singing at a very great volume. Looking upon the people's faces, I could see on some of them tears and on others great joy. Many had

their eyes closed, still more had their hands raised. It was plain to be seen that they were in heartfelt worship.

Looking toward the tent, I could see musicians and a man leading the singing from a raised platform. First, one chorus and then another; the thundering songs continued for some time.

As I was beholding the sight and trying to make sense of it, I was suddenly accompanied by an angelic personage — the same one who spoke to me at the inauguration. He bowed his head as he greeted me by name.

"Hello, Amos."

I felt the hair at the back of my neck stand straight as he looked at me. He seemed to be a kindly being, with a look of compassion on his face that calmed my fears, giving me the courage to ask what was burning in my heart.

"I know this place... it's in one of my own fields, but what's happening here? Who are all these people? How did they get here?"

"All will be revealed in time. It has been given thee to know so that ye may prepare those upon whom the end of the age will come."

"The end of... is this the future then? Who are you?"

"Thy guide, I am called Chozeq."

I HEARD mom gasp aloud as I read Chozeq's name. Reading it gave me a chill as well. I looked up at her from the open journal, remembering how she had also described receiving a visit from Chozeq after dad died. I couldn't dare reveal all the times I've spent with him myself.

"It really says that?!" she asked, peering at the page to verify it. She looked up at me in awe... "He saw him... Amos saw Chozeq too!"

I nodded in acknowledgment, doing my best to look as surprised as she was.

She continued rereading the sentence aloud — wide-eyed.

"*To prepare those upon whom the end of the age will come...* You were right; it is like Lena's vision," she noted, recalling the vision she shared with Anna's mom a few nights ago at the tent. I watched the dawning realization in her face... "That's why you were supposed to find the journal... it's for now... it's for us!"

I just nodded my head, feeling a sudden sense of foreboding as she said the words, "... *it's for us.*" The thought of our conversation with Uncle Mike briefly crossed my mind, and I breathed a prayer for a way to get through to him while there's still time. I was reminded of what Amos said when he introduced himself: *Things are about to get mighty interestin' in the world.*

I dropped my head into my hands and rubbed my hair. Despite all the excitement of the day, I was exhausted. Pushing the journal away from me on the table, I rubbed my eyes as I spoke.

"I think I'm gonna lay down for a while."

Mom felt my forehead in a kind of automatic reaction, then nodded. "It's easy to forget that you just got out of the hospital." She put her hand on my arm and closed her eyes for a second as if breathing a prayer of astonished gratitude. "You need your rest — I'll wake you up for dinner."

I DROPPED onto the bed and looked up at the familiar ceiling, releasing a deep breath. It felt good to be back in my own room. My eyes caught sight of the model ship that dad and I built together, and thoughts rushed to my mind of the way Chozeq once used it to illustrate a point. I could practically hear his voice as he had spoken to me about trials that build faith.

"Let the winds rush howling forth, and the waters lift themselves up. Then, though the vessel may rock and her deck is washed with waves and her masts creak under her full and swelling sails, it is then that she makes speedy headway towards her desired haven."

Boy, he really hadn't been kidding about stormy trials coming! Thoughts swirled in my mind of all that had happened in the months since then, including the past few days. I rubbed my hand across my undamaged chest in gratitude.

Soon after I had closed my eyes in a thankful prayer, I heard a familiar voice.

· · ·

"TODAY YE HAVE DONE WELL."

I looked over at Chozeq kneeling on one knee beside me and couldn't help but smile.

"Me? What have I done except follow where I was led?" I glanced down at my healed chest and looked back at him gratefully... "Thanks... I didn't get a chance to say thank you."

"It pleases thy Lord to bless thee. It is He who must be thanked."

His words stirred a warm joy in the depths of my soul, and I felt my heart swell with worship. Its heartfelt praises resounded inside me, finally emerging on my lips quietly, "...Amen."

Chozeq looked back at me with a heartwarming smile. Then his eyes softened to reflect the concern that he sensed in me.

"Yet, thy heart is troubled."

"Just a little," I confessed, looking down at my hands uncomfortably. "In the end of days, when all those things happen... Will a lot of people... other believers... will they be hurt?"

Chozeq paused, comprehending my concerns. When he spoke again, it was with a certain tenderness in his voice, yet it was infused with firm and resolute confidence.

"All who love Him may rest in the assurance that they abide in the dwelling place of the Most High... under the shadow of his wings. Hasn't He shown thee that He will carry thee in His own hand?"

"But it will be hard... right?" I asked. "I mean like it says in Matthew chapter twenty-four — being hated and everything?"

"Many before thee have suffered such for the Savior's sake. Many suffer thus this day."

He gripped my shoulder reassuringly, "Tho ye walk through fire or flood, He is ever with thee. Remember the safety of His hand — nothing shall befall thee except for that which He allows."

"I-I know... I'm not worried about myself, really... it's more for everyone else. Like mom and Anna and Pete and PJ and everyone... and Uncle Mike."

Chozeq gave me an understanding look.

"Trust that thy God has ordained each one's path, as he has thine own. His plan is perfect. Indeed the Lord is not slack concerning his promises. He truly is longsuffering and is not willing that any should perish. I have witnessed it over long ages and in countless lives! He has not given up on Mike — nor should ye."

His encouraging words poured strength into my soul, filling me with an unexpected fortitude. They pushed aside my worries as if they were just shadows being obliterated by noonday light. My thoughts returned to the events of the day — and my meeting with Amos.

"You knew Amos?"

"I do."

His answer gave me pause as I was reminded that time has a different meaning to Chozeq — he lives outside of it.

"He called himself a Traveler... he said that I'm one too. Am I like him?"

Chozeq looked at me with a pleased expression as he answered. "'Tis thy innocent spirit that sets thee apart child... he is likewise of an earnest heart."

"How long did he... that is... did he travel for a long time? I guess I mean — How long did he live?"

"His journeys are carefully recorded in his journal. If it is the number of his days that ye seek, then search for his resting place. It is found beside the old Hill Church."

"The Old Hill... You mean the old Methodist church?"

His answer was a mere nod, yet the look in his eye hinted that there could be more for me to discover by visiting there. I tucked the thought away with a promise to explore it further.

"How did he know to look for me? Did you bring him here?"

"The Lord knows those who are His. It is His hand that executes His plan; I serve only as a messenger... a protector."

Chozeq's humility was striking in such a powerful being. As I recalled my time with Amos this afternoon, realizing that he had the same trait — he was amazingly humble. While I was silently considering it, I recognized something else about Amos — he seemed to be able to move through time all by himself. Chozeq wasn't even with us. Somehow I hadn't considered it before.

"Amos used the word, Traveler... it was like he could move in time whenever he wanted. Was it really you doing that for him?"

"When God imparts a gift, it is given in all of its fullness. An angel's power is not required to make it complete. Thou wilt learn as he did."

"Learn? To travel in time? You mean I'll be able to do that too someday?"

"Already ye have done it."

"I've done it?! How could I? I didn't even know where I was... or when!"

"It is the Master's voice that leads thee. Ye need only to hear and follow — even through time."

My mind was swirling as I tried to comprehend what he was telling me. How could I follow through time? When did I hear God's voice leading me there?

Before I could ask him another question, Chozeq's hand touched my forehead — sending me instantly into a deep sleep.

———

MOM WAS NUDGING my shoulder as she woke me.

"You had a good nap; you must have needed it. Any longer, though, and you might not sleep tonight. Dinner is on the table."

I squinted at my bedside clock, realizing that I'd been asleep for nearly three hours. I felt incredibly refreshed.

I found myself deep in thought, trying to answer the question that I had been about to ask him — trying to recall when I had traveled on my own — when I'd heard God's voice. The conversation I'd be having with Chozeq was still fresh on my mind, but I couldn't say anything to mom about it. Mom had to repeat what she was saying before I realized that she was talking to me.

"...Anna called while you were asleep," she repeated, wondering if I was hearing her.

"What? ...Oh, thanks."

"She wanted to know if you'll be at the tent service tonight. I told her yes — you plan on going, right?"

"Yeah, definitely!"

"We can pick her up on our way. Dinner is ready; why don't you go wash up."

As I climbed off the bed, I looked back at mom, suddenly struck by how she was constantly looking out for me. I felt a sense of gratitude, thinking again about how she prayed for me the other night after I was shot.

"Hey, mom... thanks again."

"For what?" she feigned with a smile.

"For, you know... saving me."

Just like she had at the hospital, she touched the side of my face as she smiled... "You saved me first."

I looked at her curiously.

"You said that at the hospital too. What do you mean? What did I do?"

She blushed slightly as she acknowledged my question and sat down on the bed as she considered her answer.

"I don't know... it's a lot of things. You may not have realized it, but I was pretty depressed a few months ago — I guess I had been for a long time... since your father died. The O'Malleys' leaving made it worse, and then when Kelly...." She paused, leaving the sentence unfinished. She stared at her hands as she continued.

"I was in pretty bad shape. I honestly felt like I had nothing left to live for... except for you — you were the one thing that kept me going. Then, at Kelly's Memorial and afterward with Ward and Barbara at the lake when you prayed for them... and all that has happened with Mr. Van Clief and the tent." She looked up with a tear in her eye... "I feel like my life has started over... it's like it's all-new.

"That's why I prayed so hard. God had to save you... I had to try... because you'd saved me."

A small stream of tears suddenly ran down her cheeks as she finished and wiped them away with both hands. I was speechless as I stood looking awkwardly back at her, more than a little choked up. She stood and gave me a hug, kissing me on the forehead, then nudged me toward the door.

"Go on... get washed for dinner."

⌘

6

THE VAN CLIEFS

Let this be recorded for a generation to come,
so that a people yet to be created may praise the LORD
~ Psalm 102:18

While washing my face, the conversation with Chozeq repeated in my mind. *Already ye have done it...* I recalled his words again. *"...Ye need only to hear and follow — even through time."*

I shuffled through all of my memories of times with Chozeq... all of the visions — at least that's what I thought they were then. It suddenly struck me that Chozeq was with me for all of them except once.... That was the time in the hospital chapel after Kelly died. I replayed the experience in my head over and over, trying to remember hearing God's voice. If anything, that was the one time that I felt furthest from Him.

That's when it hit me... it was the overwhelming emotion I was feeling... the desperate yearning of my heart! God's voice was not audible.... I didn't *hear* it -- I *felt* it!

Despite the anger that I remembered feeling in those moments, I desperately needed *Him*. It was a stronger yearning than I'd ever known before. I needed to *see* him... not just to sense him, but to physically see him! It was then that I suddenly found myself back in Palestine on the day of his triumphal entry. He chose to bring me there — to the exact moment that was the very height of his earthly glory.

The height of His glory... that thought struck me suddenly with a profound realization. It was such an extraordinary moment... at the apex of His earthly triumph. Yet, for that moment, his focus was entirely on *me*.

The sudden realization was so overwhelming that I found myself fighting back tears and bent to splash water on my red eyes. More memories of that experience began to rush through my mind... the smells and sounds and warmth of the hot sun... it was real!

Then, as quickly as those thoughts had washed over me, they were replaced by memories of the extraordinary events that followed. The remarkable scene at Calvary — so vivid! The shattered doors of Sheol where He led captivity captive... and the horrifying stench of Hell. Its anguished cries crushed me again in a flood that shook me to the core of my soul. The horror faded as I remembered seeing Kelly in her glorious form... and hugging dad.

The words that Chozeq said to me soon after those events rose like a warm sun against my face... *"At thy hour of greatest need, it was He Himself who shepherded thy path."*

He Himself... the words impressed me suddenly with new meaning. Chozeq had not been the one directing any of those events! That's what he had tried to tell me; he was just my guide and protector, like a supernatural chaperon! One who also happened to be powerful enough to single-handedly defeat armies and sweep away legions of demons with a wave of his arm. I couldn't help smiling as I quietly considered it.

"Wow!"

That thought emboldened me further, making me realize how truly protected I was. Even a lethal gunshot hadn't taken me out! In light of this, I felt suddenly fearless and was filled with a burning curiosity about this gift of traveling — how is it done exactly? In this state of mind, it occurred to me that there was no one better qualified to explain how to 'travel' than an experienced traveler. I immediately realized that aside from Chozeq, the only experienced traveler I knew was Amos.

The idea inspired a prayer, so brief and fleeting that it was practically spoken unconsciously — but it was answered just as quickly!

I INSTANTLY FIND myself standing on the porch of the Van Clief's farmhouse. From the look of the house and its surrounding fields... and a saddle swung over a nearby rail... I can tell that I'm in a bygone age — late nineteenth century, I guess. I assume that it's during the time that Amos is living here. A quick glance over my shoulder checks for the barn — to my surprise, the structure I see is fully built and already worn-looking. It looks like it's years old. I return my gaze to the front door uncertainly, wondering what I'm going to find when I knock... wondering if anyone will even know I'm here.

My steps on the wooden porch make no sound, reminding me once again that I'm the traveler. The door is ajar as I reach to knock on it, and just as I consider pushing it open, a gust of wind from behind me does the job.

"AMOS?" I call as I step inside.

There is stirring in a tall wingback chair in the living room, and I see an older man rise slowly and turn. He smiles as he catches my eye, steadying himself with a hand on the chair-back.

"Hello Jimmy," he says in a friendly voice.

I'm struck with how much he resembles old Mister V. I'm momentarily speechless. Slowly getting my bearings, I work up the courage to continue. Amos waits patiently as if coaxing me on.

"Wh-what year is this?" I wonder aloud.

"Don't you know? You're the one who's traveled here. That's quite a good step, makin' it so soon, by the way. From the look o' ya, I reckon it ain't been long since our first meetin'."

"Same day... actually," I confess, feeling a little embarrassed to admit how much of a novice I still am.

He just looks back at me with a wise gaze that seems to recollect a lifetime of conversations between us. He smiles again like someone reminiscing over an old photograph.

"What brings you here, son?"

His question startles me. I hadn't even planned on coming, let alone thought of why I'm here.

"I-I'm hoping you can help answer that, to be honest. I think I know how I got here... I just don't know when here is, exactly... or why I'm here in particular."

"So I reckon you're hopin' for me t' tell ya what I've learned about travelin'." His shoulders rise with a subtle shake as he chuckles to himself. "Come on in an' have a seat."

I walk into the living room as he goes to shut the door and notice his journal lying open on the end table. I look back at him in surprise.

"That's your journal! It's here... not up in the barn where you hid it?"

He nods calmly with a reassuring grin. "I was just finishin' up the latest entry. Don't worry, it'll be there when you go lookin'. That's been its hidin' place for 28 years... whenever I'm not addin' to it."

"Adding? You mean you're still traveling?"

"Well, God hasn't taken me home yet... o'course I'm still."

My growing interest is evident as I take a seat and lean forward anxiously.

He stands rubbing his chin for a moment as he collects his thoughts. "You most likely already know the first thing there is t' know about it... which is that God's the one who decides the when and where. If He's sent you here, then I reckon it's because he wants me to help ya out. I imagine ya got more questions swirlin' in your head than there are stars in the heavens. Just sit tight an' listen, and I'll do the best I can."

. . .

HE SETTLES into his high back chair and pauses, momentarily closing his eyes in a short prayer for direction. His gaze is focused and intense as he looks up at me again.

"You've likely noticed that you're gettin' a fair amount of attention from some unwelcome creatures. Your gift makes you keenly sensitive to the spirit world, includin' both angelic and demonic powers. Demons are gonna have a heap o' trouble with you; they thrive in darkness and denial — havin' someone around who can recognize them on sight is a fair threat. They won't take kindly to it."

"Yeah... I've noticed that."

"Well, just remember that you're the one with God on your side — there ain't no power of Hell that can hold a candle to His mighty strength."

There's a confidence in his voice that conveys a deep well of experience with what he's describing. I get the sense that there's a great deal more that he could share on this point. After studying my eyes for a moment, however, he just nods in acknowledgment and moves on.

"O'course, there are the angels on your side as well. We have a mutual acquaintance in Chozeq, as you know."

I smile at Chozeq's name and nod in confirmation.

"In all my years, I've never had a truer friend than he is, short of the Lord Himself. He'll be the same to you if you let him be."

The sincerity in his words pours from a place deep in his soul, like a man reflecting on a profound lifelong friendship. The thought seems to remind him of a hundred adventures. He pauses for a moment, looking at his journal, as he runs his hand slowly over the closed cover.

"If you're still in the day we met, then I reckon you haven't read much of this yet." He looks up at me questioningly... "You went and retrieved it, didn't you?"

"Yes... as soon as I got back — I went right away. It was there in the barn where you showed me, safe and sound."

He nods thankfully as if his greatest worry has been assuaged.

"Jim... I ain't gonna sugar coat it — some rough times are comin'. In a way, I can't help feelin' like I owe you my sympathies, but in another way, I envy you. You may not realize it... or maybe you do, but the days you're livin' in are what's been written of for generations. You're livin' in the true End of Days, son."

His words are not news to me, but they still send a chill up my back as I hear him say them. I nod in agreement and strain to swallow. He just nods back in a gesture that conveys his understanding.... and his empathy.

"There ain't much to Travelin', truth be told. It's more a matter o' being ready than it is of planning. God has a way o' sending ya off when you least expect it, but He also will let you decide from time to time... the way you did this evenin'."

"How... how do I decide, exactly?"

"Well, now that's a fair bit of a trick to explain. It comes from bein' on the same page as Him... singing from the same sheet o' music. It takes an understanding of what He's up to."

He looks at me thoughtfully for a moment.

"I'll bet you said a prayer about wantin' to see me just before you got here."

I nod quickly in confirmation.

"Ya probably didn't ask to see me at a certain time or place. More 'n likely you were prayin' for some advice about the gift and how to use it."

I agree again, more enthusiastically.

"That was an inspired prayer... it was God's Spirit breathing in you the desire of His own heart for you. He knows best what we need before we know it. He's faithful in preparing us for what we don't know is coming."

Thoughts of the past few weeks rush through my mind as I think about his point. The way God kept preparing us and directing events was incredible! I look again at the journal in Amos' hands and nod toward it.

"What did He do to prepare you for that?"

He draws in a deep breath, and I watch his chin drop as he releases it, deep in thought.

"That's not a simple answer... nor a short one. Lookin' back over

28 years, it seems as if every journey had its own story that went before it.

"I'll say this for sure... I'm a far different man today than I was when it all started. I reckon when you read it, you'll catch that."

There's a silent pause as I wait for Amos to continue, but he just sits with his hand on the journal, as if he is reliving a hundred adventures... or is possibly lost in one that was especially profound.

I CAREFULLY BREAK THE SILENCE, noticing a family portrait over the fireplace mantle. It's of Amos as a younger man, with a wife and a son who looked to be around ten years old.

"Is that your family?"

Amos is momentarily startled by the question. He looks up and follows my eye to the portrait, then settles back as he understands.

"Yup. Marcela and our boy, Raymond — in his younger years."

"Is he your only child?"

He nods... "The only one to make it to full age."

He clears his throat after he answers as if shaking off an unwanted mix of sentiments.

I silently register the fact that Raymond has to be old Mr. V's father.

"Where are they now? I guess Raymond is grown up?"

"Marcela passed a year ago...."

"I'm sorry...."

"Don't need to be apologizin' — she's in a better place, that's for sure."

Thoughts of my brief time in that glorious place with Kelly and dad flash through my mind — it makes me wonder whether he has experienced anything like that too. I can't help asking.

"Have you seen it? Have you seen what it's like there?"

A serene look comes over his face, and I can tell immediately that he knows what I'm asking about; he nods in confirmation without answering. Then he catches my eye...

"...You have as well, I see."

"Yes... it was amazing!"

He nods several times as he agrees...

"...That it is son, that it is. I reckon all I think about these days is making it home the same as she has. God's been keepin' me here for some purpose, whatever it may be."

We sit quietly for a moment, both of us reliving our memories of that fantastic experience. I finally come back to my question about their son.

"Where is Raymond now? Does he live nearby?"

"He's doin' fine — a fine man he's turned out to be; I couldn't be prouder of him. He graduated at the top of his class at the Seminary over in Princeton. Takes after his mother, thankfully. He's servin' as Minister at the church up there on the hill. Still helps me here on the farm most days."

"Is he married?"

"Nope. Not that he doesn't have suiters; I reckon half the young ladies in these parts have heart palpitations whenever he comes 'round."

Amos notices my raised eyebrows, and he waves his hand with a smile. "He's a God-fearin' man an' busy as a beaver these days, but I reckon he'll settle down soon enough."

"Is he a traveler too?"

"Not so far as I can tell; leastwise, he never let on if he is."

"Does he know about you? About your journal?"

"My directive was to seal it up for another time. No-one's seen it, and that's how it'll be — until your day."

"My day... you mean, ***the end of the age.***"

He bows his head slightly as he nods, speaking in a sympathetic voice.

"That's right, son.... That's right."

⌘

7

MORE IN WEAKNESS

My grace is sufficient for you, for my power is made perfect in weakness...
~ 2 Corinthians 12:9

The scene in Amos' farmhouse faded around me as quickly as it began. I found myself standing once again in front of the bathroom mirror. The last thing that Amos said replays in my mind in an unending loop — *"..your day ...the end of the age."*

Staring into my reflection, the memory of the dusty farmhouse was as clear as if it had happened in just the next room. Meeting Amos in his old age had only added to my sense of awe, making it even more apparent that my travels were through time itself.

Glancing at my watch, it appeared that no time at all had passed since I left. I made my way to the table, seeing mom at the kitchen counter. She placed a full plate in front of me and then sat down with her own, looking distracted by her thoughts.

"I read some more of it while you were asleep," she said as if continuing a conversation she'd started in her head. "Amos' journal, that is."

Her comment didn't surprise me, but I forced myself to look at her curiously, being careful not to reveal any of my own insights. I quietly waited for her to continue. She gave her head a subtle shake, as if she was shaking off an unwelcome thought, and then looked up at me.

"He writes about Chozeq — he was like a protector to him. He's the one who guided him when he had his visions."

I was tempted to correct her... they're Travels, not visions. But I managed to keep the thought to myself.

"What else does he write about? What did he see?"

She looked a little nervous for a second and stared at her plate.

"You should read the entries yourself... I won't give away what they say."

The tone of her voice brought to mind Amos' own words to me a short time earlier... "Jim... I ain't gonna sugar coat it — there are some rough times comin'."

I glanced at mom's face for a second and cleared my throat, understanding from the look in her eyes that what she read still worried her. She continued with a distant-sounding voice as if she was mostly speaking to herself....

"I guess I just thought there would be more time.... It seems like it's happening so fast."

The way she mentioned time reminded me of my recent visit with Amos — I was momentarily lost in thought.

After a few moments of silence, I looked up and changed the subject.

"I feel like we should tell Juan and Pastor Wilkes about the journal. Do you think we should ask Mr. V first?"

"I don't know..." she said, hesitating. "Well, I suppose so."

I could tell that whatever she read changed her feeling about the importance of sharing it. There was something different in her voice.

"We can ask him tonight," I suggested. "I think Mr. V will agree with sharing it. After what happened to him last night... I'm sure he'll agree."

She looked at her plate as she soberly nodded her head in agreement.

Thinking of tonight brought to mind our conversation when she first woke me, reminding me that we're picking up Anna.

"Did Anna say how long she stayed this afternoon — has the service been going all day?"

"All day?! You mean all week!" mom corrected me. "It hasn't stopped for days. More and more people just keep coming."

The only thing about her comment that surprised me was the fact that I hadn't already known it. Of course, people keep coming — that has been the consistent message since I first 'saw' the tent! A flurry of memories from the past few weeks flashed through my mind, and I couldn't help shaking my head in amazement.

"It really is hard to believe this is all happening."

Mom sat silently for a brief instant and then looked down at her plate, speaking quietly:

"It really is...."

I noticed that she hadn't eaten much of her dinner — she didn't seem to have much of an appetite. To be honest, I wasn't feeling very hungry either; I was too busy feeling anxious to get back to the tent. Resting my fork on the half-eaten plateful, I pushed it away.

"Maybe we'd better get going," I suggested. "Who knows what we're missing!"

ANNA WAS WAITING on her front porch and sprinted to the road as we drove up. She had already reached the car by the time I'd climbed out to open the back door. She greeted me with a quick hug and a smile before ducking into the back seat. I settled in front and turned toward her while mom drove on.

"How long did you stay after we left this afternoon?"

"Just a little longer. There were lots of people looking for seats, so I let some people have ours. I had to get back home to finish some stuff around the house. To be honest, I was starving!"

She looked at me with a smile and nodded in a questioning gesture....

"How was your afternoon? Did you get any rest?"

[Memories of the busy day flashed through my mind in a blizzard of images as I recalled leaving the hospital… meeting Amos… finding his journal… lunch with Uncle Mike… learning how Gramps Farro died… Chozeq's visit to my room… traveling back to meet Amos in his old age…. It was all way too much to explain!]

"It was good. Yeah, I slept for a while," I said instead, abandoning any effort to describe it all.

Anna noticed the journal in my hand, remembering it from earlier.

"You still have that book that you found today… what is it?"

I looked down at it and nodded my head as mom looks over at me.

"It's a journal… like a diary. It was from Mr. V's grandfather, Amos Van Clief."

"Oh wow… really? Have you read it?"

"Just a little. It's kind of amazing — he writes about the future."

"You mean like science fiction stories?"

Mom and I shared a glance, and then I looked back at Anna; "Actually, it's more like prophecy."

Anna was speechless for a second… "What do you mean?"

"It sounds crazy, I know, but Mr.V's grandfather was sort of a prophet. His son — Mr. V's father — was the pastor of the old Methodist church."

Mom looked over in surprise; "Really? I never knew that. Did Mr. Van Clief tell you that?"

I quickly realized that I'd said too much again. I looked at mom blankly for a second and then refocused on Anna's question, ignoring mom's.

"He wrote about actual things that he saw in the future. We think he was writing about our time, right now."

"Our time?" Anna queried in surprise. "What makes you think that?"

"Well, for one thing, he mentions seeing things that he couldn't have imagined back in the 1860s, like helicopters. He even writes about our tent meetings."

"Our tent meetings?! …Get out!"

"Seriously!" I assured her as mom agreed with a nod of her head.

"But we only just started having them this week. Why would he mention them ...so long ago?"

"He wrote about events that would change things — stuff that was going to change the whole world."

"The whole world? Wouldn't that be kind of an exaggeration? It's only Center Springs — not exactly a major metropolis."

WHILE SHE WAS STILL SPEAKING, mom turned the corner onto Main Street and immediately stopped in heavy traffic. We all stared in astonishment at the sight in front of us as hundreds of cars and buses clogged the road and overflowed from Carmine's parking lot in the distance. The fields were covered with them for as far as we could see.

A news chopper swooped low overhead and circled in the sky as it surveyed the scene. Flashing lights from police cars lined the sides of the road, and teams of officers up ahead were directing traffic into the overflowing lot. There were too many to just be local police... it looked like the Sheriff called in help from the State Troopers.

"I think we'll have to walk," mom said, realizing that the traffic was not moving.

She steered off the road into the corner gas station beside us and cut back to the road we just came from. Other cars were doing the same as a stream of traffic quickly began filling the parking spaces on both sides of the street.

"I have an idea," I quickly suggested. "We can take the back way around to Mr.V's. We can park at the farmhouse."

Mom looked at me strangely, as if something was dawning on her. She appeared distracted for a moment and then agreed with a nod.

Ten minutes later, we pulled into the long driveway of Van Clief's farm. The massive scene of parked vehicles across the fields in the distance looked as if a swarm of mechanical locusts had descended on the north field, spreading into the others.

We climbed out of the car and stared at the sight open-mouthed. Besides the overflowing parking, we could see that the field all around the tent was packed with people sitting shoulder to shoulder. It was a sea of humanity, unlike anything we'd ever seen... anywhere, let alone here in Center Springs!

Anna looked over at me with an amazed expression and then down at the journal in my hand.

"Did you say that book talks about things that will change the whole world? I think I'm starting to see why this is in it."

"We should see if Mr. V. is home," I suggested, giving mom a glance. She nodded in return, acknowledging that she understood my suggestion to tell him about the journal. The nervous look in her eye made me wonder for a moment, and I could feel myself gripping the old book tightly as I climbed the stairs to the porch — still a little worried about how he would respond. It occurred to me that I never asked his permission before letting myself into his barn this morning.

THE SIGHT of the old farmhouse door took my mind off that worry. I was immediately struck with a surreal feeling as I remembered visiting this same door to see Amos just an hour ago — yet it was actually more than a century ago! The door's recent paint job couldn't hide the cracked and weathered wood patterns that revealed its actual age, still visible just beneath the surface.

When a few minutes of knocking had yielded no answer, I finally realized that mom had been calling for me and turned my attention from the old door. She gave me a curious look as I stepped off the porch, obviously wondering what had me so distracted that I didn't hear her repeated calls. She seemed to register the fact but didn't ask me about it.

"He must be there already," I said with a nod toward the tent, stating the obvious.

Mom and Anna smiled at each other, politely resisting the urge to point that out. They waited for me to put the journal back in the car, and then we set off walking toward the tent. As we got nearer, we were able to see old Bessy, Mr. V's tractor, parked at the end of the dirt road. Crowds had encircled the tent completely, considerately dividing themselves into sections, leaving isles in the grass between them.

Everywhere we looked, people were worshiping in song and prayer — many were crying. The atmosphere was charged as we slowly made our way closer to the tent's rugged platform. It was like walking closer to a powerful reactor. Each step increased the intensity of spiritual power that seemed to emanate from the place. Like we were walking toward the epicenter of God's literal presence.

Pastor Juan, Reverend Wilkes, and Bishop Bradley were part of a team praying with lines of people at the altar while the music team led a steady stream of choruses. Joyous shouts of astonished praise could be heard above the instruments each time another person was miraculously healed. The prayer team barely had time to acknowledge each healing as another desperate soul stepped forward to take each healed one's place.

Nearly everyone had tears on their faces, including us. The atmosphere was so intense that I was half-expecting to see tongues of fire suddenly appear above everyone's head at any moment.

Unable to walk any further, we stopped at the edge of the tent — overcome by the stirring in our souls. My eyes were drawn closed, and I felt my hands rise in irresistible worship, simply basking in the holy presence that was washing over us. It was a profound sense of God's presence — I could practically feel His physical touch upon my soul, making me shudder — it clouded my eyes with tears. The music team passionately belted out words that suddenly hit me with supernatural clarity:

"I am chosen, not forsaken...."

Confirmation of those words was impressed on my heart so powerfully that it melted me — I dropped to my knees, overwhelmed by a wave of gratitude.

A DIFFERENT SENSE of presence spurred me to open my eyes — it was a feeling that someone was looking at me; I strained to see through my running tears. To my surprise, I recognized that it was Amos kneeling close. His face was twisted in grief as he looked me in the eyes, then I felt his hand on the back of my head as his forehead touched mine. His words were confusing to me.

"Hold fast, boy, just hold fast! No matter what happens, trust that the Lord's plan is good and perfect. It will all be alright... just remember that — it'll be alright!"

BEFORE I COULD MAKE sense of his words, a single loud pop rang out from somewhere outside, in the field behind us. It was followed instantly by the deafening concussion of an enormous thunderbolt that shook the ground under my knees and made my hair stand on end! I immediately recognized the pop as the horrible sound of a gunshot — between that and the earth-shattering blast of thunder, my heart had skipped several beats. Through echoes of the blast, I could hear the sound of screams filling the air.

I looked again for Amos, but he was already gone. It was then that I realized someone was falling against me...

...IT WAS MOM!

⌘

8

MEMORIES OF HER FUTURE

Love never fails...
~ I Corinthians 13:8

Earlier *that afternoon...*

While Jimmy was napping, Maria sat alone at her dining room table, holding the aged journal in her hands. She was thinking about the entry that Jimmy had been reading, replaying the words that had most startled her:

"...I AM CALLED CHOZEQ."

The words stirred memories of her own meeting with Chozeq years earlier when she struggled with her husband's death. Hearing the angel's name again had given her a renewed confirmation that that meeting had been real. She had been beginning to doubt that the extraordinary event had really taken place, questioning whether it had only been a dream. Her hands were shaking slightly as she opened the journal and pressed the open pages against the table to steady them.

She scanned the handwritten entry until she found what she was looking for....

~ April 19, 1870 ~

...I felt the hair at the back of my neck stand straight as he looked at me. He seemed to be a kindly being, with a look of compassion on his face that calmed my fears, giving me the courage to ask what was burning in my heart.

"I know this place... it's in one of my own fields, but what's happening here? Who are all these people? How did they get here?"

"All will be revealed in time. It has been given to thee to know certain days so that ye may prepare those upon whom the end of the age will come."

"The end... is this the future then? Who are you?"

"Thy guide, I am called Chozeq."

"Is this real then, or am I dreaming?"

"Thou knowest."

As soon as he said this, a stiff gust of summer breeze blew across the field, rustling people's hair and garments — including mine.

"If I'm not dreaming... how?"

"The means shall become clear in time. Take heed to all that ye see and hear. Write it, as it has been shown to thee."

The sound of another flying machine drew my notice as it flew low overhead. I suspect that these fantastic contraptions must be as common as birds in this future age.

My attention was drawn to where all eyes were focused, inside the great tent. A large group of souls gathered there before half-a-dozen men. I could see that the assembled masses were crippled, maimed, and blind; many were sick with desperate diseases. The men were praying and laying their hands on them as they came, and as they prayed, they healed them.

The spirit's move was so dear that the entire multitude was moved to tears and worship. Many of them had dropped to their knees, unable even to lift their heads. Still, others stood with arms and faces raised

toward the heavens, as though they looked upon the very glory on
high. More continued to join them, arriving in a steady stream as they
gathered in ever-greater numbers in the open field.
Chozeq then turned to point toward my farmhouse, at the road
leading from it.
"See this one who walks and those who are with him," he thundered.
"The boy?" I asked, picking out a company of three who walked along
the dusty road.
"Let not his youth mislead thee — he has already endured more than
ye know. His faith makes him strong, yet that strength will be sorely
tested on this day."

MARIA WAS MOVED with a sobering swell of intuition as she read these
words. It seemed clear to her that Chozeq was talking about her son.
The fact added to her wonder about everything that had happened in
recent months. Why was this happening to Jimmy?

More importantly, what was it that would test him so greatly?
What could be an even greater test than a few nights ago, when he was
shot? She quieted her heart with a deep breath and carefully
read on....

I surveyed the peaceful crowd, wondering how such a setting could be
a place of great testing for the lad.

"What will be his test? Why am I to write of it?"

"You must write of things to come that will affect all the earth."
The angel's answer confused me. How could the testing of a single boy
affect all the world? As I pondered the puzzle, Chozeq turned toward
the field behind us and pointed out a man walking toward the tent.
He was not like the others in the crowd; his face was set with an
angry scowl, and he walked purposefully, pushing others out of his
way. I had seen men in war with that look... it was the cold, detached
look of an experienced assassin.
Dark clouds suddenly appeared above the field, rolling and folding
like smoke; the nearer the man drew, the darker they became.

As I watched, he stopped among the crowds seated in the grass and reached into the sack that was slung over his shoulder, drawing out a rifle. Without a word, he lifted it to his eye and aimed it at the kneeling boy, then fired.

His shot hit a woman who had quickly moved in front of the boy, striking her in the back. I saw her thrown forward by the force of it. Before the shooter could get off a second shot, the thick black clouds above us lit with a mighty flash, piercing the sky with the most terrific blast of lightning I ever saw. It struck the shooter square on the top of his head and blasted the rifle to pieces, sending parts of it spinning through the air. The sound of the thunderclap was so mighty that it shook the earth under our feet and sent crowds of people tumbling in all directions. When the frightful blast had cleared, there was little left of the shooter: just his shoes and the empty sack from his back. No one else appeared to have been harmed except the poor woman he shot.

That's about the time that it dawned on me who she was.

"It's the boy's mother, isn't it," I said to Chozeq without needing to look.

My kindly guide nodded to me in confirmation... a somber look etched in his brow.

Maria leaned back in her seat with a startled gasp, involuntarily placing a hand on her back. She desperately wanted to read further... to find out what would happen next, but Amos's entry ended right there. She thumbed forward in the journal, trying to find some other mention of the events or a hint of the final outcome, but couldn't find anything more.

What she did find, however, was equally unsettling.

One entry caught her eye in particular. She noted to herself that it was written by Amos a year later.

It was located about a third of the way into the book. Her scanning of the entries to this point had revealed an unfolding story that was increasingly troubling to her. This page caught her eye because of smudges in the writing — she recognized them as water stains and concluded that they must have fallen on it while the ink was wet. It might have been rain... yet something told her that they were more likely tears.

~ April 26, 1871, ~

My heart has been a tempest over what's to come. The depth of our great country's fall from doing right is a shock to me, although I guess it oughtn't to be surprising in the end times. Yet each revelation of those days weighs on me like a mountain of sorrows.

Chozeq came today at sunrise, rousing me from my morning prayers. With his touch, we found ourselves at the capital once again. Athaliah, the President's wife, was addressing a large audience of reporters with members of her staff lined up behind her. She appeared pleased with the spotlight in which she stood. Her words were as smooth as silk yet deadly as a viper's strike.

"As all of you know, the country has been besieged for far too long with the condescending intolerance and bigotry of entrenched religious zealots. These are divisive ills that my agency has worked tirelessly to weed out and eradicate. Sadly, such intolerance is nowhere better represented than by the events in Center Springs.

"I assure you that such religious bigotry will not be tolerated by this administration any longer. Today I am announcing a new executive order that was just signed by the President. Henceforth it will be a criminal offense to meet in the name of any religion that does not accept and promote the universal equality of all beliefs. We can no longer accept the biases of those who say that only their way is right.

"As we speak, a team of UEA agents is converging on the faction in Center Springs and its satellite groups throughout the country. Today their leaders are being arrested and will be held accountable for their divisive rhetoric.

"In addition, any church, synagogue, or religious group that does not adhere to these guidelines will be treated similarly. The time has come for us to close ranks as like-minded citizens and end outdated prejudices. There is no room in our enlightened society for their narrow-minded beliefs."

As we watched a roomful of hands go up with questions, the scene began to dissolve.

We found ourselves standing in the north field looking over a sorry sight. The large tent had been toppled and shredded — its ropes cut. Chairs lay strewn over the field, along with scattered possessions — shoes, jackets, and Bibles everywhere. Evidence of bloodstains could be plainly seen, some still glistening wet in the afternoon sun.

MARIA'S READING was interrupted by her kitchen phone. She left the table to answer it, letting the journal fall closed.

"Hi, Mrs. Moretti. It's Anna. I was wondering if I could get a ride to the service tonight... are you and Jimmy going?"

Maria paused uncertainly for a moment and glanced back at the journal lying on the table. She was distracted by her thoughts.

"I...I think so..." she began, then collected herself. "Yes, of course, we'll be going... Jimmy is asleep right now... he's due to get up soon. We can pick you up."

She checked the clock on her microwave, surprised to see how late it was.

"Oh! ...it's later than I thought. We should be leaving in an hour if that's okay?"

When Maria hung up the phone, she struggled with the urge to pick up the journal and continue reading but realized she had dinner to prepare. She decided to let Jimmy sleep a little longer while she got it started.

She couldn't stop thinking about all she had just read. It didn't make sense to her... why was Jimmy targeted by the gunman? Would God heal her the way He healed Jimmy? She wondered to herself as she nervously considered the scene.

She glanced back at the journal on the kitchen table, questioning whether it was really prophetic at all.

Words from the last entry ran through her mind as she pondered the question... *Athaliah, the President's wife, was addressing a large audience...*

Athaliah. The name didn't ring a bell, but Maria remembered what Jimmy said about the President who would be inaugurated. He was going to revoke nonprofit status for churches and require them to report their membership lists to the government. The same promise that Senator Sheen has been making!

She dropped her potholder on the counter and switched on her laptop, waiting impatiently for it to boot. As soon as she could open a browser, she typed a search for the Senator's name, surprised to see an article about his recent marriage. Her heart was pounding as she scanned the feature, and then it skipped several beats when she found what she was searching for. The Senator's new wife was raised in Beirut. Her name jumped off the screen and became a chill that ran through Maria's spirit...

...ATHALIAH.

⌘

9

UNSPEAKABLE GIFT

Blessed are they that mourn: ...they shall be comforted.
~ Matthew 5:4

The thunderbolt's rumbling echo was still ringing in my ears as I caught her in my arms. The look on mom's face reflected what I was already dreading. She was gasping and looked up at me with a surrendered expression — as if she expected this. She touched my face, trying to form words that wouldn't come as she searched my eyes. The hint of a smile curled the edges of her mouth, and I saw a tear roll from the corner of her eye. I watched her eyes dim, and then her head dropped backward as I felt her touch slide away from my face.

Black clouds above us were quickly dissipating; a brilliant sunbeam broke through — lighting mom's face as I felt her body go limp in my arms.

Someone behind me was screaming a plea to call an ambulance. I looked up to see Anna collapsed to her knees in front of us... she was sobbing. Pastor Juan and the others gathered around and began to pray; it was the natural thing to do, but I knew she was gone... mom was already gone.

"I saw her jump in front of him — she blocked the shot! The shooter was aiming at that boy!"

The words hit me like a second gunshot. The realization that mom shielded me explained her unsurprised expression but also amplified my pain tenfold. I held her in my arms and began to rock as the tears and panic that had been welling up inside suddenly burst loose—my cheek pressed against hers as I felt my body shake with sobs.

Within moments an ad hoc team of trained emergency responders from the audience gently laid her down and began working on her limp body. It soon became apparent that their efforts were not helping, but they kept on nonetheless.

PJ pulled me away from the hopeless scene and helped me to my feet. I found that my legs could barely support my weight; Pete helped him as I started to sink again, and the two of them sat me in a chair on the platform. Everything around us seemed to be happening in a dizzying blur. It was like they were sounds and images from a TV that had been left on in a crowded room.

That's when I noticed that my shirt and pants were drenched — it took me a few moments to realize that it was blood. An ambulance had arrived, and one of the EMTs was speaking to me through the fog, asking if I was hurt. I felt my head shaking in reply as the words refused to come. I should be hurt, but I'm not... it should have been me...

I saw them lift her. A sheet had been pulled up over her head as they carried her off. Too numb to speak, I couldn't stop staring. I watched them carry her until the scene was obscured, washed away behind a flood of fresh tears.

How did I not see this coming? Why didn't Chozeq warn me... or Amos? What good are all these travels if I couldn't even see this... I couldn't even save her! The thought was not an indictment — I realized that I wasn't angry at God the way I was at first when Kelly died. This time I just honestly wanted to know. What could God possibly accomplish through such a needless tragedy? Why was He doing this again *to me?*

I felt a gentle rebuke in my spirit that pushed me back from that debilitating train of thought.

With a slowly returning awareness of my surroundings, I looked around to notice that the crowds were thinning — people were leaving.

MY ATTENTION WAS SUDDENLY DRAWN to the sight of Uncle Mike rushing toward me. He had a frantic look on his face and was out of breath from running. When he reached me, his eyes widened at the sight of my blood-soaked clothes. I could see the fear in his eyes turn quickly to uncontrollable anguish as he collapsed to his knees.

"OH, GOD! Oh, God! It's true...! No... no... no...."

Burying his face in his hands, he broke down in sobs. His cries were so mournful that they broke me — everything within me wept except my eyes. My tears had already been cried dry. All I could find the strength to do was lean forward and hug my knees as my head hung down. Through my numbed senses, the only feelings I could recognize clearly were guilt and remorse. Uncle Mike's grief reinforced the scope of the tragedy. I was stabbed by the realization that mom would be alive if she hadn't saved me — I can't help feeling a massive weight of responsibility for mom's death.

Uncle Mike grew quiet as he got a hold of himself. I felt his hand on my shoulder, and then he hugged my head against his. His words were almost a whisper.

"Oh Jimmy... man, I'm so sorry! She wanted me ta be here — I shoulda been here...."

I lifted my face and looked at him, aggressively shaking my head.

"I-it was my fault!"

As soon as the words left my mouth, my tears began to flow again uncontrollably, and I struggled to speak through my wrenching remorse.

"H-He was shooting at me... sh-she blocked it... I'm the one...."

"Oh god, Jimmy — it wasn't your fault... you can't blame yourself!" he objected. "Your mom loved you so much... more than anything!"

My head was still shaking as I interrupted him — the words poured from deep inside me, unfiltered...

"I know now how you felt...when gramps died... I know you blamed yourself — she told me... she said it wasn't your fault. But, I know it hurt you... Oh God, I feel like that — it hurts! It hurts so bad!"

There was a stunned silence as my words seemed to hit Uncle Mike with the force of a tidal wave. I watched him squeeze his eyes closed as if they were being wrung with tears. After a long pause, he spoke again in a quiet voice, looking at me sadly with wet eyes:

"You're right, Jim... you're right about that. It hurts really bad.

"But don't make the mistake I made... don't blame yourself. It was her choice... her love. Remember that — it was a gift... the greatest gift she could give — it was because she loved you."

I struggled to be strong and bear up under the pain but couldn't help dropping my head into my hands as the grief overwhelmed me. Uncle Mike grabbed me in a hug and held tight as I drenched his shoulder with tears.

It was a few minutes before I was able to pull myself together. I glanced at him uncomfortably as I wiped the tears out of my eyes. We shared a silent exchange as we searched each other's eyes for just a moment — it was a kindred bond that conveyed a set of shared feelings so deep neither of us could express them in words.

UNCLE MIKE WAS JUST TAKING a seat next to me as he was approached by a plainclothes officer; her police badge was clipped to her belt.

"Excuse me... Mr. Farro?"

He nodded yes.

She looked at me sitting beside him and leaned closer to whisper something in his ear.

"Does it have to be right now?" he carefully asked her.

"I'm afraid so, sir. It shouldn't take long."

Uncle Mike looked at me apologetically.

"The Coroner's office needs me ta help with some papers. I guess it can't wait. Will you be okay?"

I nodded that I'd be fine. His mention of the coroner's office had left a lump in my throat too large for me to speak.

As they walked away, I began to survey my surroundings, still feeling more than a little dazed. The late-day was nearing sundown, and I could see that most of the seats had emptied. PJ and Pete were praying with Anna, seated across the platform; she was still crying.

The police were using yellow tape to block off the area surrounding where I was sitting, and I happened to notice that they were marking off a spot out in the field too. It finally dawned on me that that must have been where the shooter stood.

SHERIFF FLANAGAN DROPPED to one knee in front of me, putting his hand on my shoulder. I hadn't even noticed him coming... my mind seemed to only be processing one image at a time.

"I'm sorry, Jimmy, I truly am."

His voice was sincere, and the crestfallen look on his face conveyed his sorrow even better than his words did. I noticed a small tear escaping from the outside corner of one eye.

"Maria was a dear friend... everybody around here loved her."

He paused uncomfortably, then looked me in the eye.

"I need to ask you a few questions about what happened... is that alright?"

I nodded... Okay.

"Do you remember seeing or hearing anything? Anything unusual?"

The memory of Amos' visit immediately flashed to mind, but I quickly pushed it aside.

"N-not much. I heard the shot... like a popping sound, and then the thunderclap right after that. I was still trying to make sense of all that when I felt her falling. I caught her...." My voice trailed off as the memory overwhelmed me once again.

Sheriff Flanagan waited silently for a minute, then cleared his throat. His voice was quiet as he continued...

"This is the second shooting here this week... both shooters were targeting you. Any idea why someone would want to kill you?"

His question hit me like another blow, but it didn't inspire fear. It was the same question that I'd been struggling with myself.

"No, none." I stared out into the field at the place where the shooter stood. "Did they catch him?"

His eyes followed mine, and he shrugged. "Wasn't much of him to find. That lightning blast didn't leave much."

"Lightning blast? You mean it hit him?"

"Guess you didn't know... we have a few dozen witnesses who say it was a direct hit to the top of his head. It left his shoes and a few scraps of clothing, along with the pieces of his shattered rifle. I sure haven't seen anything like it. Those clouds came out of nowhere — then faded as quickly as they came."

His description had just driven home the fact that God knew exactly what He was doing. He could have stopped the man before mom was hit; instead, He waited until she was shot and then made sure that no one else was hurt. A piece of the puzzle seemed to surface in my mind, and I looked back at the Sheriff — maybe it was an obvious thought.

"They aren't targeting me. I mean... they're not just trying to kill me — they want to kill what's happening here."

"Who does?"

"I don't know... that's the part I can't figure out yet. But I can definitely say this... it's not just people. You're probably gonna think I'm crazy, but... what I mean is... the power that's trying to stop this is not human."

"Actually, I don't think that's crazy. I agree with you."

The Sheriff's answer surprised me. He continued to explain....

"I saw what happened the other night with the first shooter — whatever came out of him was definitely not human. There's also the fact that I saw you take a point-blank shot in the chest, and yet you're sitting here right now in one piece." He looked out again at the field as he went on: "That's not even to mention today's lightning bolt out of a clear blue sky that disintegrated a man." He looked back at me: "A person would have to be blind not to see it."

He shifted his position, grabbing a chair next to me and leaning forward as he continued.

"The trouble is... whatever it is, it's an unprecedented risk to the public safety. If it can't be stopped, then I'm afraid we can't allow these meetings to continue — it's just too dangerous."

"NO! You can't stop the meetings — not now! Not after all that's happened... a-all that's been sacrificed. Look at all the good things that are happening — all the people being healed! The people who've been...."

"Saved," he said, finishing my sentence. "I know. It's truly God's work — it's been amazing and incredible!"

A surprised look in my eyes spurred him to explain.

"I'm a Christian — hope that's not too much of a surprise. I gave my heart to Christ when I was in High School. You Pentecostals may not realize it, but Methodists are Christians too." He smiled at his own joke and then shifted in his chair as his face grew serious again, uncomfortable with the message he was compelled to deliver.

"I know how important this is... to you especially, but there are too many lives at stake. I'm really sorry, Jim... I truly am. Maybe it's just for a day or two... just until we sort out what's going on."

"WE UNDERSTAND."

I was surprised by the sound of Pastor Wilkes' voice directly behind me. Turning, I saw that Anna, Pete, and PJ were with him; Anna's eyes were red and swollen from crying.

"We'll cooperate fully with whatever you deem best. The safety of everyone here is our number one concern."

"I appreciate that, Pastor," Sheriff Flanagan answered with a hand on the visor of his cap. "We'll try to make it as short as possible... just until we can do a proper investigation and arrange for better security."

He scanned both Pastors' exhausted faces and disheveled appearance. "I imagine you both could use a break — I don't suppose you've had a full night's sleep in days."

"Yeah, I guess it's probably getting obvious, isn't it," the Pastor admitted. "I've barely noticed the time, to be honest.

PJ looked down at me with a somber expression and grabbed my shoulder. "Jim, I know this work is important to you — you've done more than anyone."

Everyone considered the unspoken ending to his comment... you've *given* more than anyone. PJ cleared his throat as he pushed the thought aside.

I could barely find the strength to lift my head. I didn't know what to think anymore. Why was this happening? If God was the one in control, how could the enemy shut down His work in this way?

My thoughts returned again to mom, and tears began to well up in my eyes. There was no fight within me — I was too drained. I just dropped my head into the arms folded at my knees and quietly let the tears flow.

Sheriff Flanagan placed a hand on my shoulder in sympathy. I heard PJ's voice as he began to pray, and other hands join theirs. In moments we were surrounded by many others who were joining them for the impromptu prayer meeting. As PJ's prayer ended, it was replaced by a cacophony of pleas to God on my behalf. They stirred my numbed soul as I gradually felt a new sense of God's presence, drawing nearer. Profoundly personal and comforting.

Suddenly, it was Anna's words that sent chills down my spine as her voice lifted above the others.

> "Thus says the high and lofty One who inhabits eternity, whose name is Holy: I dwell in the high and holy place, and am with him that is of a contrite and humble spirit, to revive the spirit of the humble, and to revive the heart of the contrite. I have seen his ways and will heal him. I will lead him also and restore comforts to him and to his mourners. Peace, peace, to him that is far off, and to him that is near, says Jehovah. Him will I heal[1]."

A stiff wind blew across the field as she finished, making me shudder. As soon as it ebbed, I was filled with the most incredible feeling of deep peace I've ever known. The oppressive sorrow seemed to fall from my shoulders, making me feel suddenly weightless.

ALL AT ONCE, I'm aware that I'm outside the tent, high in the air. Chozeq's strong hand is firmly pressed against my back. He nods at me in a signal that we are leaving here, and I watch the scene dissolve in a whirlwind of blinding light.

As it clears again, I recognize the place where I'm standing... I haven't been able to get it out of my mind since the last time I was here — it's the most glorious sight I've ever beheld. Its colors and warm breeze fill my senses as I look out over the breathtaking scene of pristine woodlands and crystal streams.

I turn quickly, anticipating what awaits us, and find mom and dad standing arm in arm with my sister Daisy. The look on mom's face is rapturous as she looks at both of them and then back at me. I can't hold back the tears as I watch them run to me and feel myself being engulfed in their group embrace. Mom touches my face as it ends, replacing the memory of her last touch with one so joyful that it makes my heart dance.

I look up to see Kelly standing beside us with an expression that absolutely glows with unbridled joy. We hug briefly, and I study her face — her eyes convey such deep wisdom that I'm quickly lost in them. I don't have to say a word; she just smiles and answers my unspoken question.

"It's begun... it won't be long now. Your work is going to bring life to countless souls. What you do will be the hope of the last generation — their final hope."

"We're proud of you, son — and you know the Lord is well pleased." Dad gives me another hug as I turn to acknowledge his words. Then mom hugs me as well. I look back at her — so glorious in her heavenly form, and I can't help feeling a renewed sense of gratitude for what she did for me in her final selfless act.

"Mom... You saved me... how can I ever...?"

She stops my words with a touch to my lips and simply smiles with a look so tender that it melts my struggle.

"You saved me first," she reminds me with a smile.

Mom's familiar kiss against my forehead is the last thing I feel as the heavenly scene dissolves in another brilliant flash of light.

⌘

10

THE EVIL TO COME

The righteous perish... consider that the righteous are taken away from the evil to come.
~ Isaiah 57:1

The crowd around us was slowly clearing as I turned to search for Anna.

"THANKS FOR THAT WORD. It touched me... more than you know."

"Me too," she admitted, sounding awestruck herself. "It's amazing how much God can change us with just a touch."

I could see that her crying had ended, and there was a peaceful look in her eyes.

"Anna, I know my mom is in Glory... there's no doubt in my mind. I don't know why God allowed this to happen, but I know she's in a better place... she's with dad... and in God's presence now."

Anna searched my eyes and nodded. I could sense that she recognized a deep change within me. She offered both her hands for me to hold. A concerned look was etched on her face as she carefully spoke.

"You're all alone now... what are you going to do?"

It was a sobering thought. I'd been aware of that fact, of course, but until now, I'd only dealt with the emotional impact. Now I was suddenly facing the practical implications. Mom had been entirely open about our financial condition. She was barely scraping by on her meager salary, even with my contribution from working at the Sub shop. Letters from the bank about late mortgage payments had been a regular occurrence. Whatever we had from dad's life insurance had been exhausted long ago, and she had no insurance of her own.

"I... well... I guess I'll need to get a better job. I could probably stay with Uncle Mike a while if I need to."

"You can stay at our house if you need to — I'm sure mom won't mind."

I thought about how close our two moms had become in the past few months. Mrs. Mirabella was likely to take the news about mom pretty hard — having me there would just make it harder. Besides, as a widow herself, I suspected that she was probably struggling as much as we were.

"Thanks... I really appreciate the offer... really. But I wouldn't want to be a burden."

Anna pouted as she listened — I couldn't help being struck with how beautiful she was, and I suddenly felt myself blushing. She picked up on my discomfort and offered a lifeline:

"I guess, come to think of it, we do have a pretty small house. You'd have to sleep on the couch."

WHILE I WAS NODDING BACK at her with a smile, there was a touch on my shoulder, and I turned to see Mr. V. looking me in the eye with a tear-streaked face.

"I'm sorry, son... I truly am."

The look on his face reflected a complex mix of swirling memories and emotions... I recognized most of them as they rushed through my own heart as well. His lower lip was quivering as he fought back the tears. It dawned on me that the inability to hold back his tears was what had kept him from coming over to me before now.

I acknowledged his sentiment with a hug while breathing a prayer for God to comfort him. As old as he may be physically, he was just a new child spiritually — a newly redeemed son of the kingdom! The tenderness in his heart was spirit-born and obviously was an unfamiliar experience for him. After stepping back and rubbing a few new tears away with his sleeve, he cleared his throat.

"Heard y' talkin'... I'd be more than happy to have y' stay with me at the farmhouse if y' need to. Got plenty o' spare rooms — just might need dustin' off, is all. Could use the help, as a matter o' fact."

His offer stirred me with a complex rush of thoughts of my own. I was reminded that the farm was great-grandpa's boyhood home, glancing at his old ring on my finger. The fact that dad worked there too added to the connection, not to mention my visits with Amos in the distant past. It occurred to me that the old farmhouse bore more of a link to my past than anywhere else. I suddenly found myself choked up and unable to answer.

"I'll take that as a yes," Mr. V. said with an accepting smile as he offered his arms for a hug.

WASHINGTON DC ~ That same evening...

BAHAL EBAZEJ IS COMFORTABLY SEATED beside a gas-burning firepit on the luxurious private terrace of his Royal Suite, atop the Four Seasons Hotel. He draws his unlit cigar from a crystal snifter, where the clipped end has been soaking in his favorite Frapin Cuvee 1888 Cognac. The same rare vintage won a gold medal at that year's Paris World's Fair. The cigar is his private brand. He holds it beneath his nose, drawing in the fragrance of its rich bouquet, sweetened by the infused cognac. Then gently warms its tip with the open flame of his lighter — careful not to scorch its perfectly aged leaves. Sitting back, he takes a long draw and breathes out the cloud of cigar smoke with a contented sigh.

Bahal is a distinguished-looking man. Life has been kind to him, for the most part. Though well into his sixties, he is fit and still sports a thick head of hair — now peppered with gray. Kindness, however, would not be used to otherwise describe him. A fact that is borne out by the presence of his elite armed security team and the suite's array of security cameras and bullet-proof windows. He waves to the guards standing nearby, commanding them abruptly to leave him; he has an important call to make.

Lifting his mobile phone, he taps the number, waits for it to speed dial, and then holds it to his ear.

"Hello, Devlon. How are you treating my beautiful daughter, Athaliah?"

"Bahal... what a pleasure," Devlon answers, not needing to fake his fondness for his new father-in-law. After all, what's not to like? His marriage to Athaliah has made him an heir to one of the world's great fortunes, not to mention providing access to a global society of powerful elites.

"If you're looking for Thali, she isn't here right now. She flew to Tyre this morning to visit with her brother — I wasn't able to get away from the Senate, unfortunately."

"Yes, I know," Bahal answers mysteriously. "It is you with whom I wish to speak."

Devlon swallows and covers the phone while he clears his throat, feeling unexpectedly nervous all of a sudden. He quickly collects himself, smiling into the phone.

"Certainly, what is it that I can help you with?"

"You have it backward, my son! It is I who want to help you; with your presidential campaign, in particular. How does one-hundred-million sound, for starters?"

There is a silent pause as Devlon processes his father-in-law's offer.

"That's incredibly generous! But, unfortunately, the laws are strict here against foreign political contributions."

"Who said anything about a political contribution? It is a gift to my daughter and her new husband — what you do with your own money is none of my affairs."

Devlon smiles as he considers what he is hearing; the image that comes to mind of the large sum filling his bank account gives him a thrill. "I don't know what to say... Thank you! Thali will be elated!"

"We needn't tell Athaliah of this. I wish it to be put to use... as you see fit — she would have it spent on god knows what."

"I'm honored, of course. I'm not sure it's wise to keep it from her, though... you know how she gets."

"I do see your point, of course," Bahal concedes. "Naturally, the fewer who know of it, the better... the laws you mentioned could, indeed, present complications. Nonetheless, if you feel you must tell her, then that is your choice. I trust that word of it will not spread further."

"Of course, as you wish. What can I do to show my appreciation? You must join us for dinner the next time you're in Washington!"

Bahal looks from his terrace at the Washington cityscape, seeing the lighted Washington monument in the distance. "When I'm in Washington... Yes, of course... I would be delighted. I'll have my secretary contact your office tomorrow to compare itineraries. I'm sure your work keeps you rather busy, as does mine."

"Of course. I understand. Thank you again, Sir."

"If you are going to be the father of my grandchildren, you must stop addressing me so formally. Call me Bahal, please."

"All right... Bahal..., thank you."

The older man nods into his phone and quietly clears his throat, preparing to change the subject.

"There is one other thing. I hate to impose upon you, but it is a matter that is most concerning — I would greatly appreciate whatever you could learn of it. An associate of mine was killed this afternoon. It was in a small town — called Center Springs, I believe. The circumstances surrounding his death are quite suspect."

"Certainly; I'll look into it at once."

"Thank you, my son. Goodbye."

MIDNIGHT ~THE MEDITERRANEAN SEA...

ATHALIAH IS SEATED at the rear of one of her father's yachts, approaching the moonlit coast of ancient Tyre in southern Lebanon. It is a quiet and peaceful night on the Mediterranean, with a warm breeze and a clear star-filled sky. She listens approvingly to the sound of distant music that is echoing from the ancient temple ruins. It carries over the water with a frantic beat — but despite its pulsating rhythm, its ethereal sound is bleak and darkly romantic... carrying an undertone of ominous sorrow.

Boarding a smaller skiff with her entourage, they speed toward the shallows. She smiles at the sight of the frenzied mob gathered in the distance; the sound of their music is pounding more loudly as the skiff draws nearer. Its pulsating rhythm and dazed, gyrating crowds might be mistaken for some sort of Gothic Rock concert — but these are not concert-goers. Their painted faces and barely clinging robes mark a more ancient purpose.

Her skiff is pulled onto the beach, and she is helped ashore, along with the others who are with her. All of them, like her, are young women in their twenties. A troop of attendants rush to meet them, helping them into ceremonial robes — the ancient dress of temple priestesses. They are quickly assembled for their entrance, with Athaliah positioned last of all. Her robe is more dazzling than the rest — she wears the horned headdress of the high priestess of Anath... the ancient Canaan goddess of love and war... sister to the god Baal.

The pounding music stops suddenly, plunging the temple ruins into total silence. All eyes turn toward the raised stone platform, and curtained columns at one end of the temple remains, as the eerie and seductive sound of *mijwiz...* ancient double-piped clarinets ...begin to fill the air. They are soon joined by the tambourine sounds of the *daff* being played by the priestesses as they dance their way onto the stage. The cheers and lustful calls of the crowd begin to rise like an aroused beast as they anticipate the arrival of the High Priestess — exploding suddenly into a deafening roar. Athaliah dances triumphantly onto the stage, turning this way and that with the fluid movements of an ancient dance... resembling the *Raqs sharqi...* that has been danced by the temple's priestesses for thousands of years. Like an ancient ballet, she kicks and spins, doing backbends and head tosses, and then slowly lowers the ritual implements that she holds in her hands, presenting them for the approval of her cheering worshipers.

In one hand, she holds a ceremonial dagger, and in the other is a golden cup. The frantically beating music begins once again, with its overpowering rhythm — dark and ominous. One of the priestesses lifts a young piglet and dangles the squealing creature by its hind legs as she holds it above an ancient stone altar. Athaliah bows, kissing the altar and then the dagger, before using it to slaughter the young swine — catching its blood in her golden cup.

When it has been filled to the brim, she holds the cup in both hands, presenting it to the savage throng who roar their approval in bloodthirsty revelry. Then she turns toward a shrouded object at the center of the stage and bows to it. The shroud is immediately thrown upward, flying into the air to reveal a white marble statue of the goddess Anath. With the cup held high above her head, Athaliah presents it as an offering.

The music stops once again, and Athaliah's voice is heard over the loudspeakers.

"Oh great and glorious Anath of the Phoenicians... goddess of love and life, and of war and death... accept our offering — this life poured out as an expression of our devotion. Grant to us your earthly pleasures and spill the blood of our enemies, just as this offering is spilled."

She pours out the cup into the statue's cupped hands, where it overflows down its white arms and drips onto the stone floor. Then she turns toward the throng and spreads her arms wide in a gesture that invites them to abandon all inhibitions and indulge their basest cravings.

The music immediately blasts forth with a beat even more furious than before, as the crowd erupts in a wild frenzy, descending into every kind of shameful, sensuous act.

Athaliah leaves the stage, accepting the embrace of a familiar man, bearded and shirtless, who offers her a flask of wine. She quickly swallows it all and smiles back at him.

"You are a senator's wife now," her brother reminds her sarcastically as he holds her in his arms. "Shouldn't you be more respectable?"

She smirks in reply.

"Americans are no less devoted to pleasure than this — with their lewd venues, human trafficking, and addictions. They worship the sun and earth as much as any of our devoted followers before them, ... even more so. The ancients sacrificed mere thousands of their babies to lord Baal, while Americans have slain sixty-million of theirs, naively calling it *choice*. Indeed, they pursue their pleasures endlessly — they merely lack an understanding of the origin of those pursuits."

Athaliah's eyes suddenly change, transforming into the eyes of a large predatory cat, bright yellow. Her voice grows deep and thunderous as she licks a splatter of blood from the back of her hand.

"It will soon be time for Americans to meet the gods they have been worshiping."

Her brother's eyes change as well, turning fiery red as he nods in approval. The pendant of Moloch that hangs from his neck begins to glow brightly as he breathes in the evil lust that seethes in the revelry around them. The two of them glance back at Anath's statue, dripping with blood, and break into a perverse peal of evil laughter.

⌘

11

UNWANTED ATTENTION

Without a word, he lifted it to his eye and aimed it at the kneeling boy, then fired.
~ Amos' Journal, April 19, 1870

"Thanks for staying here tonight."

UNCLE MIKE NODDED to me in acknowledgment. "No sweat, kid."

Until we got to the house, I hadn't realized how hard it would be to be home without her. Even though I knew she was in a much better place, I couldn't help missing her. Reminders of her absence seemed to echo from every corner. Her empty chair at the table... her favorite Afghan lying on the couch... the unwashed dishes in the sink from dinner.

Uncle Mike brought me down a change of clothes. I couldn't bring myself to go upstairs to my room; more honestly, I wasn't ready to go near *her* room. At least not yet… not tonight. Uncle Mike understood — he seemed to know exactly what I was going through and did his best to keep my mind off those thoughts.

"What's that book?" he asked with genuine curiosity.

I debated with myself whether to tell him, finally deciding that there was no reason not to. Amos said the journal was for our time — Uncle Mike was as much a part of it as anyone.

"It's a journal that was written about 150 years ago, by Amos Van Clief… Mr. V.'s grandfather. He wrote things that are going to happen in the future."

"Yeah, right," he said dismissively. "Did old man Van Clief give it to you?"

I was a little embarrassed at his question. "Well, no. He doesn't actually know about it… yet. I meant to tell him tonight, but…." I glanced down at my stained clothes, suddenly losing my voice; I stopped without finishing my sentence.

There was an awkward pause. I could tell that all the events of the last few hours were running through both our minds in a heart-wrenching blur. Uncle Mike broke the silence, clearing his throat uncomfortably.

"Where'd ya get it? What makes ya think it's about d' future?"

"Amos wrote it in the 1800s — he fought in the Civil War. But he writes about seeing things he couldn't have imagined back then, like cars and helicopters."

Looking at Uncle Mike's skeptical face, I realized that trying to convince him myself wasn't going to work. I offered him the journal instead.

"Here… read it for yourself."

Under normal circumstances, I imagine that he would have dismissed the offer out of hand, but he clearly didn't want to hurt my feelings. From the sadness written on his face, I could see that he had been just as shattered by mom's passing as I was. But aside from that, there was also another look in his eyes — a searching look. He accepted the book and waved it back at me as if conceding a point.

"Alright… okay, fine."

With a surprising amount of interest, he settled into the recliner and kicked up the footrest, switching on the lamp beside him, then cracked the book open and immediately began to read.

"I'm gonna get washed up," I said, leaving him to his reading.

"Uh-huh..." he answered without hearing, already engrossed in the journal's first entry.

STANDING at the small bathroom sink triggered a flashback of this afternoon's visit to Amos. That memory led to a flurry of others, and soon the entire evening was rushing through my mind like a recording on fast-forward. It ended with a vivid memory of Mom and Dad with Daisy and mom's last kiss on my forehead. I realized there were tears on my face as my eyes refocused on the mirror's reflection.

Shaking myself, it took me a minute to push ahead with brushing my teeth and showering, getting ready for bed. I was in a half-exhausted daze as I grabbed a few blankets from the hall linen closet and tossed one of them to Uncle Mike before settling onto the couch. He grunted a faint thank you, still engrossed in his reading.

Figuring that it was best to give him space, I turned on the TV, leaving the volume turned down, and settled into the couch, pulling the blanket up to my chin. Nothing on television seemed very interesting as I scanned the channels. It occurred to me that my own life lately made anything they could come up with in a TV studio seem blasé. Even if they did, who would ever believe it?

I was soon lost in thought again as my mind returned to the evening's events. The words that Kelly said to me sent a renewed chill down my back as I remembered them: *"It's begun...."* The phrase reverberated within me like the sound of distant thunder. The rest of her words struck me with powerful intensity:

"...What you do will be the hope of the last generation — their final hope."

How can that be true? I thought to myself. What could I ever do that would make that much of a difference for a whole generation... for the entire world?

"HEY, JIMMY — ARE YOU SEEIN' this?"

Uncle Mike's voice snapped me out of my thoughts.

"Wha...? Huh?" I half-grunted as I turned my eyes to look at him. He was pointing at the TV.

When I followed his gaze, the scene on the screen was confusing and chaotic. Images showed people screaming and running — the picture was a blur as the camera was pulled haphazardly to the ground and then raised above the heads of the ducking crowds. It was still being refocused as a blinding flash obscured everything. I managed to increase the volume in time to hear the familiar sound of a thunderclap as it shook the scene. Fiery remains of the massive lightning strike flashed brightly as the blast's shock wave sent people tumbling away in all directions.

As the reporter explained the scene, a still-image suddenly filled the screen that took my breath away. Uncle Mike froze in place and looked at me, stunned to silence. It was a picture of me... holding mom.

It showed her hand held against my face as she looked into my eyes; the photographer had captured both of our facial expressions in clear detail — mine a look of stunned sorrow, while the corners of her mouth were curled upward in a tender smile. The feelings of that moment washed over me, reminding me of every complex emotion.

Five or six more photos slid forward in quick succession, showing mom's hand dropping and my expression changing to sobs.

I felt stunned as I stared at the TV.

The reporter from our local station was fighting back tears as she described the scene. I recognized her as Caden Koller, the same reporter whose tearful conversion was captured on live TV just a few nights ago. Her wounded warrior husband was miraculously healed on the same night that I was shot. I tuned in to what she was saying....

"...Very little is known about the shooter. Incredibly, he was hit by a lightning strike after getting off only one shot. Experts are studying this unusual meteorological event, which is unprecedented on many levels, not the least of which is the fact that the sky had been cloudless just moments before.

"Authorities have released the name of the slain woman as Maria Moretti. Her son, James (Jimmy) Moretti, was the target of a murder attempt here just a few nights ago. Some witnesses are claiming that Jimmy was the intended victim in today's shooting as well; the sheriff's department has declined to comment on that claim, citing their ongoing investigation."

The TV switched off, and I realized that Uncle Mike was standing beside me, holding the remote. His face was as white as a sheet, with an expression that looked as if something had just blown his mind. He was holding the journal with his finger marking the passage he was just reading — his hand was shaking slightly.

"How much o' this have ya read?" he asked me.

I looked at the journal, then back at him…

"…Just a couple of the entries… I haven't gotten very far. Why?"

He handed me the book, open to the entry for *April 19, 1870.*

"Mom and I were reading this one this afternoon," I said, recognizing the entry. "But I only got halfway through… I was pretty wiped out; I needed to lay down."

"Ya better read it." He pointed to the place he wanted me to read and waited as I scanned what it said…

...As I watched, he stopped among the crowds and reached into the sack that was slung over his shoulder, drawing out a rifle. Without a word, he lifted it to his eye and aimed it at the kneeling boy, then fired.

His shot hit a woman who had been moving near the altar, striking her in the back, and I saw her thrown forward by the force of it.

Before the shooter could get off a second shot, the thick black clouds above us lit with a mighty flash, piercing the sky with the most terrific blast of lightning I ever saw...

I looked up at Uncle Mike with the same feeling of crashing realization that I could tell had swept over him. For him, it was an undeniable confirmation that the journal really *is* what it's claimed to be.

For me, it was the fact that a host of events have suddenly become clear — from mom's sullen mood over dinner to Amos' sudden appearance at the tent just an instant before the shooting.

Uncle Mike dropped into the chair next to me with a dazed expression.

"I-I can't believe this is really happenin'," he confessed as he rubbed his head with one hand. "How could this guy Amos have known all that?"

He leaned forward suddenly as a thought struck him...

"...Maybe he planned it! Maybe he's the one behind the whole thing!"

"Seriously? How could he have planned that lightning strike?" I challenged. "Besides, it was written over a hundred years ago."

Uncle Mike's hands clenched into fists, and he shook them in frustration.

"Well, then if that's true, it means that God saw this coming — He's the one who planned it! How could He do that to her?"

Uncle Mike's frustration reminded me of how I felt when Kelly died; I knew exactly how he felt, remembering that the pain was almost unbearable.

"There's a difference between knowing what's coming and causing it," I reminded him. "God knew what would happen today, but He didn't plan for it to happen."

"Well, He allowed it then," Uncle Mike accused.

"That's fair... yes, He did," I conceded.

I'm sitting up now — the blankets have been tossed aside.

"Remember what you said today at the shop — about how Gramps said that a time was coming when God would show Himself to the world in a way that no one could deny? He said it would be with signs and wonders — unexplainable stuff, just like what's happening here; just like it happened back in the New Testament times."

Uncle Mike's voice was shaky as he added... "He said it would be a sign of the end times... right before Jesus comes back."

"Uncle Mike... This is bigger than just us. It's bigger than just Center Springs. This is a lot bigger!"

I pointed at the blank TV screen: "What's been started here can't be stopped… no matter how hard they try or who they send. This is about a harvest… about people being saved before it's too late — you know it's true!

"So, no matter what they do, this is gonna grow — what happened today is just gonna make it grow more! If God allowed what happened today, then that's the reason why!"

Uncle Mike hung his head and nodded in acceptance. There was a different look in his eye when he looked over at me — if I didn't know better, I'd almost call it admiration.

"You're somethin' kid… I'm supposed ta' be here helpin' you an' look at ya — straightenin' me out."

He sat quietly for a minute, and I could tell he was deep in thought. Finally, he looked at the journal in my hand.

"Mind if I read some more of that?"

We shared a glance as I handed it back to him, acknowledging his unspoken search.

THE LIVING ROOM clock was striking 3 AM as I was stirred from sleep. Uncle Mike was snoring in the recliner; the lit flashlight and the open book in his lap hinted that he had fallen asleep while reading. I carefully lifted the flashlight and switched it off, and then slid the journal from under his hands and placed it on the side table.

My growling stomach reminded me that I never finished dinner, spurring me to head toward the kitchen for something to eat. The previous day's events seemed like a dream in the quiet of the night — an awful dream. However, the memories became more undeniable as I opened the refrigerator to see my half-eaten dinner plate where mom had wrapped it up. Sitting beside it, I was stunned to see a cake with the words 'Welcome Home' — mom must have baked it for a surprise celebration.

It immediately triggered a memory of seeing mom reunited with dad and Daisy, giving the idea of a *homecoming celebration* a vastly different meaning. I had to shake off the chill running up between my shoulders as I quickly grabbed my dinner plate and closed the refrigerator.

I waited beside the microwave as it finished and carefully canceled the timer to keep it from beeping. There was no sense in waking Uncle Mike. I decided to slip out onto the back deck to eat; it was a warm July evening, and stars were shining brightly in the clear summer sky. The scene triggered a flood of memories... times with Kelly when we were kids and evenings sitting here on the porch with mom. Glancing at the yard reminded me that I hadn't been doing a very good job of keeping the grass cut. The O'Malleys' old house next door looked dark and lonely, seeming to echo Anna's words from earlier in the evening: *You're all alone now...*

Laying aside my empty plate, I found myself leaning back in the chair with my feet up — staring into the night sky as my mind drifted. An earnest prayer churned within me as thoughts of the afternoon's events swirled in a chaotic jumble... *"Where did the shooter come from — who is trying to stop Your work, Lord?"*

No sooner has the prayer crossed my lips than I suddenly find myself beside Chozeq on a city street. We are standing in front of a luxury building; its large brass nameplate reads **The Four Seasons Hotel**.

While we watch, a limousine pulls up, flanked in front and behind by black SUVs. Several tough-looking men step out wearing black suits and take positions around the entrance. They form a secure perimeter as one of them opens the limousine's passenger door, and a distinguished-looking man steps out.

He is impeccably dressed and appears exceptionally fit for a man his age, with thick hair peppered with gray. He carries himself with bold confidence — from the deference of those around him, he is clearly a powerful man. The look in his eyes is sharp and unmistakably cruel.

We follow them into the hotel's palatial lobby, where they are met by a nervous-looking well-dressed man flanked by a large cadre of the hotel staff.

"It is an honor to have you with us, Mr. Ebazej. I am Adojan Caspari, owner of The Four Seasons, at your service. Welcome," he offers a handshake as he bows his chin.

"Please call me Bahal, Mr. Caspari."

"You are most kind. You may call me Adojan if you please."

He snaps his fingers, and the line of hotel staff quickly moves into action, collecting the visiting party's luggage.

"The Royal Suite is at your disposal. All of the improvements you requested have been completed."

"I am delighted by your hospitality, Adojan."

A team from Bahal's security detail boards the Penthouse elevator, departing to secure the suite upstairs. When the empty elevator returns, two guards enter and examine it carefully, waiting inside for their boss to enter. Bahal is closely followed by two more guards as he steps in and the doors close.

WE'RE SUDDENLY STANDING on an open veranda on the hotel's top floor. The morning sun shines low in the eastern sky. The sight of the Washington Monument and other distinctive landmarks in the distance makes it clear that we're in Washington DC.

Bahal's voice behind me spurs me to turn, finding him nearby with a satellite phone to his ear. On the glass coffee table beside him is an open newspaper — the photo at the center of the page is already familiar. Bahal seems uncharacteristically charming as he speaks, obviously probing for information.

"Thank you, doctor. His remarkable recovery is unexpectedly good news. I'm very pleased to hear it. You say he checked out just moments ago? That's wonderful, certainly a testament to the competence and skill of your fine care facility. Thank you very much."

I watch as he hangs up the call, and the facade of charm quickly leaves his face, filling it instead with anger. He presses a speed dial button, and his call is answered immediately.

"The events in Center Springs are becoming troublesome. Be assured that I am not paying you to fail me!"

He appears annoyed as he impatiently listens to the reply, cutting it off in mid-sentence.

"I tire of these excuses. The Moretti boy has just been released from the hospital. The longer he remains, the greater the danger grows that he will pose a threat to our plan. I suggest that you take care of it quickly... put Corvo on it; he's the best we've got."

Bahal doesn't wait for a reply, hanging up the call and tossing the phone onto the couch. His face is set in a fierce-looking scowl as he turns on his heels to head inside.

———————

IN A FLASH, we're suddenly standing beside a bare metal table in a large room with concrete walls. The men seated all around are wearing orange jumpsuits with numbers on the back — it's a prison cafeteria. A pair of men come into focus; one is older, probably in his fifties, and the other is at least a decade younger. The older man is speaking in a low voice....

"Tell yer boy we got orders from upstairs. He don't need ta worry 'bout bein' caught — the client's got connections, ya know what I mean?"

"What's the job?" the younger inmate asks in a voice so gruff it sounds like he's been gargling nails.

"Get dis..." the first one says as he pulls out a folded newspaper page and opens it on the table, then pokes the picture with a thump. "It's a kid. Jus' take 'im out an' then shoot up the place — make it look random, ya know?"

"Where at?"

"Center Springs. Can't miss it... jus' tell 'im to look fer a big tent."

From the older man's words, it's not hard to guess whose picture he's pointing at. I'm more interested in the date on the newspaper, but a closer look only reveals that the date header has been cut off. Nonetheless, from all that we've just seen, it's pretty obvious what day it is.

Scanning the room, I notice a clock mounted high on the wall and note the time: 11:41 AM. Just about the time that I was first meeting Amos... at the tent.

"Why...?" I ask myself aloud, finishing the thought silently: *...Why me?*

To my surprise, the men suddenly turn and look in my direction. A familiar pain pierces my shoulder, and their eyes reveal the reason for their sudden attention. I see them morph into vertical slits and flash red as they flit back and forth like the eyes of a snake. Although they clearly sense my presence, they apparently can't see me. Their noses flare as if sniffing the air, and one of them waves his arm, searching the space where I'm standing — it passes right through me.

Both men quickly jump to their feet and step backward, and the glow of Chozeq's flaming sword can be seen reflecting in their eyes as they return a hateful glare. From the table behind me, I suddenly hear a familiar voice:

"What's 'a matter, boys? I've seen that look before... looks like you've seen an angel."

My head snaps around to see Chase looking at the men with a confident smile. He has had his hair cut, and his beard is neatly trimmed — he looks healthy and rested. PJ's Bible is open on the table in front of him. The men curse and wave at him with their arms, then walk away. Chase watches them leave, waiting for them to exit the door before turning his gaze in our direction and scanning the area. While unable to see us, I can see a look of gratitude in his eyes and watch as he breathes a thankful prayer. Looking down at his open Bible, he seems amused at what he sees, pointing at the words as he reads them aloud:

"...God, you make your angels winds, and your ministers a flame of fire."

He nods as if acknowledging Chozeq's presence and searches one more time with his eyes before returning to his reading. I can't help staring at him, amazed at his transformation since the day I saw him delivered from his own demonic bondage.

CHOZEQ PLACES his hand on my shoulder, and we instantly find ourselves in the prison visitors' area. The clock on the wall reads 2:00 PM as a visitor takes his seat at a window opposite one of the men from the cafeteria. Both of them grab the telephone handset on their side of the glass partition, lifting it to their ear. I can hear every word.

"Is the line clear?" the visitor asks cautiously.

"It ain't tapped, if that's what ya mean," Billy assures him, nodding toward the attending guard with a signal that he's an ally.

"Did ya get the envelope I gave the guards for ya?"

The visitor retrieves an unsealed business envelope from his pocket and opens it, pulling out the newspaper clipping.

"Check out the article," the inmate instructs in a gravelly voice. "You'll find him at those tent meetings that it describes... it gives the location there. The client wants a spectacle... but make sure ya take care o' the kid first. Ya ain't gotta worry about nothin' — our client, has... you know, connections."

"What's the purse?"

"Fifty G's. The account number is written inside the envelope — your usual password... after the job."

I turn to Chozeq with a mix of emotions welling up within me...

"He's the shooter...." I swallow, waiting for my racing heart to slow enough to speak again.

"...Who is he?"

Chozeq draws my attention to the printed paper label that serves as his Visitor's Pass: **Ed Corvo**.

The name burns indelibly into my mind.

⌘

CALM BEFORE A STORM

Bear one another's burdens, and so fulfill the law of Christ.
~ Galatians 6:2

A loud ringing stirred me from a deep sleep. It took a while for me to realize that it was the doorbell — its repeated rings sounded more like a runaway alarm clock. I had no idea what time it was, noting that sunlight brightly filled the living room, stinging my eyes. The chair where Uncle Mike slept was empty, and his blanket had been neatly folded and laid aside. I could see the journal sitting on the end table beside it, lying closed with a bookmark tucked inside, marking the book's midpoint. His suitcase was lying open in the middle of the floor, and it looked like several things had been removed, but Uncle Mike was nowhere to be seen. However, the faint sound of singing coming from the shower gave a pretty good clue to his whereabouts.

All of this processing had taken my groggy mind a full minute, during which the doorbell had not ceased its ringing. I finally kicked my way out of my tangled blanket and climbed to my feet, stretching with a wide yawn, then stumbled to the front door. Through the peephole, I was surprised to see Anna and her mom standing on the porch holding food containers. I ran my fingers through my unkempt hair self-consciously, then quickly checked the condition of my badly wrinkled pajamas before clumsily pulling the door open a crack.

"Hi!" Anna said with an apologetic smile as she saw me. "Hope we didn't wake you?"

"I... ah... sorry... I guess I overslept. What time is it?"

"We waited till eight o'clock but didn't want you to eat before we got here. We brought breakfast!"

"Oh... thank you," I said in surprise, finally remembering to pull the door open. "Sorry. Come on in... wow, breakfast... what a nice surprise."

Anna slid past me, giving my pajamas and unruly hair a once-over as she smiled warmly.

Mrs. Mirabella stopped and put her hand on the side of my face, giving me a sympathetic look.

"You poor dear... you look like you haven't slept a wink. Who could blame you? Such a terrible thing, just terrible."

I cleared my throat to shake off its sudden tightness before speaking... "Here, please let me help... we can put these in the kitchen."

WITHIN MOMENTS ANNA and her mom had started the oven and were busy preparing to reheat their trays of pancakes, bacon, scrambled eggs, and muffins. It looked as though they planned to feed a small army. The thought made me suddenly nervous — I rushed to the kitchen window and scanned the driveway.

"Is anyone else coming?"

"No, don't worry!" Anna reassured me. "We might have gotten a little carried away with all this," she acknowledged with an embarrassed nod toward the counter full of food.

"It looks delicious," I admitted honestly. Smells of bacon and warm muffins had begun to fill the room.

"I'm afraid it's cooled down a bit," Mrs. Mirabella confessed. "But a little reheating should help... just give it ten minutes or so."

I caught Anna smiling again at my pajamas and bare feet.

"Uhh… that's perfect — sounds like more than enough time for me to run and get changed. If you're okay here?"

"Oh yes, of course," Anna's mom readily agreed. "You run along… we can find our own way in the kitchen just fine."

As she was still speaking, Uncle Mike's voice bellowed from the next room…

"HEY JIMMY, are you cooking? That smells awesome…."

The sound of Mrs. Mirabella's sudden high-pitched "OHH!" was more like a yelp, causing Uncle Mike to stop abruptly and lower the towel that he was using to dry his hair. Both women were turning a rosy shade of crimson as he stood in the kitchen doorway in just his boxer shorts.

"Lena!" he echoed as he wrapped the towel around himself. "I-I didn't… I'm sorry… Better excuse me." He exited quickly and made a fast getaway.

Anna's mom was using the oven mitts to fan herself as she regained her composure. "I suppose we should have called before dropping in like this. I hope Mike will forgive me." She was blotting her cheeks and forehead nervously as she apologized.

"Are you kidding? Just put a plate in front of him, and he'll forget all about it," I joked, trying to reassure her.

I hadn't realized that Uncle Mike and Mrs. Mirabella were on a first-name basis. Anna shared a smile, hinting that we were each thinking the same thing — that both of their surprised reactions may have revealed more chemistry than regret between them.

AN HOUR LATER, our breakfast plates were empty, and we were seated around the table talking. Mrs. Mirabella and Uncle Mike were well past their embarrassed awkwardness and were smiling broadly as they shared stories. He was regaling her with childhood exploits while growing up in Brooklyn. She matched his stories with surprisingly entertaining adventures of her own from the small farm community where she was raised. Anna kept chiming in with: *"You never told me that!"* and *"I never heard about that before!"*

A KNOCK DREW OUR ATTENTION, and I turned to see Pete standing at the door — he was holding an enormous arrangement of flowers that partly obscured his face. As I opened the door, he stood silently looking at me for a moment, as if he was at a loss for words.

"Sorry doesn't seem like enough," he finally offered in a low voice.

He spread his arms wide, holding the giant arrangement in one hand as easily as if it were a single flower. I felt flowers engulf my head as he wrapped his arms around me in a hug. There was a small tear at the corner of one eye as he stepped back again.

"Mrs. M was kinda like a mother to me too, ya know?"

His comment was striking. When he was five, Pete lost his own mother and had a pretty rough home life; but I hadn't realized how much he had come to lean on mom for the stability that he never had himself. I nodded back at him sadly in acknowledgment.

"Come on in, we're having breakfast. There's plenty left and a fresh pot of coffee."

The others greeted him warmly as he entered.

WHILE I WAS STILL HOLDING the door, I noticed Sheriff Flanagan's patrol car pulling into the driveway. Without a second thought, I left the porch and ran to his car.

"Did you find out who the shooter was?" I anxiously asked as I rounded the front bumper.

He hadn't heard me. He was leaning into the passenger seat, where he retrieved a large basket and presented it to me as he stood. It was filled to overflowing with fruit, cheese, and crackers, with candy bars mixed in.

"The men all chipped in for this," he explained. "Figured you might be able to use it… for guests and all."

"Wow, thanks… really," I said, honestly touched by the gesture.

"We're real sorry for what happened, Jim. Your mom was a good woman... one in a million."

There was a sincerity in the Sheriff's voice that conveyed genuine sorrow — the kind that's felt by a true friend. He leaned his head down like he was paying respects as he looked at me through his eyebrows and handed me the basket. I wasn't sure what to say and just nodded back as I lifted it from his hands, surprised by how heavy it was. I quickly leaned it against the hood of his car and laid it down.

"Is that too heavy? Here, I'll...."

"...No, it's fine," I interrupted, raising a hand for him to wait.

The question I'd just asked him was still burning in my mind.

"The shooter... have you found out who he was yet?"

He placed a hand to his forehead and shook it as he answered....

"Look, Jimmy. You don't need to be worrying about that — it will just make you crazy. We're following up on all the leads we're getting; there were plenty of witnesses who saw him and even some news footage...."

"He was Ed Corvo!" I blurted, interrupting him.

"W-what? What are you talking about?"

"The shooter's name was Ed Corvo," I repeated. "He was hired by a man named Bahal Ebazej."

Sheriff Flanagan seemed stunned, staring back at me with a disbelieving look.

"Who... h-how do you know that?"

I turned to make sure no one from the house was near us....

"I can't tell you that exactly... but promise me you'll check it out?"

"Look, Jim, if you have a lead, we need to talk to them; you could be getting in over your head."

I stopped to think about his comment for a second — there was no way I could tell him that I traveled back in time and witnessed it first-hand. He'd never believe me. He'd never follow up on the lead then.

"I really can't tell you. But please — just do me a favor and check it out? Corvo visited someone at Stockslock yesterday afternoon. It was at 2:00 PM; there should be a record of his visit."

"Stockslock — you mean the penitentiary? How...?"

"...Find out who he met with... that should lead to the others behind it," I interrupted. "Ebazej is behind it all — he's the one who hired them."

There was a stunned silence for a moment as the Sheriff tried to process what he was hearing. He finally placed his hands on both my shoulders as he released a sigh.

"You've been through a lot, Jim." He sympathetically looked at me as if I had three heads. "Take a few days and just rest. Let us do our job."

"Do it then!" I insisted. "Just promise me you'll check with Stockslock?"

He sighed and nodded reluctantly. "Okay fine, I'll call them and check it out. Okay?"

I nodded gratefully, and he patted my shoulder. "Need a hand with that basket?"

"No, I got it," I hugged it against my belt and turned to look at him with imploring eyes. "Thanks again... Really."

His eyes searched mine for a moment, and then he nodded accept-ingly and opened the driver's door. He waited for me to reach the front walk before starting the car and backing it out.

THE PHONE WAS RINGING as I walked through the door. Uncle Mike answered and talked quietly for a moment to whoever it was. I presented the basket to Anna and the others.

"This basket is from the police. They all chipped in."

Pete's eyes widened in surprise, and Mrs. Mirabella placed her hands on her cheeks in admiration.

"Oh my, It's beautiful! How nice of them to do that!" she exclaimed.

I handed the basket to Pete, noticing that a place had been found for his flowers near the front windows.

"They look good there," I complimented Anna, expecting that she had something to do with the choice of location.

"Thanks. They do, don't they." She smiled as she not-so-subtly congratulated herself.

We were interrupted by Uncle Mike's voice calling from the kitchen. He was holding out the phone for me.

"It's Barbara O'Malley," he explained as I got nearer. I could tell by the look on his face that she was pretty upset.

"Oh, Jimmy, it's so awful! You poor dear!" She sniffled, and her voice cracked as she struggled to hold back tears. "Pastor Wilkes just called us with the news. How could this have happened? ...such a senseless tragedy. It's good that your Uncle Mike is there — you shouldn't be alone at such a terrible time. Ward and I are coming out to see you just as soon as we can get a flight; he's booking it right now."

She finally paused for a breath and collected her thoughts, then spoke in a softer voice.

"Are you alright?"

I had to clear my throat before answering... "Yeah. I'm fine. I guess it hasn't totally hit me yet... you know... like with dad. But I know she's in a better place, really. She's with dad now."

The phone was silent until I began to hear Mrs. O'Malley quietly weeping on the other end. I hadn't intended my comment to sound heartbreaking, but I guess it came out that way.

The room behind me had grown quiet as well. I glanced around to see Anna hugging her mother while they both wiped tears from their eyes. Uncle Mike was sitting on the edge of the couch with his head hanging down, and Pete was pacing the floor with his hands clasped on top of his head.

"Anyway," I said, turning back to the kitchen and trying to gently lighten the mood, "It'll be really nice to see you guys. Don't get too mad when you see how high the grass is next door — I haven't done a very good job with that lately."

The line was still quiet, but I could hear just enough to know that we hadn't been disconnected. Finally, I heard Mrs. O' compose herself the best she could.

<Sniff> "You always do such a nice job on the lawn. I'm sure it's fine. <sniff, sniff> Don't you dare worry about that right now." There was another short pause, and she sounded like she was fighting back a few more tears as she continued. "You've been like a son to us, Jimmy.

You know that. Please remember that we're here for you... no matter what."

———————

UPON HEARING that the O'Malleys were coming, Anna and her mom decided that the house needed a top-to-bottom cleaning. They worked at it for most of the day, enlisting the help of Pete and me for the heavier efforts — mostly Pete. The only room that escaped their attention was mom's bedroom, which we all avoided disturbing — especially me. I was quick to offer my room for Mr. & Mrs. O', making the case that I was doing just fine on the couch. Uncle Mike made it clear that he wouldn't need a bed — he'd be returning home to his apartment above the sub shop as soon as they arrived.

He replaced the standard 'Closed' sign on his shop with a note explaining that the shop would be temporarily closed for the rest of the week. He returned an hour later with a week's worth of food, explaining that it would only have gone to waste sitting at the shop.

LATER IN THE AFTERNOON, Uncle Mike and Mrs. Mirabella worked together in the kitchen, cooking up an amazing pasta and Italian sausage dinner with home-baked bread. The way the two of them seemed to be hitting it off was perhaps the one bright spot in all of this.

"Where did a Scandinavian farm girl learn how to make Italian marinara? That tastes outstanding!" Uncle Mike complimented her.

"...Mirabella?" she hinted, reminding him of her last name. "My husband was very particular about his Italian food."

"Ahh," Uncle Mike accepted. "He did the world a service... he taught you very well."

"It was his grandmother, actually. Enrico liked to *eat* Italian food... he didn't have a clue how to prepare it."

"Even better! Italian grandmothers... God's gift." Mike declared, holding up his glass of wine for a toast. Mrs. Mirabella clinked it with her own and took a small sip, smiling in agreement.

. . .

THERE WAS a knock at the door, drawing my attention away from the kitchen entertainment. PJ was standing on the porch with his wife Baibina, holding a large tray of cookies.

"Thanks for coming over," I said to him sincerely, giving him a long hug. I turned to his wife and shook her hand as she caught my eye with a sympathetic gaze.

"Mes condoléances, Palanqueta, (Our condolences, Jimmy)" she offered sincerely.

"Come inside; we're just getting ready to sit down. Please join us."

Everyone echoed the invitation, waving with their hands for them to join.

"We have plenty!" Mike insisted. "Gotta confess I might've gotten a little carried away... I have trouble cookin' small portions."

A look at the table confirmed his point. It was loaded with four huge heaping platters, along with an assortment of bowls of steaming vegetables and two overflowing baskets of hot sliced bread.

PJ and his wife finally agreed to join us, and he held a chair for his wife as she took a seat.

"Pastor, would you like to say a blessing for our meal?" Mrs. Mirabella asked hopefully.

"Of course," he quickly accepted, bowing where he stood.

> "Father, we are thankful to you for the bounty of this feast and
>   for the love of dear friends at such times of great sorrow.
>   You entreat us to comfort one another, and we admit that
>   each of us needs the comfort that comes from friendship.
>   But more importantly, from the friend who sticks closer
>   than a brother — You are that one who is the source of all
>   comfort — our Lord and Savior.
> "We thank you also for the beautiful life of Maria. She lived
>   your love in everything that she did, always providing a
>   shining example of your grace that lived within her, espe-
>   cially in her most heroic and selfless act of all, which
>   brings us together tonight in remembrance.

"We lift Jimmy to you, Lord, and ask that you wrap him in
your heavenly embrace — may You cover him with Your
pinions, and under Your wings may he take refuge.
"Draw all of us nearer to You in this difficult time and help us
to honestly confess to You our need for Your continued
forgiveness, Your Mercy, and especially, Your presence. In
the wonderful name of Jesus, we offer these petitions before
Your holy throne. Amen."

Everyone echoed PJ's "Amen." Uncle Mike was uncharacteristically silent and brushed a tear from his cheek. I breathed a silent
prayer of my own for God to complete the work He had started in my
Uncle's life. He looked preoccupied for several minutes before
settling back into the conversation, accepting compliments for the
amazing meal.

"This credit belongs to Lena," he insisted. "She is an Italian
Master!"

The table raised their glasses to Mrs. Mirabella while she blushed
and bashfully thanked Uncle Mike.

The enthusiastic conversation continued throughout the meal. I
was happy to sit quietly and enjoy the entertainment. Anna seemed to
be doing the same; we shared kindred glances as the laughter and
noise level steadily rose.

When plates were finally empty, Baibina joined Anna and her
mom in clearing the table, adding coffee cups and dessert plates. Her
platter of Brazilian cookies was soon unveiled and presented on the
table.

"These are traditional Brazilian cookies from Baibina's home
country," PJ explained, pointing out the different varieties as he introduced them.

"These with the chocolate and nuts on top are Brazilian Jubilee
Cookies; they're made with brown sugar and coffee, with Brazil nuts.

"These white ones are Biscoitos de Maizena, with cornstarch,
vanilla, and coconut.

"The ones that look like little sandwiches are Bem Casados —
Brazilian Wedding Cookies, which are sponge cakes made from

potato starch, with different fillings — egg coconut custard cream, lemon curd, walnut cream, and chocolate ganache."

Everyone's mouth was watering, despite the huge meal we'd just eaten.

"But first!" Mrs. Mirabella interrupts. She was holding mom's cake from our refrigerator.

"I believe all of us here were invited by Maria for a celebration of Jimmy's homecoming from the hospital — that invitation was for tonight. I know that she would have wanted that celebration to go ahead with or without her, and since we're all here — it is only fitting." She placed the cake on the table as everyone nodded sincerely and clapped.

"Jimmy, your being here is a great miracle; we can't lose sight of that," PJ offered. "Yes! Let's celebrate it!"

By THE TIME I finished a slice of cake and half a dozen cookies, I felt as stuffed as could be. Anna's mom happened to be standing closest to the kitchen when the phone rang and went to answer it — returning a moment later with her finger pointed at the TV.

"It's Chrissy. Turn on the news, quick!"

"What channel?" Pete asked as he rushed to grab the remote.

Mrs. Mirabella repeated the question into the phone... "What?" she said, not sure if she had heard correctly.

"Any channel... she says it's on every channel!"

"W-what is...?" I started to ask.

My question was answered the moment the TV came on. Footage from last night's local news had gone viral. Channel after channel had interrupted regular programming to report on the shooting and mysterious lightning strike. Many were also candidly reporting on the past week's events — giving tallies of the number of people healed and showing interviews with several of them, including the studio interview with Caden Koller and her husband, with their doctor and PJ.

Interspersed throughout the coverage on virtually every channel were the zoomed-in closeups of those still images of me holding mom. They took my breath away, but I couldn't pull my eyes off them. Despite the heartbreaking scene, they didn't fill me with sorrow... instead, I found them inspiring an immense degree of love for mom and pride for what she did.

Mrs. Mirabella had just hung up the call with Chrissy when the phone immediately rang again.

"Hello?" She looked up at me as she listened and then placed her hand over the phone... "It's The Times — they want to do an interview."

While she was still speaking, my cell phone started to ring, then Uncle Mike's, then PJ's. We all looked at the caller ID labels and glanced back at each other — the calls were all from major networks.

"H-hello?" I answered nervously.

Mrs. Mirabella saw me answer my phone and lifted the receiver to her ear... "He's on another call. Can I take a message...?"

"Yes, th-this is Jimmy Moretti. Y-yes... yeah... that was me... and my mom...."

PJ and Uncle Mike are doing the same.

The calls didn't stop. As soon as we each hung up our phones, they rang again. After an hour, we just started letting the calls go to voicemail.

"I... think I agreed to do an interview on national TV tomorrow night," I confessed, looking up with trepidation.

⌘

13

BEGINNING

All these things are the beginning of sorrows...
~ Matthew 24:8

S unrise revealed an army of reporters gathered around our
doorstep. They filled the front yard, trying to cram onto the
porch. Vans from the news networks lined both sides of the
street with satellite dishes pointed skyward. They looked like flowers
in a strange metallic garden as I stared at the scene from an upstairs
window.

Flashing lights marked each end of the block as patrol cars arrived
to turn away more network vans that were still coming. We were
grateful to see Sheriff Flanagan pull up in front of the house. He and
several deputies made their way to our porch and began to move the
reporters back, forming a semi-circular barrier on the lawn.

Mr. O'Malley welcomed him.

"Hello Ward," the Sheriff said as he shook Mr. O's hand. "It's good
to see you; I'm sorry for the circumstances." Mr. O' nodded in thanks
as he held the door open for the Sheriff to step inside.

"Thanks for coming right over, Connor," he answered. "I was afraid they'd overrun the house."

Sheriff Flanagan handed Mr. O' the morning newspaper. I could see from across the room that the entire front page of the tabloid was filled with a closeup of the image that had gone viral; me holding mom. Mr. O' shook his head sadly and offered it back.

"Keep it," the Sheriff said as he turned to look outside. "What are you going to tell them?"

"That's a great question. Reverend Wilkes and Pastor Rodriguez are on their way — they offered to help."

"That's a good idea. I'll see that they're cleared through." He squeezed his radio and conveyed the information, hearing both checkpoints respond with confirmations.

"Hello Connor," Mrs. O' said, greeting the Sheriff as she came alongside her husband. Her eyes were red from crying. The Sheriff hugged her, offering his condolences. The three of them had been friends since college — part of a close group that included my parents.

"Who would have ever thought that Vinny and Maria would be the first to go..." he said absent-mindedly. He quickly caught himself when he saw me standing in the kitchen doorway and bowed his head regretfully.

"Good morning Jimmy."

"HI, SHERIFF FLANAGAN." I pretended I hadn't heard his comment as I shook his hand and glanced out the window at the growing crowd on the front lawn... "How many are out there? I didn't realize there were this many news networks in the whole world."

He chuckled. "They all want to see you... feel up to it?"

"Not really. Some leg braces would help to keep them from wobbling so much."

He gripped my shoulder with his hand, giving it a slight shake. "You'll do just fine. You don't have to talk if you don't want to." He looked me in the eye and then leaned closer, speaking in a low voice to avoid being overheard...

"By the way, keep yesterday's conversation between us. Stockslock confirmed Corvo's visit — it's an open investigation now."

His words were reassuring. I looked back at him gratefully and nodded that I understood. "Thanks for checking... and believing me."

His expression was serious-looking. "I'm going to need to know how you knew that. We'll talk later — after all this."

I felt myself swallow nervously, turning my head toward the crowded lawn to avoid eye contact. It was a relief to see Pastor Wilkes' church van pulling into our driveway. PJ retrieved a lectern and carried it over to the front steps. Within minutes it was surrounded by microphones. A dozen cameras were being hastily arranged, with their crews jockeying for position.

Mr. O' held the door open as he greeted them both.

"I'm so glad you called," Reverend Wilkes said sincerely. "I've never seen anything like this. I do believe God is opening a door."

PJ hugged my shoulders. "How are you doing?"

"Okay, I guess. Still can't believe this is all happening."

LITTLE RYAN O'MALLEY thumped down the stairs in his feet pajamas and ran across the room to his mom. She lifted him into her arms as he rubbed his eyes and looked around in confusion at the sights around him.

"Scares me...."

She hugged him close and kissed his cheek. "I know, honey, but it's okay." She points to me... "We're at Jimmy's house — you remember him!"

His feet had already begun to move before he reached the floor as she set him down.

"Jimbee!" he yelled excitedly as he raced across the floor toward me and jumped into my arms. He clapped his hands against both my cheeks playfully as he smiled at me, then he pointed out through the front door at the crowd on the lawn. "Whatz 'at?"

"Those are reporters... they like to ask lots of questions. Like you do!"

"Porters?"

"Yup. Maybe you'll be one too someday."

I set him back down... "Porter!" he repeated as he ran back to his mom.

SHERIFF FLANAGAN GENTLY INTERRUPTED, asking for everyone's attention.

"If everyone is ready, we should get this show on the road... so to speak. Who plans to speak?"

The pastors and Mr. O' raised their hands; everyone looked at me.

"I-I don't really have anything to say," I replied uncertainly. "But I can stand with you if that's alright?"

"They'll have questions for you," the Sheriff warned, "Okay with that?"

I nodded yes, unable to imagine what anyone would want to ask me.

"I'll open it," Sheriff Flanagan volunteered. "Who should I hand off to?"

Mr. O' raised his hand... "I have a prepared statement... from the family," he said, looking at me briefly, then he turned his gaze to the pastors... "Then I guess I can hand it to either of you?"

PJ quickly deferred to Reverend Wilkes, who accepted with a nod.

"It's best to keep remarks short — they'll be edited down to unrecognizable sound-bites anyway," the Sheriff advised from experience. "The real reason they're here is to ask us questions." He looked again at me as he said that.

"I can help answer those," PJ quickly offered, putting his arm around my shoulders supportively.

The sheriff looked at each of us, gauging everyone's readiness. "Okay... if we're ready then... let's pray!"

All of us welcomed his suggestion with enthusiasm. PJ took the lead while we bowed our heads.

THERE WAS a wild rustling in the crowd as the front door opened, and we made our way down to the lectern. A moment later, there was silence, punctuated by the clicking of a hundred camera shutters.

"I'm Sheriff Flanagan. I'd like to say thank you on behalf of our Center Springs community for your orderly and respectful conduct here this morning. It is a painful and challenging time for all of us, and especially the Moretti family.

"The events of yesterday are the subject of an active investigation, and facts are still coming to light. I can tell you what we know so far. Last evening, a man entered the grounds where an outdoor church service was being held. At approximately 7:30 pm, this man was seen drawing a rifle out of a sack that he wore strapped to his back. He then proceeded to aim the gun at members of the audience before shooting a female victim in the back. The identity of that victim, as you already know, was Maria Moretti, 42 years old. Immediately after that event, the shooter was fatally struck by lightning.

"At this time, I'd like to introduce those who are with me. Mr. Ward O'Malley, a close friend of the Moretti family, will give a statement on their behalf with Jimmy Moretti. Beside them is Reverend Rodriguez of the First Avenue Assembly and Pastor Wilkes from the Community Bible Church.

"We will open for questions following their remarks. Thank you."

THE SHERIFF STEPPED AWAY, and Mr. O' took his place.

"My name is Ward O'Malley... my wife and I have been close friends of the Moretti's for most of our lives — Jimmy is like a son to us."

"On behalf of the family, I'd like to thank you all for coming. We are focused this morning on a remarkable woman." Mr. O' glanced at me as he continued.

"After Maria's husband, Vince, was lost in a tragic accident three years ago, she persevered in the face of overwhelming odds. She never complained or shared her challenges with others, even though she worked two jobs in a struggle to pay off large medical bills while keeping a roof over their heads. Jimmy worked as well, after school and on weekends, contributing all he earned to help with the family's expenses.

"Earlier this year, our own family suffered a tragic loss as well. Our daughter Kelly was taken from us after a battle with brain cancer." Mr. O's voice broke slightly as he pressed on... "Jimmy was *such* a comfort to Kelly and to us during that terrible time — exhibiting the remarkable strength of character that shines so brightly in his life. Since then, with a strength and inspiration that I think has only come from God, he has helped turn Kelly's tragedy into something truly good and astonishing. What you see happening in Center Springs is the result of that work... a move of God's spirit that has already saved countless souls and has allowed hundreds to find healing.

"My wife Barbara and I have been preparing to launch a Charitable Foundation in our daughter Kelly's name to help families who are struggling with tragic losses. We'd like to announce that we are renaming that foundation to honor these friends who have given so much to help us. It will be called the *Kelly's Friends Foundation.* We pray that it will be used to provide at least a small portion of the comfort that we have received from Maria and Jimmy."

I couldn't stop a few tears from escaping and running down the side of my cheek as Mr. O' turned to hug me. He moved away from the lectern, and Pastor Wilkes stepped up, waiting for a moment as the applause slowly died down.

"I'M REVEREND WILKES. I've had the pleasure of knowing this fine family for more than twenty years... I've seen Jimmy grow up since he was born and am truly inspired to see the young man that he has become."

He stood quietly for a moment, signaling that he intended to change subjects.

"I feel it important to recognize exactly what is happening here. The Bible speaks clearly of a final period of human history. Scripture uses several names for it, calling it the End of the Age, the End of Days, the Great Tribulation... or as Jesus simply referred to it in chapter 24 of the Gospel of Matthew, 'The End.'

"Jesus told his followers how this final age would *begin*. He called it the Beginning of Travail... literally, the *Beginning of Sorrows*.

"I'm not here to give a Scripture lesson. I'll encourage everyone listening to read that chapter in Matthew for yourself... chapter 24... and look for the signs that Jesus described. It may well be the most important learning you will ever do. The recent events here in Center Springs are a portent of that time. This past week we have witnessed severely disabled children, and adults made whole, blind receiving their sight, and those with terminal illnesses being cured. We're seeing an outpouring of the Spirit that is drawing souls by the hundreds each day.

"We also know that there will be enemies of God's saving work. Those forces have already been responsible for terrible and tragic acts, one of which has claimed Maria's life. These threats cannot stop the work of God nor slow His calendar of world events. Just as light shines more brightly in the darkness, so God's work will shine all the brighter as darkness increases. We shine as His lights in that darkness whenever we reflect the love of Christ. That light is never brighter than in selfless acts such as Maria's."

The pastor looked directly into the camera as he finished... "I feel impressed to leave you with this admonition: Today is the day of salvation, now is the acceptable time. I encourage all who are listening to heed God's invitation. Today, if you hear His voice, do not make the tragic mistake of hardening your heart against Him. He invites you to come — everyone who is laden with the cares of the world. He is the only one who can give you the rest that you desperately seek."

The Pastor offered the lectern back to Sheriff Flanagan as he stepped away.

⌘

14

VENGEANCE

God sees your pain...

Sheriff Flanagan stepped back to the lectern and quickly cleared his throat. "Thank you, Reverend Wilkes.

"At this time, we will open it up for your questions...."

Hands shot up across the audience, and dozens of questions were shouted out together. The Sheriff pointed to one reporter.

"Do you know the identity of the shooter?"

The Sheriff responded: "An active investigation is underway; We are questioning a large number of witnesses."

ANOTHER REPORTER SHOUTED OUT A FOLLOW-UP... "Are you focused on any suspects? Who do you think is behind these shootings?"

The Sheriff was steadfast: "We are not prepared to discuss that at this time."

. . .

A YOUNG WOMAN in the first row had an angry expression as she questioned accusingly: "Why was the shooter allowed to carry a gun into a crowded venue like that?"

The Sheriff sighed sadly. "As with most peaceful gatherings, whether at churches, concerts or supermarkets, we are used to people entering freely. Security procedures were not in place to screen everyone."

SOMEONE A FEW ROWS back yelled out: "Is it true that the shooter was aiming at Mrs. Moretti's son, and she blocked the shot?"

[Sheriff:] "Some of the eyewitness testimony seems to suggest that."

I COULD FEEL a hundred sets of eyes bore into me and knew that my face was reddening... I stared at my shoes and took a deep breath to calm my racing heartbeat. PJ gripped my shoulder, providing some much-needed support.

"I HAVE a question for Reverend Wilkes... Are you saying that this shooting is a sign of the end of the world?"

Pastor Wilkes stepped back to the microphones. "No, I'm not suggesting that at all. I'm only pointing out that the recent events hint to a spiritual awakening that is consistent with the Bible's description of the end times — when God's Spirit will be poured out in the last days."

The Pastor called on a man near the back who was waving his hands.

"REPORTS on social media say that the shooter was killed by an energy blast from an invisible alien spaceship. What do you say about that?"

The Pastor looked dumbfounded. He turned to Sheriff Flanagan for help, who simply pointed to the next reporter — "Next question!"

"THIS IS FOR THE SHERIFF. Notwithstanding Alien theories, what *do* you make of the unusual lightning strike? Since no remains have been found, is it possible that the shooter escaped?"

[Sheriff:] "I'll leave the weather analysis to professionals. I will say that I was there and saw what happened firsthand. I can assure you that he did not escape."

A COLLEAGUE of the first reporter piped up: "Then it's true that he was vaporized? How is that even possible?"

[Sheriff:] "That's definitely a question that should be directed to a scientific expert. I can only say that it happened... and I'm not alone in saying it — a thousand other people saw it too."

A WELL-KNOWN reporter from one of the national networks was standing in the front row. Her sophisticated appearance distinguished her from many others; she was dressed in a professional business suit with an earpiece barely visible in her ear. She removed her sunglasses as a separate camera crew focused on her.

"I have a question for Jimmy," she said with a charming smile as the Sheriff called on her. He stepped aside and offered me the lectern - my knees were shaking.

"First, let me say how sorry I am about your mother... our hearts go out to you."

"Th-thanks... thank you," I replied awkwardly.

"We have been looking into the background of your tent meetings — they began with a group of high school students... isn't that correct?"

"Yes... FCS — Fellowship of Christian Students."

"Interesting. Is it true that many of the members of this group are former drug addicts or had gang affiliations?"

I paused uncomfortably, taken aback by the sudden change in the tone of her voice. "I... well, I guess... yeah. It's really incredible how God has been changing lives."

"Indeed." Her tone of voice seemed increasingly dismissive and judgmental. "Isn't it also true that Reverend Rodriguez himself is a former gang member?"

I glanced back at PJ and saw him standing calmly with his eyes closed... his head was bowed in prayer. I looked back at her without answering.

"Experts have said that the group hysteria and claims of miraculous healings in these tent meetings are indicative of drug-induced hallucinations. Do you deny that gang activities are feeding this drug use? Are you a gang member yourself, as some have reported?"

"Wh-what? No... that's crazy."

"Isn't that the real reason you have been targeted by shooters — twice in just one week? Aren't you, in fact, a gang *leader*?"

I could hear a flurry of camera shutters as objections in my defense were raised by everyone standing behind me. I remained stunned to silence, trying to process her accusations. All I could think to do was breathe a prayer...

"Lord, where is this attack coming from? Show me how to respond!"

The most unexpected thing possible happened in response to my prayer. A sudden flurry of images flooded my mind — they were of a young girl being mistreated by a man in a collar... a clergyman. The images continued in a near blur as I could see the girl growing older while the abuse continued. It soon became clear that the girl was this reporter. An intense feeling of pain and shame-filled my heart, along with rage — a deeply vindictive spirit! I realized that I was being allowed to feel the complex emotions swirling within her.

I looked her in the eyes and noticed a shadow covering her face. It was a ghostly-looking veil that lingered over her eyes and stretched over her head, wrapping around her neck and piercing into her heart. I sensed its presence... its overwhelming shame and rage. It seemed to be moving... undulating like a hellish parasite that was feeding on her spirit.

The crowd had fallen silent, waiting for me to respond. Cameras were live-streaming the action, and I was faintly aware of the continued clicking of still cameras firing continuously, sounding like inappropriately-timed applause.

"GOD SEES YOUR PAIN," I heard myself saying. She looked at me strangely.

"He hasn't forgotten you or abandoned you — you don't have to feel ashamed — it was never your fault. God can take the pain from you... He can heal you."

Her face twisted into an ugly, insulted expression as the piercing in her spirit was suddenly amplified.

"Wh-what are you talking about? D-don't try to make this about me!" She touched the front of her neck as she shook her head, looking around self-consciously.

"*Molly*... that's your name, right?" I said, lifting a hand toward her in a conciliatory gesture. There was a flare of recognition in her eyes — she had never revealed to anyone that Molly was the nickname her grandmother used for her as a little girl. It was the name she used when they prayed together — the name she always used for herself when she privately prayed as a child.

"God heard every prayer you prayed as a little girl. He heard every time you cried to him in pain, Molly."

ALL AT ONCE, She lost her professional demeanor and screamed back at me as the rage suddenly exploded. "HOW DARE YOU!! YOU KNOW NOTHING... **NOTHING** ABOUT MY PAIN!"

She realized what she was saying and stifled her outburst, trying to regain her composure. The oppressive spirit writhed as it tightened around her head and throat, driving itself deeper into her heart.

"It's okay! I'm sorry!" I quickly said, apologizing as I made my way around the lectern toward her. One of the men from her crew blocked my path, pushing me back. I could feel the surging pain and rage that she was feeling... the shame was overwhelming. Tears began to flow down my cheeks as I struggled to reach her.

"I just want you to know that God hurts for you too — He feels all of your hurt... He loves you!"

"HOW DARE YOU CLAIM GOD LOVES ME!! HOW DARE YOU! He did NOTHING to help me — NOTHING! He LEFT me alone! He... he LET it happen!"

There were suddenly tears streaming down her face. I could see that the ghostly veil that held her prisoner was bubbling and writhing, making her face twist with vindictive anger... I could feel it within her — she wanted vengeance against God!

Immediately I knew the spirit's name! The searing pain in my shoulder ignited with an intensity that nearly drove me to my knees. I could practically hear the crackle of Chozeq's invisible flaming sword as its heat warmed the side of my face. With an outstretched hand, I stared into the ghostly apparition...

"SPIRIT OF VENGEANCE, I BIND YOU IN THE NAME OF THE LORD OF HOSTS! You are commanded to leave her in Jesus' name!"

THE GHOSTLY BEAST immediately screeched in a loud wail that could be heard by everyone. People were turning and looking all around for the invisible source of the terrifying sound when, all at once, it materialized like a black ooze, covering the woman's head and neck. The muffled sound of her terrified cries could be heard from beneath the ugly mass — they were a high-pitched scream...

"HELP MEEE! HELP ME PLEEEEEASE!"

I could feel PJ and Pastor Wilkes laying hands on my shoulders as they interceded for the woman. The man blocking my path had staggered back, drawing away from the women in fear. All of those standing nearby had done the same, horrified at the horrendous sight. I had a clear view of the vile beast, and my eyes bore into it as I repeated Heaven's decree against it....

"SPIRIT OF VENGEANCE, YOU ARE BANISHED FROM THIS REALM IN JESUS' MIGHTY NAME... LEAVE HER... NOW!"

THE CREATURE SCREECHED MORE LOUDLY than before and flew into the air, trying to escape, but was caught by a force that it could not resist. Mouths hung open in astonished terror as the entire crowd looked upon the flailing leather-winged demon before it was pulled roughly to the ground. Its monstrous cries were finally snuffed out as it was dragged beneath the sod.

The woman had fallen to her knees in the grass, still screaming hysterically. I quickly knelt in front of her, carefully putting my hand on her shoulder. I saw another woman's hand reach down at once — it was Caden Koller, the reporter who gave her heart to Christ a few days ago. Caden looked at me as if to say, 'I've got this,' and then knelt to embrace the woman — holding her as they cried together.

While I watched the fantastic scene, ...while *all of us* watched... Caden led her to the Lord with a simple and heartfelt prayer that the woman repeated eagerly. It was the second time in a week that well-known newswomen had given their hearts to Christ on live TV.

⌘

15

SALT

You are the salt of the earth...
~ Matthew 5:13

I gotta say, Jimmy, anytime you people are on TV, it sure ain't borin.'"

The dry wit was unmistakable in Mr. V's voice over the phone as he commented on the morning's news conference. "I reckon those Network folks are scramblin' ta figure out what in tar-nation just happened in front of their own cameras. You're probably watchin' the TV same as me... this thing's taken off like a tsunami all 'round the world."

"Yeah, I think you're right," I admitted, watching the non-stop coverage. "You'd think it was a moon landing or something."

"I suppose it's a fair-stretch bigger than that. Between the Pastor's words about the end of the world and then you tanglin' with that demon right in front of everybody.... Well, that's gonna get folks' attention; no two ways about it."

'...*Events that will change the whole world....*' The words from Amos' journal rang in my mind.

I could see investigators from several government agencies combing the lawn outside our front windows. They were all wearing white bodysuits with face masks like it was a new kind of pandemic. Some took measurements, while others drew core samples of sod and took readings with odd-looking instruments.

By now, all of the news vans had been expelled by an army of State Police. The entire block had been sealed-off to traffic. News choppers hovered overhead at a safe distance, making our quiet neighborhood rumble like an action movie. I suspected that our neighbors were becoming pretty annoyed with it all.

A pair of agents interviewed everyone at the dining room table while Sheriff Flanagan stood nearby looking on. I was supposed to be with them if it weren't for Mr. V's phone call. They had just looked over at me for about the sixth time, making it clear that they wanted me to rejoin them immediately.

"I'd better get back to the table; they're calling for me."

Mr. V. cleared his throat and agreed, growing more serious as he spoke. "My offer still holds — if ya need a place to hide-out from all those folks... well, ya know my door is open."

"Thanks, Uncle Jim."

He grew quiet... "You take care o' yerself, Jimmy. I ain't been much of a prayin' man over the years, but I'm learnin'... I'm prayin fer you son."

"Thanks... that means a lot."

PLACING the kitchen phone back into its charger, I took a deep breath to steady my nerves before turning toward the agents, who were growing increasingly impatient. A moment later, I was sliding into a chair beside PJ.

"Sorry about that...," I apologized as I leaned my elbows on the table, then dropped them awkwardly into my lap.

Agent Frank DeMassi was a crusty detective who looked like he might have done a few tours in active duty. His crew cut and a small tattoo of an eagle, globe, and anchor on the side of his neck suggested it was probably in the Marines. His regulation black suit and white shirt were neat and clean, with bulges that hinted of huge biceps and a likely pistol holster strapped to his chest. A pair of mirrored sunglasses hung from the outside of his jacket's lapel pocket.

"So let's get this straight," he immediately started in, sounding incredulous. "You claim to have been shot in the chest at point-blank range and then released from the hospital in just three days, with no signs of injury."

"A-actually, it was two days... well, one and a half, to be exact." I looked to PJ as I compared notes with him... "I was shot on Sunday night... then I was in the hospital all day Monday and Monday night, then got out on Tuesday...."

DeMassi smacked his notepad against the table in frustration, interrupting my train of thought. "What kind of fool do you people take me for? Either you're lying about the first shooting, or you must have been wearing body armor." He leaned forward suspiciously... "Now, what would a kid your age be doing with that kind of hardware?"

Sheriff Flanagan spoke up from where he was standing behind me: "I can vouch for the shooting — the shooter is still locked up back at my station if you want to interview him. The paramedics and hospital doctors can confirm the rest."

Agent DeMassi leaned back and tossed his pen onto the table, acting like he had just uncovered a massive conspiracy. "I'll get to the bottom of it — don't you worry about that! In fact, yes... I would like to interview the shooter... *and* those paramedics!"

Agent Sharma cleared her throat, pausing for her partner to cede the floor. He gestured with his open hand for her to go right ahead.

"Jimmy... I'm very sorry about your mother." She looked at me intently with evident sincerity as she paused for a moment. "Who do you think would be trying to kill you?"

I looked to Sheriff Flanagan, and he nodded that I should go ahead and answer.

"I don't know much about him... but his name is Bahal Ebazej.

He's the one who ordered it. The man who shot my mother was named Ed Corvo."

The two agents looked at each other with serious expressions and leaned forward.

"Corvo... Are you sure?"

"Do you know him?" the Sheriff asked, picking up on their sudden interest.

"He's a professional hit man — top notch. A real pro." DeMassi looked at his partner... "Why would Corvo hit a church service in the middle of nowhere?"

Agent Sharma glanced at me and then back at Frank. "Why would he be sent after an unknown kid?"

DeMassi's eyes bore into me again — I was dreading the question that I knew was coming....

"How do you know all this?"

I looked around the room at PJ and Pastor, then glanced at the Sheriff nervously.

"I-I can't tell you... I promised I wouldn't."

"Look, kid," Agent DeMassi said, getting annoyed again. "This is serious business... it's a murder charge. Even if we take your word for it, that would never hold in a court of law."

"He can't be convicted anyway; he's already dead," I pointed out. I looked imploringly at Agent Sharma, who seemed like the friendlier of the two. "Just check out the lead, see if he's missing. He must have had a car or an apartment or something — see if he's really gone!" I looked up at Sheriff Flanagan again... "He met someone at the penitentiary yesterday... it was at 2:00. That's when they gave him the job."

The sheriff's expression was stone-cold serious as he looked at me and then back at the agents.

"I called the penitentiary, and it checked out. Corvo visited one of the inmates at 2:00 yesterday afternoon. A guy named Billy Mansell."

DeMassi and Sharma wrote the name in their notebooks. DeMassi looked back at me with an expression as serious as the sheriff's — except his look implied a threat and a warning at the same time.

"I don't know what you've gotten yourself into, kid, but you need to watch out. You're in over your head with this crowd — these are dangerous guys."

He looked back at his quickly scrawled notes... "What about this Bahal guy?"

"Bahal Ebazej," I confirmed as they both wrote it down. "Like I said, I don't know much about him. He's pretty rich. He has an accent... middle eastern, I think."

The agents looked at each other with a critical glance.

"You heard him talk?"

"Just a few words... he was on the phone." My answer wasn't a lie... he actually *was* talking on a phone. I just left out the detail about me standing invisibly beside him while time-traveling.

Agent DeMassi looked at his partner and then back at me.

"Dare I ask how you happened to hear his phone conversation?"

I looked back at him blankly and swallowed hard — realizing that I had talked myself into a corner again.

Agent Sharma held up her hand in a stopping gesture and looked at her partner. "Illegal wiretaps are not admissible evidence. I think it might be best to end it here to avoid compromising our investigation."

DeMassi reluctantly agreed. He looked at me sternly. "You're playing with major fire here, kid! My advice is to back off and stay as far away as you possibly can. Leave the investigating to us!"

He reached into his jacket pocket and pulled out a business card. "Call us right away if you hear anything else. Keep away from whoever this informant is — it could be a trap."

I nodded my head, accepting his advice as I realized that it was best to play along. Secretly, I was thinking that Chozeq — my informant — is the furthest thing from a threat that I can imagine.

As the agents got up to leave, the Sheriff's radio squawked with a call from one of his deputies.

"Sheriff... There's a news crew here saying that they have an appointment to do a TV interview. They're insisting that they're expected."

Sheriff Flanagan looked at me for confirmation.

"NNN... Yeah, that's true, I guess. I almost forgot about that."

"Let them through," he answered into his mic.

AGENT DEMASSI OFFERED me a handshake at the door on his way out; there was a friendlier look in his eyes as he leaned closer.

"Sorry if I was rough on ya' back there — it's my job. You're a good kid. Some friendly advice... keep this stuff we talked about between us. The fewer who know, the better. And I was serious about backing off — stay away from this."

"Thanks," I nodded, accepting his advice. "I won't say anything."

He searched my eyes as we shook hands, and I sensed that he was sizing me up. Agent Sharma offered her hand as he moved on.

"Good luck with your interview, Jimmy... be careful. Be sure to call if you need us."

THERE WAS a collective sigh of relief as the door closed.

"Well, now that they're gone, who wants lunch?" Mrs. O' asked, emerging from the kitchen with a platter of sandwiches. "I used the rolls and cold cuts you brought us, Mike... I hope that's alright?"

"That's what they're for! Saved me the work o' makin' em myself!"

Sheriff Flanagan grabbed his hat. "I'll be heading out now, too — I need to get back to the station."

"Are you sure you can't stay for lunch, Connor?" Mr. O' challenged him.

"I'll grab something downtown — I don't eat lunch much normally. There's usually something or other keeping me busy."

"I'll bet you don't get many days like this, though," Mr. O' challenged with a smile as he offered a handshake.

"That would be correct for sure, thankfully." He looked outside at the news van unloading broadcast equipment. Production crew members were preparing to carry it inside. "Maybe I'll stop back later for the main event."

"Please do!"

Uncle Mike made his way to the sandwich platter and grabbed

one, taking a bite. He raised one finger in the air… "Jus' needs a little oil 'n vinegar… an' maybe some oregano…."

Before Mrs. O' realized what was happening, Uncle Mike lifted the platter from her hands and carried it back into the kitchen. She was standing with her hands on her hips in disbelief as Mr. O' put his arm around her waist and gave her an understanding smile. Her offended expression softened as she gradually smiled back at him.

"Here we go!" Uncle Mike announced mere minutes later, reemerging with his enhanced versions. "Barbara did all th' real work — I jus' added a few embellishments."

"I should have known better than to make subs with a professional in the house," Mrs. O' retorted with a smile.

Uncle Mike used his free arm to hug her shoulders while balancing the platter in his other hand. The gesture was an apology of sorts. At least, that's how Uncle Mike viewed it, judging by the humble expression on his face.

"Let's see… I'm guessin' you wanna say grace." Uncle Mike suggested in a respectful voice. "Would one 'o you Reverends like ta do de honors?"

Pastor Wilkes rose to the challenge, and soon we were all seated at the table, eating happily. Looking around the room, I couldn't help thinking how much mom would have loved this — especially seeing Uncle Mike being part of it. Having the O'Malley's back made it easy to forget that they ever left… until I stopped to remember all the things that will never be the same. For a moment, I could imagine Kelly bumping elbows with me, half expecting to hear mom chiding us for stealing each other's food. I was surprised by a sudden attack of tears as my eyes welled up unexpectedly.

Mrs. O' was quick to notice, sitting across the table from me. Mr. O' was sitting beside me, and she caught his eye with a subtle nod; a moment later, I felt him put his arm around my shoulders. It took a minute for me to get my voice; I cleared my throat.

"It's really great having you guys here… thanks for coming."

Mr. O' gave my shoulder a reassuring squeeze and then returned both hands to his sandwich, not wanting to let himself get choked up.

Watching the scene, Ryan scrambled out of his mom's lap and

crawled under the table, instantly appearing by my side. I stood him in my lap, and he mimicked his father's gesture, putting his small arm around my neck and patting my shoulder.

"Thanks, buddy," I said, messing up his hair, while Mrs. O' pouted at us sentimentally.

⌘

LIGHT

You are the light of the world...
~ Matthew 5:14a

A knock on the door announced the arrival of the NNN crew. Uncle Mike was the first on his feet, answering it protectively, like a backstage guard greeting a bunch of groupies. A guy in jeans and a sweatshirt flashed his *National News Network* ID and was eventually allowed inside, setting down a bunch of laptop and camera bags that were hanging from his shoulders.

He was followed in by a man in his late thirties, wearing designer jeans and a blazer. He removed his sunglasses as he scanned the room.

"You are...?" Uncle Mike asked.

The man placed his hand on his chest in surprise. "Berith Gruner," he announced, expecting everyone to recognize his name.

"I-I'm the Producer," he added as he saw the blank expressions on everyone's faces. "I don't usually come onsite for remote work, but this is quite a unique case." He looked around the room again, taking its bearings as he continued to explain... "We're expecting record viewership for this one. It's being carried live by all of our affiliate channels and has syndication deals around the world."

A few more crew members entered with arm-loads of equipment, followed by a set of furniture movers in coveralls. Berith began pointing at the room's furnishings, directing the movers to clear an area in front of the fireplace. At the same time, large screens were positioned to reflect light, and a pair of 'Interview' chairs were strategically placed.

Cameras were being positioned at several angles, each on impressive-looking mechanized tripods.

"Set up the control room in there," he said, pointing at the dining room table as crew members arrived with a large industrial carrying case. The movers began grabbing empty dining room chairs, including the one where Uncle Mike had been sitting.

"ALL RIGHT, THAT'S IT!" Uncle Mike yelled, stopping the action. "Can't ya see we're havin' lunch here? Ya can't jus' barge in an' turn de house upside-down."

Berith looked at him aghast as if he'd never heard anyone speak to him that way before. Uncle Mike didn't back down; he pointed at the living room....

"Do whatever ya gotta do in there fer now. Leave the family to eat in peace — we're in mournin' here... have some respect!"

Berith raised both hands in surrender, directing his crew toward the living room with a quick nod of his head.

Soon, rows of neatly placed wires ran around the room, waiting to be attached to the control board. Berith spoke quietly to his crew supervisor, giving him instructions before disappearing outside. He could be seen pacing back and forth on the lawn holding his cell phone to his ear.

A SHORT WHILE LATER, everyone was helping with clearing the table when a woman entered, dressed in a business suit. She held up a folder containing papers, presenting it to no one in particular.

"James Moretti?" She queried, scanning the room.

"Over here," I answered from the empty table. Ryan was still sitting in my lap, enjoying one of Baibina's cookies.

"Hi. I'm Candice, the Programing Director? We spoke last night on the phone... Nice to meet you. I have some paperwork I need you to sign for tonight's interview."

Mr. O' stepped out of the kitchen with perfect timing. "I can take a look at that if you'd like," he offered.

"Yeah, thanks..." I gratefully agreed, "...that'd be great."

Candice smiled at him and handed him the folder. "We just need signatures in the places marked. The check there is already made out."

A check? The words registered in my mind, surprising me. I didn't remember talking about a check-in last night's phone conversation.... Come to think of it, I didn't remember much of anything from last night's calls — the scenes on the TV all by themselves were more than I could take in.

Mr. O' took a seat beside me as he opened the folder and looked up at her in surprise. He pulled out the check and handed it to me — it was for $5,000. I was stunned as I stared at it, holding a hand to the back of my head as I slowly shook it in disbelief.

Candice seemed to grow nervous after a moment and began to explain.

"That's our standard honorarium for a national interview...."

"I-I can't accept this," I stammered as I interrupted her.

She looked down at her small briefcase with a resigned expression, as if she expected my reaction. To my surprise, she pulled out a second check and handed it to me.

"Let's not beat around the bush... This is our final offer."

The sight of it made my head spin. I was unable to respond as I tried to comprehend the amount I saw printed on the certified cashier's check in my hands. Mr. O' looked back at her as if there had been a mistake.

"This is for fifty thousand dollars!"

She nodded, giving us a satisfied smile.

"You don't understand," I objected as I regained my voice. "I can't take this... I can't take anything — not for this... not after mom...."

Candice looked at me nervously and turned quickly to Mr. O', speaking in a tone that seemed a little more anxious than business-like. "I assure you this is customary for an exclusive with this kind of national profile. You can be certain that the network will make many times that amount."

There was an awkward silence as I felt everyone waiting for my response. An idea surfaced suddenly.

"I want it to go to the foundation," I blurted, looking at Mr. O. "The Kelly's Friends Foundation."

"Jimmy... this is a lot... You have college to think about... and this house. You shouldn't decide right now."

"That's what I want — I'm sure of it. I can't do the interview otherwise."

Candice's eyes grew large, and she stood frozen, looking like her entire career was hanging in the balance. She didn't dare speak — she seemed afraid even to breathe.

Mr. O' nodded at me quietly and stopped arguing. He turned his attention to the contract and began reading it carefully as Candice released a deep sigh in relief. She did her best to recover her composure and pulled out a chair, taking a seat across the table.

"I'll stay right here... in case you have any questions."

THIRTY MINUTES LATER, MR. O' had grilled her over a dozen points and requested a half-dozen mark-ups. The two of them were on a first name basis as he finally told me to sign a few of the pages and then initialed them himself, keeping one set and pushing the folder back across the table. Candice stood and offered her hand, smiling as she shook mine.

"You're going to do great Jimmy, I'm really looking forward to your interview." She looked over at Mr. O' and nodded gratefully, "Thanks for all your help Ward."

As soon as she was out the door, Mrs. O' walked up behind her husband and hugged his shoulders. "I'll bet they didn't plan on there being a lawyer at the table," she quietly said with a smile.

"Just a corporate lawyer," he added with a grin. "But I guess that's the worst kind."

———

PJ AND PASTOR WILKES approached all of us after conferring quietly for a moment. Pastor Wilkes looked to PJ and then spoke for both of them — his voice was soft-spoken.

"When you're ready to discuss arrangements for a memorial service... the church is at your disposal."

His suggestion was not unexpected but still rolled over me like a cold wave that momentarily took my breath away. Mrs. O' rubbed my back briefly as she saw my reaction. I cleared my throat and managed to reclaim my voice.

"Is Uncle Mike here?"

He emerged from the kitchen with a pained expression in reaction to the Pastor's question.

"Excuse me... are you finished in here?" The NNN crew member who posed the question looked at us uncomfortably. Several others stood behind him, anxiously waiting to finish getting set up for tonight's broadcast.

"Knock yourselves out," Uncle Mike agreed with a wave toward the Dining Room. He turned and motioned for the rest of us to head into the kitchen, where we gathered around the small kitchen table.

The pastor started by gently probing for information about mom's funeral arrangements. "Will there be an interment?"

"No..." Uncle Mike answered after clearing his throat. "It'll be a cremation."

There was an awkward silence, and I could tell that they were all eying me sympathetically. PJ nudged my arm and quietly spoke near my ear. "It's okay if you don't want to stay for this."

"No, it's okay... I want to."

Pastor Wilkes nodded and carefully continued. "In that case, the

Memorial could be done any time you're ready. Are there family or friends who need time for travel?"

"Just the O'Malleys," I said, looking across the table at them.

"Yes, of course," Pastor acknowledged. "How long are you planning to be in town?"

"Well… I'm not sure," Mrs. O' said, looking at her husband. "I suppose we'll need to get back in a week or so."

"I can talk to Ed about working remotely for a while if needed," Mr. O offered.

"Alright, we don't need to decide the date right now," Pastor advised. "We can assume that it will be held at the church for now, if you'd like. The location can be revised if needed."

"How would you like the service to be conducted? Did Maria have any favorite songs or verses…?

"…God Will Take Care of You," I quickly answered, nearly interrupting him. "That was her favorite song."

The pastor wrote it down. "Would you like to have anyone speak?"

"I would…" Uncle Mike blurted out loudly, looking surprised by his own voice. "I-I would… I'd like to say a word," he added in a quieter voice.

"Of course, Mike, that's wonderful," Pastor acknowledged as he wrote Mike's name. "I can give you a passage if you'd like to do a reading….."

"…No — th-that's okay… I have my own. I have something to say… something I need to say… in her honor."

Mr. O' gave Mike's shoulder a firm grip, and Mike nodded to him appreciatively. He and Mrs. O' both raised their hands, offering to speak as well.

"Maria and I were best friends since nursery school…." Barbara said, wiping her tears.

"That's a fact," Uncle Mike agreed. "You two were tight… there's no doubt about it."

Everyone looked at me with the unspoken question.

"You can sit this out, Jimmy… no one will blame you," Pastor assured me.

I took a deep breath and released it, steadying my nerves the best I could.

"I think I'd like to try... to talk. I really want to try."

———————

A SHORT WHILE LATER, PJ and Pastor Wilkes announced their goodbyes, saying they wanted to ease some of the chaos in our cramped house. Members of the growing broadcast crew seemed to be milling around everywhere.

"We'll be in prayer for your interview Jimmy, we've alerted the church prayer chain," Pastor Wilkes said. He shook my hand and patted me on the back with an approving nod.

PJ stepped up right behind him and gave me a hug. When he stepped back again, he stopped to look at me, then patted me on the chest to remind me where to look for my words.

"Just remember what Jesus said in Luke 21:15. 'Settle it in your heart not to meditate beforehand how to answer: for I will give you a mouth and wisdom, which all your adversaries will not be able to withstand.' I'm praying for you, Jimmy... for that."

"Thanks," I said sincerely as I gave him another hug. I stood on the porch watching until they pulled out of the driveway and headed away down the street. It was just after 2:00 PM. The interview wasn't until 8:00, leaving plenty of time for the butterflies to multiply.

———————

THE CREW WASTED no time converting the dining room into a control room, complete with several computers, an enormous mixing board, and an array of monitors reaching practically to the ceiling. As I reentered the front door, a half-dozen engineers were hovering over the controls and testing camera feeds while others milled around the living room, adjusting lighting and shifting items that would be on camera.

Wandering back to the kitchen, I decided to give Anna a call and stepped out onto the back deck for some peace and quiet.

She started off talking a mile-a-minute as soon as she answered....

"Jimmy! I've wanted so much to call you, but mom said you were probably too busy with all those reporters and people at the house. We saw the press conference this morning — Oh my gosh! Are you okay?! What was that thing? — how is that reporter? — she gave her heart to the Lord on TV; that was so unbelievable! Are you sure you're alright? That was SO scary!"

I smiled as I waited for the flood of her pent-up emotions to subside.

"Yeah, it's been kind of nuts around here today," I confessed, finally getting a word in. "PJ and Pastor Wilkes just left; things have quieted down for now."

"They've been showing commercials all day about your interview tonight. All the news shows have been talking non-stop about what happened this morning."

"Wow," I said, honestly surprised. "Must be a slow news day, I guess."

"No, it's crazy! People are saying it's the end of the world. An Italian channel even interviewed the Pope about it."

"Really? What did he say?"

"Just that this morning's events were nothing new. He acted like he'd seen it all before, but I don't think he really had."

While she was talking, a news chopper flew over the house and then suddenly looped around and hovered overhead.

"Are you out on your deck?" Anna asked.

"Yeah, why?"

"I'm looking at you on TV... Oh my gosh, I can't believe it!"

A moment later, several other Helicopters arrived as well.

"Well, I'm glad I'm not in my pajamas."

Anna laughed at the inside joke. "Better in pajamas than boxer shorts," she added, giggling hysterically at her own version.

"Now I *am* feeling uncomfortable," I admitted, climbing out of the deck chair. I turned to the choppers and waved before heading back inside. Anna was still laughing her head off.

"Speaking of clothes," she said as she finally settled down, "what are you going to wear for your interview tonight?"

The question threw me — I honestly hadn't thought about it. I ducked my head to look out the kitchen window, trying to see if the choppers had moved on.

"I don't know, haven't thought much about it. Does it matter?"

"Yes, of course, it matters! You don't want to look like a dork, or like you're crazy or a fanatic or anything. But you shouldn't be too dressed up either like you're going to a wedding or a prom or something." She paused, thinking about it for a moment.

"You should look kind of business-like, but approachable... and sincere, not fake. I think maybe just some nice slacks and a plain dress shirt, with a simple tie; no jacket. That sounds about right."

"Thanks. That's actually really helpful," I admitted honestly.

"You're welcome... I wish there was something else I could do to help."

"You've done plenty already — all your work here yesterday was incredible. You'd go nuts if you could see what a mess the NNN crew has made of the place.

"...But if you really want to do something, you can pray for me. I'm trying not to think about tonight and all the people who'll be watching, but have to admit it makes me a little terrified."

"You're gonna do great. Just remember how much God wants to use this for His glory; keep thinking about that and let Him give you the words to say,... you can't go wrong."

"That's pretty much the same advice that PJ gave me."

"Well, there you go... *In the mouth of two or three witnesses...*" she said, using a verse to make the point.

"I'm pretty sure that verse is about using witnesses to confront a guilty brother," I added nervously.

"It is? Okay, never mind that one then... but, you're going to be great... just like always," she quickly added with a laugh.

Her voice grew more serious. "Jimmy, I'm really impressed with the way you're handling all of this. If it was me... I don't know what I'd do. When you talked the other night about knowing that your mom is home in glory, I could almost see it; it was so real. That was so beautiful. Just keep that in your heart. Remember she's watching too... remember the cloud of witnesses who are cheering you on."

I could practically hear the sound of dad's voice echoing in my mind: *We're proud of you, son — and you know the Lord is well pleased.* The memory of it choked me up for a moment.

"But if it helps for you to hear me say it," Anna continued — "I will definitely be praying for you."

I waited silently, letting that last promise wash over my soul like clear fresh water. My voice was quieter but moved with feeling:

"I'm glad I called you... I'm really glad."

"Me too," she quietly agreed.

⌘

SHINING

...so let your light be shining before men
~ Matthew 5:16

The makeshift control room that filled our dining room was alive with streaming broadcasts. Each of its dozen monitors flashed from station to station in a continuous rotation. I was honestly surprised that most of the networks were still focused on the events here in Center Springs.

Commentators were interviewing an array of purported experts — from legitimate scientists to New Age spiritualists. They were all trying to offer explanations for the events of the past few days and frequently contradicted one another. The sound was turned up for just one of the channels, the one on their large central screen, which of course, was NNN.

A subtitle across the bottom of the screen introduced the current guest as Dr. J. Leopold, Ph.D., Professor of Religions at a well-known secular university.

. . .

WELCOME, Dr. Leopold; thank you for joining us on today's program. We'd like to get your reaction to these comments made this morning at the press conference in Center Springs...

The clip is a short excerpt of Pastor Wilkes' comments, advising people to read Mathew 24.

The Professor was glancing down at his own notes while the clip played.

[*Host*] Professor, what do you make of those remarks?

[*Dr. Leopold*] It is classic fanaticism to associate every unusual event with the end of the world. Religious groups — particularly of the Christian persuasion — have been pointing to the end of the world for thousands of years. Modern scholars of the New Testament are more enlightened than that. It seems far more likely that Jesus was making a prediction about Palestine in his own time -- and the Jewish Temple, in particular -- which was destroyed by the Romans in the year 70 AD.

[*Host*] I see. In fairness, we should point out that the Reverend clarified that he was not saying that these events were a sign of the end of the world. Be that as it may, it sounds like you do believe that Jesus was able to foresee the future....

[*Dr. Leopold*] Foresee... foreknow... forecast... These are terms for merely observing the political, military, and societal conditions of the day and having the foresight to anticipate their natural conclusions. Jesus clearly had a gift for connecting with people and understanding societal dynamics. He was very good at predicting the likely outcome of any actions that these dynamics would elicit. Indeed, it would not have been difficult to predict that the freedom-aspiring Jews would eventually clash with their Roman occupiers. This would be met with brutal military force by the Romans.

[Host] Fascinating.…

Reverend Wilkes also referred to something he called "The Beginning of Sorrows." What is that, exactly?

[Dr. Leopold] Well, Christian eschatology…, or the doctrine of last things, speaks of a final period of human history, which is believed to be notable for an abundance of supernatural manifestations and great calamities befalling the earth during this time. The Beginning of Sorrows is simply the beginning of this terrible time.

I would like to point out that this beginning has been assumed many times in the ensuing centuries, particularly during the first and second world wars. Naturally, such predictions have always proved unwarranted.

[Host] Dr. Leopold, you have certainly been adamant in your writings and lectures that you believe spirituality is merely the manifestation of emotional and chemical impulses. You have said that there is no such thing as a spiritual realm. How would you explain this clip that was captured during this morning's press conference?

The screen suddenly filled with a close-up shot of the black-winged demon as it screeched and hissed before being dragged into the ground.

As the scene cut back to the Professor, he appeared to be staring at the monitor with a startled look.

[Dr. Leopold] …Wh-what is that? Some kind of joke?

[Host] No, sir… that is footage from this morning's live press conference. I assume you have seen this?

There was a blank stare on the Professor's face, which was turning white. He looked down, fumbling with his notes.

[Dr. Leopold] I-I don't know what kind of game you are playing, but this is highly unconventional and, frankly, unprofessional. That is an obvious trick of special effects.

[Host] No sir, ...that was captured live just hours ago — dozens of reporters witnessed it in person.

The Professor suddenly removed his earpiece and walked off the set in a huff.

———————

"HARUMPH..." I heard Uncle Mike intone from just behind me. The sarcasm in his voice was typical for its understatement as he added... "That interview went well."

He was shaking his head as I turned and looked at him. He continued...

"I guess I wouldn't have believed it either if I hadn't seen it for myself. I can just imagine what that guy would say about Amos' journal."

Looking him in the eyes, it was pretty obvious that his resistance was weakening. With everything that had happened recently, the Spirit's call in his heart must be deafening. His eyes seemed to confirm that his fight against God was nearing its end. Something else in his look was also different — he was looking at *me* differently.

"I've been wantin' ta ask ya something. This mornin' when you looked at that reporter — it was like you could see that thing... even before it turned visible. Is that true?"

I debated for a moment what to reveal. Uncle Mike's sincerity was apparent, and the searching look in his eyes made me feel like I owed him an honest answer. I finally decided to answer frankly.

"I could sense its presence; you're right. At first, it was just a feeling, then it became clearer — like a ghostly thing. It looked sort of like a veil."

"Has that ever happened before?"

"You mean, can I see if demons are hiding in the furniture and stuff like that?" I joked.

He looked at me seriously. "That ain't funny. I'm serious — it scares the livin' daylights outta me. How come you weren't scared? How did ya' know ta do what ya' did?"

I was about to answer when he continued — he had more to say.…

"Maria told me what happened at the tent the other night… when you were shot, but I didn't believe it. I figured with all the stress and all, that she jus' imagined it. I gotta say… it's pretty hard to disbelieve my own eyes."

I looked at him thoughtfully. "Which thing is harder to believe… that demons are real, or that Jesus has authority over them? The reason that the first thing doesn't scare me is because of the second thing. I think what might really be scary for people is realizing that both things are true… realizing that it really matters what they think about God."

Uncle Mike blew out a lungful of air like he was a locomotive releasing stream. He didn't answer, staring in the direction of the TV screens — I'm pretty sure he wasn't looking at any of them.

AFTER A FEW MINUTES of watching more nonsensical explanations for the morning's events, I'd had enough.

"I have a ball and a few gloves out in the garage," I said, nudging Uncle Mike in the arm. "What do you say we get out of here and play catch?"

He smiled, looking grateful for the distraction, and slapped his arm across my shoulders.

"Hey Ward — game of catch!" he shouted toward the kitchen as we made our way out.

Mr. O'Malley popped his head through the doorway with a smile. "Great idea!"

Mrs. O' joined us, with Ryan in tow, as I led the makeshift entourage out into the garage. The baseball gear was stacked in the corner, just where Kelly and I left it at the end of last fall's season.

Kelly's glove was sitting right at the top, with her signature initials 'KO' scrawled on the side. A rush of memories washed over me as I held it, and after a moment, I realized I'd been gripping it tightly with both hands.

"Sorry..." I said as I handed it to Mr. O' with a self-conscious nod. "...Maybe this will fit Mrs. O'."

As he took it, I realized that he had already recognized it in my hands... apparently, they all had. There was a palpable quiet among them. He didn't answer — he just held it for a moment himself. Mrs. O' had Ryan on her hip as he offered it to her, and the two of them shared a sad glance. She hugged the glove close as she looked at Ryan and gave him a kiss.

The service door from the garage led into our backyard. I was embarrassed at how tall the grass was as we slogged through it. To be honest, in fact, I was mortified but did my best to make a joke of it.

"Hope we don't lose the ball in this... it's like the wild frontier out here."

"You ain't kiddin'," Uncle Mike jabbed — never one to miss a friendly dig. "Maybe we'll see some gazelle or water buffalo."

"A couple of hungry goats wouldn't be a bad idea," Mr. O' added with a wide grin.

Mrs. O' smiled at me and shook her head, insisting that it was fine.

A quick scan of the sky confirmed that the news choppers had finally left. I guess there was actually some real news happening somewhere else.

"POP FLY!" Uncle Mike yelled as he slung the ball high into the air. My legs kicked in automatically, racing deep. I was able to get under it just in time with a stretching catch. Mr. O' was holding his glove toward me for the cut-off, and I zinged it to him, hearing a loud pop as it slapped his glove.

"Good arm!" he yelled, pivoting to fire the ball back to Mike, who caught it and then lobbed one to Mrs. O'. She carefully tossed it to Ryan, who *almost* caught it. He scooped it up and ran to his dad with it.

It was speeding back to me again a minute later, and then I lobbed it high for Uncle Mike to field. The next time Mrs. O' threw it to

Ryan, he caught it in both hands. There was a look of surprise on his face that quickly turned to pure joy — he ran toward Mr. O' again shouting: "Dadda, catched it, catched it!"

Pretty soon, I was having such a great time that I'd forgotten how surreal the week had actually been. Uncle Mike and Mr. O' did their best to keep me running, including a few throws that only the Flash could catch, making me hunt in the tall grass.

Mrs. O' finally looked at her watch and announced it was time to start cooking dinner.

"Looks like we'll be squeezing around the kitchen table," Mr. O noted as she handed him her glove.

Mrs. O' stopped with her hands on her hips, "What about all the crew… should we offer them something to eat?"

Uncle Mike spoke up, "Let's eat out here on the deck! There's plenty o' room for all of 'em if we push the picnic tables together. There are still meatballs in th' freezer."

"I'll warm the oven and start the pasta," Mrs. O' agreed, scooping up Ryan.

The rest of us got the tables and benches set up, and then Uncle Mike headed inside to help in the kitchen. Mr. O' motioned toward a pair of deck chairs and took a seat, looking winded. I settled into the chair beside him with a comfortable sigh.

"The arm's still got it, but the legs aren't what they used to be," he complained as he stretched.

A moment later, Mrs. O' appeared with Ryan and released him onto the deck, where he scrambled into his dad's lap. Mr. O' gave him a hug and carefully laid Kelly's glove on the table.

"You guys should take that back with you; it's yours," I said as I looked at it.

He just nodded silently and stared at it for a moment before looking back at me with a quick thanks.

"It's hard to believe she's only been gone a few months," he said with a sigh. "So much has happened."

The flurry of events from the past few months rushed through my mind as I nodded in agreement. I was struck with the incredible privilege I've had of seeing her, not once but twice, since that day. The mere thought of those experiences sent a thrill through my soul that made me shudder.

"I have to say, Jim, you're not the same kid we knew a few months ago either. I'm truly inspired to see how strong your walk with the Lord has grown."

"I don't feel like I can take any credit at all for that. To be honest, it feels like God just decided to chase me despite myself," I confessed.

"He does that with all of us... none of us deserve it."

I nodded in agreement, although I was privately thinking that not everyone has an angel guardian who accompanies them on trips through time. Nonetheless, some of Chozeq's earliest words to me came to mind: *Better or worse are meaningless peculiarities when all are equally condemned, and all who ask are freely redeemed.* There really was no explanation for God's choosing me for this amazing work. I absolutely didn't deserve it — the only thing I'd ever done was to be willing, and I hadn't even been consistent in that.

I shook myself from deep thought.

"Hey, by the way, thanks for the chairs for our tent... that was really amazing!"

"That was God's hand, without a doubt," he admitted. "I heard about what you were doing in the same hour that the Seminary asked me whether I knew anyone who needed them. The timing couldn't have been better."

"You need to come to see the tent before you go back. They look amazing!"

"I hear you could use more."

"You're not kidding... we could use a bigger tent!"

"I'll keep that in mind in case we get any Circus clients!"

———

It was a little before 5:00 as we settled at the picnic tables, filled with bowls of spaghetti and meatballs and warm garlic bread. Uncle Mike found a few clean plastic tablecloths and supplied plenty of plates and silverware. The entire crew accepted our invitation to dinner.

Mr. O' stood at the end of the table and raised his hands to get everyone's attention.

"It's great to have you all here with us; thanks for joining us for this meal. The food looks and smells incredible... I'll say a quick blessing, and then we can have at it!

"Lord, you understand that we sometimes need to see the love you have for us with not just our faith, but sight as well. Thank you for the amazing demonstration of that love you have revealed for us here in Center Springs. When we recall the reason for our gathering here tonight, we humbly confess that we need to feel your embrace in this difficult time. Maria was a beloved friend, sister, and mother who gave the greatest measure of her devotion. Our hearts are thankful for her life, and we pray that her sacrifice will resonate throughout this country for the glory of your kingdom. Amen..."

His amen was echoed by voices all around the table.

There was a hushed atmosphere — I could feel crew members looking at me sympathetically, afraid to talk.

"I don't know if anybody else is hungry, but those meatballs smell awesome!" I said as enthusiastically as I could, grabbing for the closest platter. "These are my uncle's specialty — he owns Farro's Subs... check it out!"

"Yo, thanks, Jimmy!" Uncle Mike yelled from the other end of the table. "If ya wanna sneak in a commercial for the shop on yer interview, that'd be great too!"

The crew started to laugh and add their own jokes, accomplishing the job of lightening the mood.

ALMOST AN HOUR LATER, I was sitting with Uncle Mike, feeling pleasantly stuffed. The crew members had gone back to their preparations, and Mr. O' was helping with cleanup in the kitchen.

"Have ya thought about what you're gonna say in the interview?"

"Not really," I admitted. "I've kind of been deliberately avoiding thinking about it."

"You got some guts, kid... Vince was like that. He had nerves o' steel."

I stared up into the late afternoon sky and quietly released a deep breath. It felt good to hear my dad's name, but I definitely wouldn't compare myself to him on this point. I mulled over the words and repeated them silently to myself... *Nerves of steel.* In my case, it was more like nerves of tinsel — I was feeling a little like a leaf in the wind, to be honest. Uncle Mike looked over at me, seeming to sense my anxiety.

"Hey," he said, leaning forward in his seat. "It's in you... it's right inside there. If anybody's got what we need in this world right now, it's you. Just give *that*. That's what we all need."

The look in his eyes was searching — he was speaking from his heart... about the need in his own soul. It was just the message I needed to hear. I suddenly knew exactly what I needed to say tonight.

After a minute or so of silence, he sat back and continued, sounding uncertain.

"I was thinkin'... it might be best to keep quiet about that journal for now."

I hadn't planned on sharing it — I was already thinking the same thing. But the tone of his voice made me look over at him curiously.

"You've gotten through more of it than I have. Want to tell me what you read?"

He lowered his gaze uncomfortably. "Just sayin'... I think ya aught'a read it first."

His remark reminded me of the way mom had answered a similar question last Tuesday afternoon. It leaves me with an ominous feeling.

"O-kay... alright, fine... I won't mention it."

He acknowledged my promise with a nod of his head, still staring blankly toward the deck, obviously deep in thought.

⌘

CITY ON A HILL

A city set on a hill cannot be hid.
~ Matthew 5:14b

By 6:30, I had taken a much-needed shower and was working on my necktie. Thankfully, Mrs. O' had taken it upon herself to iron a shirt for me and picked out a tie from my dad's old collection. Mr. O' rescued me after my fifth failed attempt at tying a Full Windsor, producing a tidy knot with the length just right.

Uncle Mike yelled up from downstairs: "YO! Jimmy... There's a makeup crew down here looking for you — they're supposed to make you beautiful."

I honestly hadn't expected that.

I was led into the kitchen and seated in a chair in the middle of the room, then wrapped in a barber's cape as the makeup crew quickly got to work. Someone trimmed my hair, then stepped away as two more grabbed my hands and started filing my fingernails, while a third began rubbing something on my face. I was struck by the realization that the woman doing my face had a pierced nose and purple hair. There were no mirrors, and as far as I knew, she could have been making me look like Beetlejuice. After a few minutes, someone shined a bright light in my face, and the makeup artist studied her work seriously, making one final adjustment. When all was finally done, she held up a hand mirror for me to admire her handiwork. I was relieved to see that I didn't have clown lips.

"Thanks, nice work," I complimented... not knowing what else to say.

"Thanks, kid," she answered in a matter-of-fact response as she collected her gear and packed up.

A small entourage was arriving as I made my way from the kitchen; in the center of it was an impeccably dressed woman in her early forties. I recognized her from TV.

"VANESSA FILMER," she said, introducing herself with a handshake.

"Hi. I'm Jimmy," I answered uncertainly.

She placed her hand on my cheek and patted it. "Oh, I know who you are, my dear." The smile on her face was not patronizing, but it didn't really look warm either. It looked like someone thrilled to have just won the Lottery. She leaned close and pointed at the kitchen, speaking to me as if she was saying something confidential....

"My turn for a touch-up, then we'll talk."

She rushed off, giving me a chance to scan the house for the first time. The makeshift control room was buzzing with action. Several engineers worked the controls and a few others hovering over them wearing headsets and giving orders like, *'Break,'* and *'3...2...1...Fade'.*

Berith Gruner, the Producer, was walking around the room ordering people to make various adjustments. He didn't take much notice of me.

I was surprised to see Caden Koller and her husband standing at one end of the living room. She gave me a friendly wave from across the crowded room. That corner seemed like a safe place to go, and I quickly made my way over to them.

"I'm Nyle," her husband introduced himself with a broad smile. His handshake was firm and steady — no one would ever know that he had been a paralytic in a wheelchair just days ago.

"They want to interview us too," Caden explained. "I'm so nervous. I'm not used to actually *being* the news!"

Someone touched my arm, and I turned in surprise to see Trudi Staring, the reporter from this morning's press conference — the woman who was oppressed by *Vengeance*. She was fighting back a swell of emotion as she looked at me. Before I had a chance to raise my hand to shake, she wrapped her arms around me in an impromptu hug and squeezed tightly. I found myself patting her carefully on the back in surprise. She stepped back, dabbing the bottoms of her eyes with a tissue to keep the welling moisture from ruining her makeup. Her voice cracked with emotion as she strained to speak...

"What you did this morning... I never thought I'd *ever* feel this way again... this *free*. I want you to know how grateful I am."

"Thanks... but I can't take any of the credit. God did it — He set you free."

"I-I know... I know..." she was fighting back tears and fanning her face with her hands as she struggled to maintain control. A burst of moisture welled in her eyes, and she dabbed them quickly.

"Praise God!" I answered spontaneously, watching her nod her head in grateful agreement.

A pair of familiar voices behind her drew my attention. Pastor Wilkes and PJ had arrived, followed closely by Sheriff Flanagan, who happened to walk in at the same time. Trudi hugged them as she continued struggling with her tears.

"Hi, Juan. It's good to see you again," Caden said as she hugged PJ. Nyle offered him a firm handshake and wrapped his other strong arm around PJ's back with a friendly slap.

"IF THERE ARE NO OBJECTIONS, I'd like to offer a word of prayer for this evening," Pastor Wilkes said, scanning our faces.

"We can go over here... in the corner," I suggested. The rest of the crew ignored us — or pretended to, as we took each other's hands and bowed our heads together. Pastor Wilkes led first...

"Heavenly Father, we know that none of the events in recent days have been a surprise to You. You guide our steps and order our ways, and You have destined this evening in Your Divine plan for the world. As we honor Maria's memory, we invite your Spirit to be the master of all that we do tonight and ask that Your angels keep watch over this place while the message You have prepared is delivered from this room and beamed throughout the world. Guide every answer and inspire each thought as we commit our hearts lovingly and gratefully to you."

PJ then quietly lifted each one of us to the Lord by name, ending with me. He finished by quoting the verse he shared with me earlier in the afternoon...

"...We hold to Your promise Lord: *I will give you a mouth and wisdom, which all your adversaries will not be able to withstand.*"

"WELL THEN..." Vanessa said uncomfortably from right behind me, daintily clearing her throat. "If you're ready?"

She bid me follow her with one hand while pointing with her other arm toward the interview chairs, making me feel a little like an airplane being guided into the gate. They had me sit down under the bright camera lights, and someone clipped a mic to my necktie. A large microphone also hovered above my head on a long boom.

Vanessa smoothed the page on her small notebook and smiled at me.

"How are you feeling?"

I had to clear my throat before answering. "Fine... I'm okay, thanks."

As my eyes focus on the surrounding set, I realized there were 60-inch screens on either side of us, just off-camera. They were showing the opening credits, with a large headline that read: SPECIAL REPORT. Behind the headline were images from Tuesday night at the tent, including a slide show of the now-familiar shots of me holding mom.

"You can call me Vanessa," she offered informally in a friendly voice. "I'm very sorry for your loss. Your mother must have been a very special woman."

"She really was. She was pretty special."

[VF] "Tell me about her."

I was momentarily thrown by the question. There was so much I could say about her; how could I sum it up in a few sentences?! As I was struggling, a single word suddenly came to mind...

[A] "...*Devoted*. That's the word that stands out the most about her. It's hard to imagine a more devoted parent or friend. We could be talking about anything, and she always hung on every word — like it was the most important conversation in the world, no matter how trivial. She was definitely an awesome mom, but she was also a lot more than that... she was a genuine friend. Not in an artificial way, like she was trying to fit in; it was just real. I guess maybe it was because we'd been through so much together... after dad died. We just had *each other*, you know?"

[VF] "I can see that the two of you had an extraordinary bond."

[A] "We did. It grew over time... especially this year.

[VF] "It sounds like this was a big year for changes in your life. What happened, exactly?'

Her question triggered a flurry of memories... most of which involved Chozeq. I did my best to sort through them all, pushing aside the big list that I knew I couldn't speak of. What remained were poignant images of Kelly and mom at the most difficult points in both their lives.

[A] "I had a friend... Kelly. We grew up together; I guess she was like a sister, except more, we did everything together. We were more than just friends."

I was surprised by a stray tear running down my cheek and quickly wiped it off, pausing for a moment before continuing.

"She had a brain tumor, and… uh… and ah…we… we lost her."

I wiped away another tear. There was another pause as I collected myself again.

"I took it pretty hard, and so did mom. Kelly was like a part of our family… all the O'Malleys are, including her parents and her little brother. Anyway, through that experience, God started to show me what's really important in life.

"It forced me to admit that we really have no control over whether we live or die. We can do our best to keep fit and avoid some dangerous things like smoking, overeating, or not wearing seat belts, but ultimately there are a trillion cells in our bodies that carry on millions of processes that we have no control over. One out of four people will get cancer; we can't change that. Ultimately, God is the one who controls that."

"CUT!"

It was Berith Gruner's voice. "Great work… that's really great; we can work with that."

Vanessa explained what was going on, noticing my confused expression. "That was being recorded. It will be edited into teasers — fifteen-second commercials and sent to all the affiliate stations." She glanced at her watch. "We have about 30 minutes before we start."

I felt like I'd just been through the first few turns of a wild roller-coaster that has suddenly lost power. I couldn't help wondering how wild the rest of the ride would be.

HALF AN HOUR LATER, we were finally given the cue that we were about to go back on-air. It had been the longest 30 minutes of my life. I hadn't moved far, afraid to disturb all the careful positioning of the mics and lights.

This time we could hear the opening soundtrack, which started with several soundbites from the earlier teaser. Then the show's theme music kicked in. Vanessa had settled into her chair and looked as comfortable as ever; she was obviously a real pro at this. The camera zoomed in on her as we went live.

[VF] "Welcome, and thank you for joining us for this special edition of America Tonight. I'm Vanessa Filmer.

"Our guest tonight is James Moretti, the boy at the center of a media firestorm. The heartrending images seen here, of Jimmy holding his dying mother after she was tragically shot, have been shown world-wide. As we have all been learning, there is a great deal more to the story of what is happening here in the small town of Center Springs, which we will explore together with you tonight."

I COULD SEE that the camera had zoomed out; it was now showing both of us. Vanessa turned to me and began with her first question of the live interview.

[VF] "Jimmy, tell me about Tuesday night in your own words. What do you remember?"

I needed to pause and take a deep breath, waiting for my heart to settle down.

[A] "We arrived late for the service. The roads were backed up with traffic, and we walked part of the way. I remember the crowd… it was huge; the tent has a thousand seats, and it was full, but there were still twice that many outside.

"The pastors and elders from local churches were praying for people who were crowded in around the altar. Amazing miracles were happening — I remember meeting a man as we got closer — he was walking toward us with tears. He was telling everyone he met that his eyesight had been restored. He kept saying: *I can see... I came here blind, but now I can see!* A pile of discarded crutches and wheelchairs was being collected — it was huge… it was hard to fathom all that was happening.

"The music team was leading a song… *Whom the Lord sets free is free indeed... and thousands were singing.* We passed many people who were just kneeling in the grass and praying or crying. There was a powerful feeling in the air. You'd have to have been there to know what it was like — it felt like God himself had descended on that field... like it was holy ground."

VANESSA SEEMED to flinch a little uncomfortably and pressed past my last remark.

[VF] "In your statement to the police, you say that you made your way to the tent and stood beside the stage. What happened next?"

Her question forced me to focus on the part of the story that I was dreading the most. I looked down at my hands, realizing that I was wringing them together. Pausing for a breath, I forced myself to put them down, gripping my legs above the knees.
[A] "I... I was kind of overwhelmed — by the song, the atmosphere, the call to worship. I remember being drawn to my knees."

[VF] "Is that when the gunman opened fire?"

The image of old Amos immediately rushed to mind as he appeared with his tearful words. I pushed the thought aside....
[A] "I heard the gunshot. It sounded like a pop in the open air, but I knew that it was a gun from the screams. There was another blast before I had a chance to move — a thunderbolt; it shook the ground where I was kneeling. I was still trying to understand what was happening when I felt her fall against me... I caught her."

[VF] "Your mother."

Fresh tears welled up in my eyes as I relived the events. I brushed them away with a closed fist and continued...
[A] "Yeah... I knew what had happened from the look on her face."
A few more tears escaped. I did my best to ignore them.

"She looked relieved… I'll never forget it. She couldn't talk, but she held my face with a look of relief that I was okay."

I wasn't able to stifle the brief flood of tears that suddenly overwhelmed me. I sat silently for a moment with my eyes tightly closed and felt my body shake.

[VF] "It's okay, take your time."

Her voice was sympathetic, and it helped me refocus and get a hold of myself. When I opened my eyes, she was offering me a handkerchief.

The best I could do was to nod in thanks and offered an unspoken apology, as I used the handkerchief like a towel to mop up my face. Most of the make-up artist's careful work was quickly transferred to it.

Music began to play, and Vanessa read from her TelePrompter into the camera…

[VF] "We'll be right back after these messages."

⌘

19

___

PAIN

Pain is a warning of danger...

___

The makeup crew rushed onto the set, and the woman with purple hair gave me a wink as she knelt in front of my chair.
"I should-a used the waterproof stuff on you kid," she joked, lightening the mood. "Good as new," she declared after a minute of work. She gave me a wink and offered me a clean handkerchief, just in case, and then scrambled away.

The music signaled that we were back on the air.

[VF] "Thank you for being with us for this special edition broadcast of America Tonight. I'm Vanessa Filmer. We're speaking with young Jimmy Moretti."

She turned back toward me with a sympathetic expression as she prepared to ask her next question.

[VF] "These are difficult things for you to talk about... I appreciate that. The authorities have confirmed witness accounts that the shooter was aiming at you. Your mother blocked that shot, didn't she."

[A] "Yeah... y-yes. That's what they say. It makes it worse to know that."

[VF] "Does it frighten you that someone was trying to kill you?"

[A] "Frighten me? Not really. My life is in God's hands... I'm ready to go if it's my time."

[VF] "Do you believe then that it was your mother's time? Some would say that God chose to take her life — how does it make you feel to think that that could be true?"

I looked at Vanessa, searching her eyes for a moment. Something in her voice almost sounded like cynicism. I could sense that she didn't mean to be hurtful but had the feeling that she couldn't accept the idea of a divine creator.

[A] "He didn't choose it. It might have been in His perfect timing, but that doesn't mean he caused it. In fact, I'm more convinced than ever that God doesn't cause or use evil. But he has an incredible capacity to bring something good from anything — even from something that was intended for evil."

Vanessa was uncharacteristically silent for a brief moment as if my answer had triggered a powerful memory. She let her notepad hang to one side as she leaned slightly forward.

[VF] "But an all-powerful creator could prevent evil if he wanted to, couldn't he? Atheists frequently point to pain as a reason they can't believe in a loving God. You obviously believe in God — why do you think He allows pain in the world?"

I wasn't surprised by her question. In fact, I was more surprised at how clearly I suddenly expected it. An answer was on the tip of my tongue before she had finished speaking...

[A] "...It's funny that the ones who bring up that question most often usually claim to be atheists."

Vanessa looked at me quizzically.

[VF] "Why is that?"

[A] "Well, when you think about it, the question implies a moral judgment — that allowing or causing pain is immoral. Yet, the idea of morality only makes sense if there is a higher law to measure behavior against. It requires that there is some sort of absolute definition of right and wrong that everyone agrees with. The recognition of right and wrong is an admission that a higher law exists, but not only that — it's a confirmation that it is written inside us from our earliest moment."

[VF] "I was following until the 'written inside us' part. Why do you feel that that proves God's existence?"

[A] "Think about it; even small kids know that fairness is important and that causing pain to others is wrong. But more importantly, people know that putting oneself at risk to help someone else is right and good. That can't be explained by evolution or natural selection because it's the opposite of self-preservation. Yet, it's a universal human trait.

"The Bible explains why it proves God created us, and it's the most logical explanation that there is. In the creation story, we see that love existed *before* humanity. Love was already at work in the Godhead before there was human life. That's why Jesus said that Love is the greatest commandment — it's the ultimate moral law. It happens to be the essence of what God is, and he wrote it into our human hearts."

[VF] "Alright... but if love is written in all human hearts, why is there hate and pain in the world?"

Once again, an answer to her question bubbled up inside me as if it was being poured into my mind.

[A] "To answer the question about pain, I think we have to understand that pain and evil can't be separated. The fact that pain exists in the world is evidence that evil exists. If the essence of God is love, then evil must be his opposite — an opposing force that seeks to undo all the good that God does. God isn't the cause of evil, but he can use even our pain for good; to change us — even to save us."

An unexpected memory suddenly came to mind that seemed to illustrates the point perfectly...

"I saw a report a few months ago about a little girl who was born with a rare disease that made her body insensitive to pain. It's called CIPA, I think. It sounded at first like that might be a blessing, but it turns out that she lives under the constant threat of serious injury from wounds or burns that a normal person would quickly recoil from. She has to be watched constantly because she could easily hurt herself in a way that could end her life. When they interviewed her mother, she said something that struck me. She said *I pray every night for my little girl, that God would give her a sense of pain.*

"Stop and think about that for a moment, and put that thought together with the fact that God's essence is love. It becomes easy to see that our ability to feel pain was given to us for a reason. Pain is a warning of danger, but not all danger is physical. Sometimes the danger is much greater than physical harm — sometimes, it warns of eternal harm. It's our deepest inner pain that shows us our need for a savior."

VANESSA LOOKED STUNNED FOR A MOMENT, and a glint of moisture began to well in her eyes, but then she quickly collected her thoughts and stared down at her notepad. She subtly cleared her throat, touching the small of her neck as she carefully swallowed...

"...I must say, Jimmy, you are a surprising young man...

[VF] "If you don't mind, I'd like to shift gears just a bit. The Sheriff's department has confirmed that Tuesday night was not the first attempt on your life."

The screens began playing a clip from Sunday night, showing paramedics as they lifted me on a stretcher and rushed me away in an ambulance.

[VF] "Last Friday night, you *were*, in fact, shot. Is that correct?

[A] "Yes, that's right.

[VF] "Help our audience understand what happened.

[A] "Well, it happened so fast... I remember walking up the aisle... the service was about to start. The man was wearing a long coat, like a raincoat. He was sweating and had a tormented look on his face — desperate looking. He stammered, and his voice gave me an uneasy feeling — he said my name, and I answered him. Then he apologized... saying that they were making him do it, and that's when he pulled out a sawed-off shotgun and shot me."

[VF] "He shot you at point-blank range. How badly were you injured?"

[A] "The EMT's said that my heart stopped and I wasn't breathing. It broke three of my ribs."

[VF] "And yet, you were discharged from the hospital on Tuesday morning, just over a day later, with no sign of injury. How is that possible?"

Her question brought a thrill to my soul as I remembered the moment that Chozeq's sword touched my chest. I could feel the thrill bubbling inside me like a geyser as I attempted to answer.
[A] "It's pretty obvious that nothing is impossible to God. The doctors couldn't believe it either; they ran a bunch of tests and rechecked me about six times."

[VF] "You provided NNN with a release that allowed us to review your medical records — they confirmed your account. I'd like to come back to that in a moment.

"First, I want to get back to the shooting. Why would someone want to kill you — Who do you think is behind these attempts?"

I happened to look past Vanessa and saw Sheriff Flanagan standing just off the set behind her. He shook his head subtly in a reminder that I shouldn't share any of what I told agent DeMassi.

[A] "I think, whoever it is is, they are more likely to be trying to stop what's happening here — they're really after that and not me."

[VF] "You think the shooters were both trying to stop the tent meetings? What's so special about these services?"

My thoughts suddenly took me back to a discussion at the tent with Pete and PJ on the morning after our first all-night service. PJ was telling us about the Latter Rain — his words replayed as clearly as if he'd just spoken them:

> "God is doing something here — right here... something
> incredible! We just have to keep doing what we're doing
> and make sure nothing gets in the way. There are souls at
> stake... thousands- maybe millions of souls!"

A curious look in Vanessa's eyes signaled that she had picked up on the surge of emotion the memory triggered. She waited for me to speak.

[A] "All throughout history, God has marked important points in his plan with special demonstrations of his power. Those times have been profound milestones in human history — the Israelites' deliverance from Egypt was when God gave the covenant law to Israel. The miracles of Elijah's prophetic ministry marked judgment over Israel's breaking of that covenant. The miracles that Jesus performed were a sign that God was making a new covenant with the whole world through the gift of his own son. The birth of the early church was marked by a period of profound miracles that began on Pentecost.

"Another period in history has also been promised, when God will pour out his spirit like never before. The prophet Joel said it will be on 'all flesh'... it will be global. It'll be a great harvest when huge numbers of lives will be radically transformed and saved. This period of miracles will be like nothing we've seen in 2,000 years, and it will be on a scale that has never been seen in the world before. It's sometimes called the Latter Rain, and it happens shortly before Christ's return."

[VF] "So you believe that these tent meetings mark the end of the world?"

[A] "No, definitely not. But I do believe they are the beginning of something important. What's happening here is the first spark in a fire that will soon sweep the whole world."

[VF] "What makes you think so?"

I was tempted to explain by saying that Chozeq told me... but, even though it's the truth, I was pretty sure that an explanation involving an angel suspending me in midair might not be very convincing. I decided to point to recent events instead.

[A] "Just look at what's happening! My own healing wasn't the first miracle we've seen. Since the first night of services at the tent, there have been continuous miracles. To be honest, that first service never ended... it continued around the clock until last Tuesday night. Hundreds of people have been healed of cancer and other diseases. We've watched crippled people and paralytics jump and walk... deaf people have regained their hearing, and blind people have received sight! Even more importantly, more than a thousand have received new life and forgiveness at those altars!

"This is just the beginning of what God is starting throughout the world. We've already seen the same thing beginning to spread to other towns and cities. It will start happening in other countries — this is going to spread around the world."

THE SET DIRECTOR signaled that we were going to a commercial break. Vanessa turned toward the camera and read the prompter:

[VF] "When we return, we'll be talking to a couple whose lives have been dramatically changed by those events. You won't want to miss this... We'll be right back."

⌘

20

GLORY

...they may see your good works and give glory to your Father in heaven.
~ Matthew 5:16b

There was a flurry of activity as crew members added two more chairs to the set. Caden and Nyle were quickly ushered in from behind the cameras. Caden gave me a smiling thumbs up and silently mouthed a few encouraging words as she took a seat beside me.

Vanessa greeted them and accepted Nyle's handshake.

"It's good to see you again, Caden. How are you both?"

The couple shared a glance and smiled broadly. "Never better," Caden answered.

The set director yelled: "Thirty seconds!"

Vanessa offered a last-minute instruction... "I'll introduce the clip first, then back to you."

They both nodded with a look to each other and held hands. Caden looked comfortable in front of the cameras, but it was clear that Nyle was as nervous as I was.

The music signaled once again that we were back on the air.

[VF] "Thank you for tuning in to this special edition broadcast. I'm Vanessa Filmer, and this is America Tonight.

"We have been speaking with Jimmy Moretti about the events in Center Springs that tragically claimed his mother's life last weekend. We're joined now by a husband and wife pair who have recently had a dramatic experience at one of those services themselves. The clip you are about to see will be familiar to you if you were watching the news last weekend."

The clip of Nyle's healing began to play, showing Caden looking into the camera with tears streaming down her face. The tent, packed with people, was visible in the background.

"What's happening here is like nothing I've ever experienced," Caden could be seen saying as she wiped a tear from her cheek.

"It has not been shared publicly that my husband is a wounded warrior... he suffered a head injury that left him without the ability to speak or to use his right arm and leg — he's been in a wheelchair for two years." She wiped more tears from both her cheeks as she continued, obviously struggling to hold herself together. "The footage we want to show you is real..." she cried for a second with a few gasps of joy and then managed to continue, "... I want you to see what just happened..." She lowered her mic and nodded to the crew to play the clip.

The scene showed the news camera panning across the expansive crowd as everyone was praying. Many people were crying and lifting their hands when it suddenly looked like a wave was sweeping through them, knocking many of them to the ground or to their knees. As the camera followed what was happening, it panned toward Nyle seated in a wheelchair near the back — he had a deeply moved expression on his face and sat with one arm raised and the other lying limply in his lap. When the wave struck him, he fell from his wheelchair onto his knees. Then he could be seen looking down in surprise at his legs and suddenly moved the fingers in his limp arm. He grabbed his disabled leg with both his hands in shock and then climbed to his feet and stood, then began clapping his hands and leaping and praising God... "I-I CAN WALK!!! P-PRAISE GOD I CAN WALK!!!!" Caden could be seen running into the scene and throwing her arms around his neck, screaming and crying in joy as he spun her around and around.

As the cameras cut back to a live shot of the set, Caden was wiping away fresh tears of joy, clearly reliving the fantastic event once again. I handed her my unused handkerchief.

[VF] "Nyle and Caden, welcome, and thank you for being with us tonight. Nyle, if I may start with you… You were injured in an IED attack, is that right?"

[A] "Yes. Our company was on patrol at dawn. I had the turret — that was the gun turret on top of our armored vehicle. The blast lifted our AV into the air and shattered my helmet. I don't remember anything else until I woke up three weeks later in a field hospital. Part of my skull had been pulverized, and fragments of it were driven into my brain; I lost hearing in my right ear. The doctors said I'd never walk or speak again."

[VF] "To see you now, that seems hard to believe. Yet your discharge papers and medical records all confirm it. How long was it before you were able to leave the hospital?"

[A] "I spent a month overseas before being flown to Decatur, Georgia, where they did five operations to implant a stainless steel plate in my head and do reconstructive surgeries. I was there for six months."

[VF] "Caden... When Nyle came home, he must have been in pretty bad shape."

[A] "Yes. He was bedridden for the first four months. After that, he used a wheelchair and remained unable to speak with extensive paralysis."

[VF] "Such severe injuries. How were you able to cope?"

[A] "I didn't cope very well, to be honest. I became bitter and angry — mainly toward God. I couldn't bear to look at other couples walking hand-in-hand or sitting in a restaurant together. The sight of mothers with their babies was so painful because I knew we would never have that ourselves.

"I guess I coped with my pain by immersing myself in my work; I tried to block it out but spent most nights crying myself to sleep."

[VF] "Tell us about Friday night. What made you bring Nyle to that tent meeting?"

[A] "It really started a few nights earlier. I had been at my wit's end. When the station...."

[VF] "...You're a news reporter for our local affiliate WCST...."

[A] "Yes, that's right... When WCST assigned me to cover the church tent meetings, I was annoyed, to be honest. I really hadn't been much of a churchgoer — in fact, I hadn't been in a church in years. Not since Nyle was... well, like I said, I was angry with God.

"But when we got there... my cameraman and I, it was different from anything I expected. We started interviewing people... primarily high school and college-aged kids, and I couldn't help noticing how different they were. They had this incredible peace about them and joy. They all kept telling us about these extraordinary experiences they'd had — they said they'd met God. It wasn't figurative — they really meant it. Then we started seeing people being healed. I saw a small child in a wheelchair with severe cerebral palsy... she stood up, completely healed — a normal young girl! I watched her parents both collapse to their knees, just weeping in joy.

"I knew it was real... it was undeniable. I knew that I needed what these kids had found — I knew I desperately needed it! My cameraman was kind of surprised when I knelt down right there and accepted Jesus as my savior. He broadcast the whole thing on live TV, but I didn't care — I was changed. Something inside me was changed that night; I was a new person. All of my bitterness and anger melted away.

"My first thought was that I wanted Nyle to know what I'd found — I just wanted him to know. I knew I had to bring him and show him... I had no idea what would happen to him!"

[VF] "Nyle, what do you remember of that night?"

[A] "It's a little patchy, to be honest. Caden told me where we were going, but I didn't understand why she was so anxious to go to a church service. It was my fault that we arrived late, I suppose. Her camera crew was waiting for us when we arrived, and they seemed upset that Caden had missed something. They pointed to an ambulance that was speeding away."

Nyle looked at me sheepishly as he explained... "It was taking Jimmy to the hospital — he'd just been shot.

"Caden was undeterred. She pushed my wheelchair closer and parked me at the end of one of the rows near the back, half outside the tent where she could keep an eye on me. Everyone was praying — I mean, they weren't just bowing politely; they were really praying! It was intense — there was such a spirit in the place... kind of an awe-inspiring presence. I'm not sure why, but I started to cry.

"Then, suddenly, there was this sound — it was like a whirlwind or tornado or something. It swept across the people there like it was blowing them over. Then it reached me, and I felt this extraordinary presence — incredibly welcoming and forgiving. The next thing I remember is being on my knees, and... well... you saw the rest."

[VF] "That is a truly amazing story. Was your hearing restored as well? Is it as if the injury never happened?"

[A] "My hearing is perfect — that was the first thing I noticed, in fact, and yes, my speech and motor control are as good as ever. I still have a steel plate in my head — I like to think of it as a reminder of the miracle God performed. …I also get to use it as an excuse for being a hardhead sometimes." He glanced at Caden with a quick smile.

[VF] "It sounds like everything we're hearing about these services, if true, is only good. Why do you think anyone would want to stop them?"

[A] "That's honestly beyond me. I can't imagine who would want to stop it!"

VANESSA LOOKED to all three of us, and her eyes narrowed in a serious expression.

[VF] "What would you say to the skeptics who have a hard time believing what you're describing? Unfortunately, there is a long history in the world of groups that brainwash their members into believing in miraculous events. Is this a cult?"

Caden and Nyle both looked at me with flabbergasted expressions, unable to believe Vanessa's question in light of all that we had just discussed. I was relieved to realize that an answer had suddenly popped into my head….

[A] "This has happened out in public… not in a secret basement or some foreign wilderness. Our local hospital is full of medical proof of the miracles we've seen. The people who have been leading the services are longstanding Pastors and leaders from churches throughout the area. The cult explanation just doesn't work.

"To the skeptical people… I can understand that; they're more than welcome to come and see for themselves. If that's not possible, then they only need to ask God to meet them where they are. He's not far away... God is the one who is seeking and pursuing *them*. The restlessness they feel was placed there by Him... that's his invitation. He is inviting them to come to Him. We don't need to be perfect to come; we can come with all our pain, our shame, and emotional wreckage, and He takes all that and exchanges it for forgiveness and genuine rest. This is the time to finally come... now is the time."

There was a short silence as Vanessa searched my eyes. I was able to catch a brief glimpse of the struggle that was raging deep inside her. After a moment, she glanced at her notes and then leaned back in her chair, taking a deep breath. Quickly regaining her professional voice, she looked away from me and straight into the camera....

[VF] "Healing miracles and forgiveness are one thing, but demons are something else entirely. When we return, we'll be speaking with Trudi Staring. Don't go away."

From the monitors, the screeching sound of the vengeance demon began to play, as its black leathery face filled the screen, then faded as the scene dissolved to a commercial break.

⌘

21

BEAUTIFUL DAYLIGHT

...it was like a horrible darkness was being ripped away...
~ Trudi Staring.

C aden and Nyle quickly stood and gave me a smile as they started to make their way off the set while Trudi arrived. A set crew member lifted one of the chairs to remove it, and Trudi held up her hand, asking him to wait.

SHE LOOKED AT CADEN.

"Would you stay? C-can you stay on with me?"

Caden looked to Vanessa, who did not object, although there was very little warmth in her eyes for Trudi. Until today, the two women have been bitter professional rivals.

Trudi was invited to take the middle chair as they sat down. She leaned over to me and whispered....

"You're doing fantastic — you're a natural at this!"

I nodded in thanks, honestly grateful for her encouragement, although, on the inside, I was just as terrified as ever. Something was amazing about Trudi; she seemed to emanate peace and appeared to be filled with wonder, like a child. There was a joy in her spirit that reminded me of someone who had just emerged from a long cold winter into the warmth of the summer sun.

The set director yelled a five-second warning, and the show's theme music began to play. Vanessa spoke into the camera.

[VF] "Thank you again for joining us for tonight's special edition broadcast of America Tonight. I'm Vanessa Filmer.

"We have been talking with Jimmy Moretti about recent events here in Center Springs. In our last segment, we spoke about miraculous healing that has been reported. Now we will shift gears once again to look into a darker side of things here in Center Springs. We are speaking with Trudi Starring, who suffered an astonishing experience in a press conference here this morning."

VANESSA TURNED toward Trudi and welcomed her.

[VF] "Trudi, thank you so much for agreeing to join us tonight. How are you doing?"

[A] "It's a privilege to be on your program Vanessa; thank you... I mean that sincerely. I'm doing great... I honestly don't think I've ever been better."

[VF] "Well, that shows remarkable fortitude in light of this morning's events. Is it alright if we show our audience what occurred?"

Trudi nodded acceptingly.

The clip showed the morning's scene from several cameras at various angles, clearly capturing the extraordinary sight of the huge leathery black creature. When it ended, Vanessa was staring unbelievingly at the screen. She seemed to catch herself and glanced at her notes before looking back to Trudi.

[VF] "While many people may have a hard time believing reports of miraculous healing, it is even more difficult for most of us to accept the existence of actual demons. I honestly don't know what to make of this morning's events... what do *you* think that was?"

[A] "Who could blame you for being astonished! If I hadn't experienced it, I wouldn't have believed it myself. There is no doubt in my mind that the thing we saw was a demonic creature. For me, it wasn't just the sight of it... I felt it!

"When it left me, it was like a veil over my heart was suddenly lifted — all of a sudden, I could see the world as it actually is. A gigantic weight of bitterness and pain just fell away!"

[VF] "Jimmy, you spoke to the creature — you called it Vengeance. Why did you use that term?"

[A] "That's what it was — a spirit of vengeance. I just felt it... it's hard to say why or how."

Trudi met my gaze and reached over to take me by the hand. There was a growing mist in her eyes.

"Jimmy... what you did was so incredible!" Her eyes welled with tears. "I don't know how you knew... how you did what you did....." She looked back at Vanessa.

"Jimmy has an amazing gift... it's amazing...." A few tears ran down her face, and she ignored them. "I knew something special was happening when he called me Molly." She looked at me again and squeezed my hand as if gripping it for support, then turned back to Vanessa. "That was a name my grandmother used for me. She told me that in our heritage, it meant: 'Wished-for child' — my grandmother was Jewish." She looked back at me and searched my eyes as she continued. "No one else knew about that name... no one."

She glanced down at the floor for a second and then back at Vanessa, continuing nervously.

"I was a victim of abuse as a child... it was someone our family trusted, a priest.

"...We were raised in an orthodox Christian Church — my father was orthodox," she added, feeling compelled to explain.

"The abuse started when I was young — probably only five or six years old. It continued until I was in High School." Her tears were falling steadily now as she struggled to go on. A few more handkerchiefs appeared, and she accepted them gratefully, releasing my hand as she dabbed her eyes.

"I tried to tell... no one took me seriously. I grew more and more bitter and rebellious until my parents finally sent me away to a boarding school." She stared downward... "My pain became what defined me. It made me hard... and, I suppose, a little cruel. I was driven to do whatever it took to never be vulnerable again. I didn't care who I had to fight... or who I hurt," she looked at Vanessa as she said this, and the two of them shared a knowing glance that seemed to melt them both.

Trudi quietly cleared her throat and swallowed with some difficulty. She looked back at me as she finally continued.

"When you started speaking this morning, it was like I'd been awakened inside a prison. I could hear your voice, but something else had the rest of me. I could feel it stabbing at my heart and squeezing me harder than ever — it was pure rage. When you called it by that name and did what you did... the only way I can describe it is that it was like a horrible darkness was being ripped away, suddenly freeing me and leaving me in beautiful daylight."

More tears rolled down her cheeks as she silently mouthed the words *thank you* to me. I realized that there were tears on my face, too, and nodded back at her as I wiped them off with the back of my hand.

[VF] "That's an incredible story. Thank you for being willing to share it. I have a feeling you are helping many others who can relate to the pain you described."

VANESSA TURNED TOWARD CADEN. "You were quick to console Trudi. Did the two of you know each other?"

[A] "Only professionally," Caden answered, giving Trudi a quick smile. "Call it intuition, I guess... I just knew what I had to do. I didn't even think about it — I guess I just reacted."

[VF] "You prayed a prayer together?"

[A] "Yes... the Sinner's Prayer."

Caden caught the expression on Vanessa's face and explained, "That's what they called it when I prayed the same prayer — when I was led to the Lord. It's a prayer of confession, accepting forgiveness."

Trudi interjected...

"It was more than that... more than a prayer. It wasn't just words; it was an **encounter** — I could feel God's presence... he was actually there with us! It changed me forever."

VANESSA STUDIED Trudi's face for a long moment, her eyes acknowledging that she recognized the change. "I can see that it did," she admitted quietly, with more than a little wonder in her voice. She finally collected her thoughts, glancing back at her notes, then she laid them aside and turned to me.

[VF] "Jimmy, we spoke about pain earlier, and I understand what you said about God being able to make something good out of tragedy. Wouldn't it be more loving if He prevented evil altogether? Couldn't God have stopped what happened to Trudi and so many others like her?"

I considered her question silently for a brief moment as a response flooded my mind.

[A] "You mean by striking the priest dead or removing him some other way? I suppose He could have. It's difficult for us to know all the parts of a puzzle that big. What that man did was truly evil, but could he have also done some other things in his life that helped people? Few people are entirely evil, and none of us are completely good.

AN ANSWER suddenly formed in my mind with incredible clarity — it gave me a chill as I considered the implications of it.

"The answer goes deeper than people hurting others, though. Most people understand the value of real love. It's a beautiful thing to see two people who are genuinely in love. Yet, what kind of love could that couple have for one another if they didn't also have the freedom to **not** love each other? Without free will, it wouldn't be love at all — there can't be love without free will.

"Love is so valuable that God has deemed it worth all the pain and evil that result from our free will. Jesus was not exempt from that pain. In fact, his whole reason for coming was to suffer and bear the consequences of our sin. He endured the cross, not just for nameless humanity, but for me and for *you, personally.* His life, death, and resurrection provided a bridge to an eternal life where suffering will only be a memory, but its lessons will shape eternity. There are no more tears in Heaven because love will be the only law, ruling in every heart.

As I considered eternity, my mind was suddenly filled with the shocking image of Hell's terrible gates. The wailing screeches of condemned souls made me shudder and quickly brought tears to my eyes. I looked back at Vanessa, moved with an urgent appeal that surged from within me.

I felt a tear roll down my cheek as I looked at her, adding in a quieter voice:

"Hell is the exact opposite. A place where evil, hatred, and free will exist in the absence of love. For those who reject the bridge that Jesus provided, any suffering experienced here will be nothing compared with the terror that exists there."

⌘

22

SAVED

Whoever calls upon the name of the Lord...
~ Romans 10:13

After the lights had dimmed and the cameras were shut off, the crew wasted no time in beginning to dismantle their equipment. The makeshift control room was the last thing to be shut down after Berith Gruner was satisfied that the interview had been properly saved and the Network's regular programing resumed.

Trudi, Caden, and Nyle were waiting with the others as I walked off the set, finally free of microphone wires. It was an incredible relief to be out of the hot lights and away from the cameras.

Vanessa was talking to Mr. Gruner in the dining room. She shook his hand as he congratulated her and smiled broadly when she made her way toward us.

"The ratings were through the roof," she eagerly explained, "... nineteen million viewers, and that's just on *our* network."

Trudi's eyes widened; "Wow! That's like a Superbowl!"

"Yup," Vanessa affirmed, "and the syndication deals will ensure that it's replayed on other networks... probably a dozen times at least."

My knees felt suddenly wobbly as I thought about all those people. I couldn't even picture that many people. As a matter of fact, the largest group I could remember ever even *seeing* at one time could only have been a few hundred-thousand or so, and that hoard of jagged-winged creatures wasn't even human.

Uncle Mike slapped me on the back, startling me. "Way ta' go, kid... ya done real good."

I turned to thank him, and he threw his arms around me in a congratulatory hug. As I stepped back, the others all patted me on the back and echoed his sentiments. Mr. O. shook my hand with both of his.

"That was really something, Jimmy. You should be proud."

It hadn't occurred to me to feel proud over it. Relief is what I mostly felt, plus the bittersweet realization that none of this would be happening if it hadn't been for the tragic events on Tuesday night.

VANESSA WAS the last to shake my hand. "Thanks, Jimmy... that was a fantastic interview."

Her eyes hinted that there was something else on her mind; it was a conflicted look — there was turmoil in her eyes. She took my arm and gently led me a few steps away from the others, speaking in a low voice so as not to be overheard: "Can I talk to you... off the record?"

"Sure. What is it?"

"Can we go somewhere... outside, maybe?"

I nodded. "Out on the back deck... it's over here."

I looked back over my shoulder at the others and caught PJ's eye... "Just gonna get some air," I explained, holding up a hand to ask them not to follow. PJ quickly understood and pressed his Bible into my hand, urging me to take it, while he motioned with a subtle gesture that they'll be praying.

Vanessa stopped as she stepped through the door, and her eyes surveyed the backyard before scanning the night sky carefully, apparently checking for spies. I suggested a few chairs, but she sat at the picnic table instead, keeping her back toward the house; I took a seat on the opposite side, across the table from her. The light from the house was at her back, making it hard for me to see her eyes, but I could detect a sniffle and noticed her wiping her cheek with one hand.

"Sorry for dragging you out here. I don't mean to seem mysterious. I guess I'm just not as brave as Trudi and Caden." I nodded that I understood.

"What you said in there... in the interview, about God being real and His essence being love... do you believe that? I mean, really, truly believe it?"

"More than anything."

"I've never believed in God... honestly never. My father was a devout atheist. Everything I ever learned in school convinced me even more that God was just a made-up idea. I was planning to use tonight's interview to prove that point — I was sure that the idea of a personal God was indefensible.

"I-I'm honestly not sure what happened. As soon as you started talking, it was as if something started pulling on my heart. It wasn't even the words you said — it was something else... something I've never felt before."

"That's the Holy Spirit," I explained. She didn't answer, but I saw her head tilt to the side as if she was having a hard time disagreeing.

"When Caden described what happened to her..." she paused as if searching for words. "Somehow, I knew she was telling the truth... that it was real." Vanessa put both of her hands on her head and pulled her hair back like she was trying to wrap her brain around the idea. "I've known Caden for years; we weren't especially close, but we started around the same time at the Network. I remember when she married Nyle, and I remember how devastated she was when he got hurt. Seeing him tonight... well, that just made it even harder to deny.

"But, Trudi...." She took a deep breath and released it, sounding as if she was trying to lift a two hundred pound weight. "The Trudi I spoke with tonight is not the same person I've known before — not at all! And I can't deny that the clip from this morning's press conference is hard to explain in natural terms."

She sat quietly for a moment, struggling with the implications of her own conclusion.

"Those things you said about pain, and love, and free will... I've never heard before. It never occurred to me how inseparably they're all connected. And you were right — it does point to God... all of it... it only makes sense if there is a loving God at the center of it all."

"The part about Jesus dying for you is true too," I added quietly.

She sat silently, I couldn't tell if her eyes were open or closed, but it soon became clear why she wasn't talking... she was weeping. I reached over to the center of the long table and grabbed the basket of napkins, pushing it in front of her. She seemed too distraught to notice. Through tearful gasps, she began to sob in lament...

"I-I've done things... hurt people... I've been God's worst enemy. I don't deserve his love — h-how could he love me?"

"None of us deserve it," I assured her. "Even when we try, the Bible says that all of our attempts at righteousness are like filthy rags. Here, let me show you...."

There was enough light coming through the house windows for me to read by. I opened to Isaiah chapter 53 and began to read a few verses.

"These words were written eight hundred years before Christ but were part of a prophecy about Jesus...

> 'He was despised and rejected by men; a man of sorrows,
>   and acquainted with grief: and as one from whom
>   men hide their face he was despised; and we
>   esteemed him not.
> Surely he has borne our griefs, and carried our sorrows;
>   yet we did esteem him stricken, smitten by God, and
>   afflicted.
> But it was for our transgressions that he was wounded,
>   he was bruised for our sins; the punishment needed
>   for our peace was upon him; and with his blood we
>   are healed.

Vanessa had begun openly weeping as she listened, covering her eyes with her hands as she leaned her elbows on the table. I softened my voice sympathetically as I continued reading.

> All of us are like sheep who have gone astray; we have turned every one to his own way; and God has laid on him the iniquity of us all.
>
> He was cruelly abused, yet he didn't open his mouth; as a lamb that is led to the slaughter, and as a sheep that before its shearers is dumb, so he opened not his mouth.
>
> By oppression and judgment he was taken away; and as for his generation, who among them considered that he was cut off out of the land of the living for the sins of others to whom the stroke was due?
>
> They made his grave with the wicked, and with a rich man in his death; although he had done no violence, neither was any deceit in his mouth.
>
> Yet it pleased God to bruise him; he put him to grief: when he made his soul an offering for sin…
>
> He will see the travail of his soul, and be satisfied: by himself shall my righteous servant justify many; and he shall bear their iniquities.
>
> Therefore I will give him a portion with the great, and he shall divide the spoil with the strong; because he poured out his soul unto death, and was numbered with the transgressors: yet he bare the sin of many, and made intercession for the transgressors.

By the time I finished reading, Vanessa had leaned her head into her arms on the table and was weeping bitterly. I could feel her shaking as I stood and put my hands on both of her shoulders, beginning to pray.

"FATHER, thank you for the presence of your Spirit here with us now. The work you're doing in Vanessa's heart is a great gift, the most amazing gift of all. You are melting her heart from cold stone and transforming her, at this moment, to new life. It is an act that only the Spirit of God can perform in a human heart."

I LEANED an elbow on the table, speaking quietly.

"Vanessa, the Bible tells us that it's with our heart that a person believes to gain righteousness, and with our mouth confession is made unto salvation. If we confess with our mouth that Jesus is Lord and believe in our heart that God raised Him from the dead, we will be saved.

"It's so simple, and yet it's impossible to truly do unless the Holy Spirit first begins the transforming work that you're feeling right now. Jesus said *I stand at the door and knock; if anyone hears my voice and opens the door, I will come in to them and be their friend.*

"He's knocking on your heart right now. Are you willing to open your life to Him?"

Vanessa nodded her head several times, barely able to speak the words that flowed tearfully from a place deep inside her.

"I'd like to help you if that's okay?" I offered. She anxiously nodded again.

"...Y-yes... please!"

"I'll lead, and you can follow what I say; just listen to the words and repeat them if you agree.

> "Father, thank you for sending your son... to take the punishment for my sin... I believe that Jesus died for me... and that he rose again from the dead with resurrection life... I accept your forgiveness... and am willing to make Jesus the Lord of my life... from this moment on... I commit my life to him... and invite him to be my friend... and my Savior! Thank you, Lord, for forgiving me! Amen."

Vanessa was still weeping, but after a moment, there was a clear difference in her cries. Her sobs of remorse had changed to tears of joy. The depth of her emotion was contagious, and I began to cry myself as we continued together for several more minutes in prayerful worship.

When I eventually looked up, PJ and some of the others were standing near the door. I nodded my head, acknowledging what just happened, and he smiled a broad smile, lifting his hand in praise.

Caden and Trudi pushed past him, and before he could stop them, they ran to either side of Vanessa and threw their arms around her. The three of them cried and laughed together while Nyle and the rest of us looked on in joy and amazement over what God had done.

I NOTICED Uncle Mike standing inside the house, watching us all through the door. Pastor Wilkes walked up behind him and put a hand on his shoulder. I couldn't tell what they said to each other but was only partly surprised to see Uncle Mike wipe a tear from his cheek. Moments later, they walked through the door together, and Pastor called PJ over to join them; the next thing I knew, the three of them were suddenly kneeling on the deck. I could barely move fast enough as I jumped up from the table and rushed to join them, quickly inviting Mr. O and Nyle to join us.

Tears were running down Uncle Mike's face, and I could hear him telling Pastor that he didn't think God could forgive him. I nudged my way in, kneeling right in front of him, and looked him in the eyes.

"Remember what you told me about what mom did? You said it was the greatest gift... an act of her love. You told me not to blame myself. You were right!

"It was the same with Gramps... he saved you because he loved you — it was his choice... his gift to you. He wanted you to live — I know he'd want you to accept forgiveness! He never would have wanted you to blame yourself for what happened."

His tears were streaming faster now, and he squeezed his eyes closed, doing his best to acknowledge that I was right. I looked to Pastor, asking him to take the lead, and he began leading Uncle Mike to Christ.

Through my own wet eyes, I recognized Amos' familiar figure

standing just behind where my uncle was kneeling. He nodded to me with a kind and grateful expression and then looked at Mike earnestly. It was impossible to miss Chozeq beside him. He stood head and shoulders taller than Amos and towered over the men kneeling in front of him — not to mention the fact that his entire personage was glowing intensely in the surrounding darkness. He looked at the scene with a joyful expression and then lifted his hand, beckoning me to look up at the sky around us.

As I followed his gaze, I was suddenly able to see that the sky was filled with bright hosts of angels. More than I could count. Some were standing beside Vanessa, with Caden and Trudi — ministering to them as the women sat together with their heads bowed. Tears of joy flooded their eyes at the angels' ministering touch. The throngs of angels covered the sky over our small deck like a dome, extending higher in row upon row, far into the clouds.

Looking back at Uncle Mike, I could see that his struggles were weakening — his heart was surrendering as wall after wall of his defenses were finally toppled. His cries had become sobs — remorse and repentance had replaced his resistance, and mercy now covered him like light.

I closed my eyes in thankful prayer....

Suddenly, Uncle Mike and I found ourselves kneeling at the apex of eternity... at Calvary. Uncle Mike was kneeling beside me, and I could see him bowing low as Jesus' loud cry shattered the darkness with a blast of light — He cried out: *It Is Finished!*

Uncle Mike's filthy rags were transformed into bright, clean robes, and I watched as Jesus called his name. His face was filled with wonder and astonished awe.

Mike was still shaking at the fantastic sight when a hand touched his shoulder. He turned to see mom, holding out her arms to hug him... beside her were Gramps and Grandma. I couldn't stop the tears from flooding my eyes as I watched them welcome him.

While Mike hugged his parents... especially his dad, mom

turned to me with a loving look and then hugged me close — I held her for as long as I could.

As the scene faded, I could feel the deck beneath my knees and recognized the sound of PJ's voice as he finished praying.

Uncle Mike looked up at me through tear-filled eyes and studied my face, searching for the shared memory that he knew was there. I subtly nodded yes; I saw it too... I saw *them* too. Recognizing my answer, he grabbed me by the back of the neck, pulling me close in an emotional embrace. I could feel him breakdown in sobs... of joy.

⌘

23

DEFENDED

And he answered, Fear not: for those with us are more than with them.
~ 2 Kings 6:16

T he mantle clock was chiming midnight when I finally pulled the sheet up to my chin, settling down into the living room couch. The house was quiet for the first time in 18 hours, and all of those hours were replaying in my head... repeatedly.

It had certainly been a day to remember. The morning press conference all by itself would have been memorable enough. The thought of Trudi's deliverance in our front yard sent a thrill through my soul as I thought of it. The recollection of Mr. V's words about it afterward made me smile...*anytime you people are on TV, it sure ain't borin'.*

Thoughts careened through my mind of the conversation with agents DeMassi and Sharma. I couldn't help wondering whether they would really follow up on Corvo and Bahal. I had to admit that the evidence I offered would have seemed pretty light to me if I was in their shoes.

My thoughts raced through all the craziness of the night's interview experience. It honestly seemed surreal, except for the parts where Vanessa and Uncle Mike both gave their hearts to the Lord. Those were *very* real!

A familiar, thunderous voice suddenly broke the room's silence....

"THIS DAY STANDS as a great light in eternity."

I lifted myself onto an elbow and turned toward Chozeq; it was good to see my old friend.

"I can hardly believe it," I admitted to him. "Trudi, Vanessa, and Uncle Mike — all saved in the same day!"

"They are only three of many," Chozeq revealed. "Greater than a hundred thousand souls have found redemption this day because of thy obedience."

My mouth dropped open in astonishment at his words. For a moment, I was unable to move as the power of his message left my body numb and took my breath away. Mom's sacrifice immediately came to mind, bringing a tear of realization as I understood that she saved many more than just me. Chozeq nodded silently as he grasped my thought.

"Ye have done well in honoring her memory," he said, placing his massive hand on my shoulder reassuringly, "...and also in glorifying thy Lord."

"What now? The tent services have been shut down... is that all there is? Does the work God is doing move somewhere else now? You said that it would spread like a great fire."

As I was asking the question, the vision that Anna's mom had on the first night of tent meetings came to mind — it was a fiery whirlwind that grew tall and then exploded outward.

"That vision that Mrs. M saw... was that about tonight? Is this what her vision described? All those people who were saved tonight, is that the explosion that she witnessed?"

Chozeq looked at me kindly and smiled. "Ever thou art an impatient Lad. In this desire tis good for thee to be so; thy fervor for the Lord's work is indeed noble. Nevertheless, remember that God is long-suffering and abundant in mercy. Tho his plans are immutable, yet he will gladly stay them to await the last soul to find shelter beneath his wings.

"Tonight is but a beginning and not an end. There is much more that He calleth thee yet to do."

At that, he rose to his feet and reached out his hand, bidding me get up. I threw off the sheets and quickly stood in pajamas and barefoot to take hold of his huge hand.

IN AN INSTANT, we have become lost in the swirling vortex of time and space. Then, just as suddenly, we find ourselves in an ornate paneled room, looking at Bahal as he sits behind an imposing desk.

Seated across the desk from him is a younger man, powerful-looking in his own right and elegantly dressed. On his face is a look of deep distress.

"HOW ARE you connected to this man… this shooter? Do you know what it would mean to my candidacy if this were to be discovered?"

"Relax, Devlon," Bahal urges the Senator in a calm, smooth voice. "How could it be discovered? I've never met the man, and besides, he was vaporized without a trace by that lightning blast — quite conveniently, I must say."

"But you told me he was an associate of yours. Did you have anything to do with the attack?"

"Of course not! Not that I find it objectionable either… such religious movements must be dealt with swiftly. Popular uprisings of this sort must not be allowed to grow — it would set back our cause by decades. You, of all men, surely realize this."

Devlon hesitates, appearing conflicted. "Y-Yes, of course. It's just that there are other ways… politically, and through our control of the media — why resort to killing as the first option?"

"You have your ways, and I have mine," Bahal insists dismissively. "I'm not sure you fully understand the gravity of the situation. This is no ordinary church group... something far different is happening here."

Devlon looks at his father-in-law with a confused expression. "H-How is it different?"

Bahal lifts a remote and aims it at the large TV screen across the room. It switches on with images from the tent — news coverage from Caden's conversion, followed by the night I was shot and Nyle's healing. The clips continue, showing scenes from Tuesday night of miraculous healing and Corvo's attack, followed by the lightning strike that killed him. Bahal shuts off the TV.

"Does that look like your typical Sunday School?"

The degree of venom in Bahal's voice surprises Devlon. He hadn't been paying attention to any of these news clips before now and struggles to make sense of them.

"What is that?" Devlon asks sarcastically. "Those people are obviously acting... that could be a scene from any B-Movie."

Bahal stands to his feet and looks down at his son-in-law — Devlon notices the older man's eyes flash with fire for a split second and flinches nervously.

"You would do well to keep up," Bahal admonishes him. His voice is purposefully calm and reserved but hints at a burning anger just beneath the surface. "Take my advice... this movement must not be allowed to grow."

Devlon holds up his hands in surrender. "Alright! Alright! I'll take care of it. Just promise me you won't get involved."

"Why would I involve myself?" Bahal lies.

Devlon knows that he is lying but pretends to accept his word. It is more convenient than arguing, and he knows it will provide viable deniability. But there are other loose ends.

"At your request, I made calls about the shooter... I sent agents. How do I explain my sudden interest in this assassin?"

Bahal lifts his hands as he speaks in a gesture that looks as if he's holding a large globe in front of him. "You are a powerful Senator with access to government secrets... you were obviously investigating a crime of utmost importance for national security. Simply claim that the rest is classified."

I FEEL Chozeq's hand touch my back in a signal that we are moving again. Seconds later, we are standing beside a car that has pulled onto the shoulder of a large highway. The huge green road sign in the distance announces the exit for a town that I recognize — we're on the local interstate, not far from Center Springs. Apparently, the car has broken down; I can hear the starter whirring, but the engine isn't starting. *No spark... or maybe out of gas,* I tell myself, subconsciously diagnosing the trouble.

A man gets out of the passenger side and pops the hood, checking a few wires.

"It ain't overheated, and da' battery's good," he yells back to the driver. "Must be a clogged fuel line or somethin'."

Yeah, or that... I agree to myself, checking off 'enough gas' from my mental list.

The man walks back to the passenger door and looks inside. "Come on, Lorenzo, ya ain't supposed ta sit in a disabled vehicle. We gotta stand behind da' guardrail."

"Screw dat," Lorenzo retorts. "Anybody hits me an' I blow their brains out."

The man outside shakes his head and mumbles under his breath: "Sure provided ya' got any brain left yerself...."

"You say somethin'?" Lorenzo challenges.

"No, nothin'. Suit yerself."

"I'm callin' Zharov," the driver yells through a curse-filled rant. Seconds later, a man with a thick accent can be heard over the car's speakerphone. Lorenzo lays into him...

"Anatolii, wuttaya doin' givin' us a broken down piece-a-garbage car. We're stuck on the frickin' highway. Ya' better be ready ta explain ta da' boss why we couldn't make the hit!"

"That is a brand new car — I just got it in!" the man on the phone objects. "S-O-B cheats... that is the last time I fence a car from those bums!"

"Yeah, yeah, right," Lorenzo interrupts impatiently. "Jus' get here with a replacement... pronto!"

As the phone disconnects, Lorenzo yells to his partner: "What's dat address again? I'm puttin' it in my phone in case the next car don't have a Nav system in it."

"32 Granite Drive," he yells back.

I swallow hard and look back at Chozeq, "That's *our* house!" I'm suddenly looking everywhere for clues… "When is this happening? Is this the future? We have to warn the O'Malleys!"

Chozeq calms my racing heart with a touch. "Rest, Lad. Thou art safe in thy Father's care. No harm shall befall thee, nor shall any come to those in thy house." He nods back toward the men, encouraging me to listen as they speak.

"Why do ya think they want this kid dead so bad?" Lorenzo asks his partner.

"Beats me. I jus' know that the client is way up there — real connected, ya know wut I'm sayin'?"

"What do ya think really happened to Corvo?" Lorenzo asks nervously.

"Must'a been a coverup - nobody gets disintegrated by lightning. That's crazy."

"Had ta be a real pro to take *him* out. What's this kid's angle… think he's connected to somebody?"

"We ain't paid ta ask questions."

"Come on, Mac, this is *me* you're talkin' to. We go way back, right?"

"All's I know is the contract ain't exclusive — it's like a bounty, know wut I'm sayin'? First one that gets the kid takes the purse."

Lorenzo pounds his fist on the steering wheel. "Here we are stuck on the highway… Damned car!"

He suddenly opens his door and steps out, inches from moving traffic. His partner yells in surprise.

"What are ya doin'?! Yer gonna get killed!?

"I ain't waitin!" he yells as he waves his arms at a coming car. That one speeds past, blasting its horn as it swerves to avoid hitting him. The driver shakes his fist at Lorenzo, who ignores him and waves to the next car approaching. That one slows down and pulls over. A middle-aged man gets out; he's wearing janitor's blue coveralls — it looks like he just got off work.

"Car trouble? Can I give y'all a lift somewhere?" he offers.

Lorenzo pulls a gun from the back of his belt and aims it at the man, who quickly raises his hands. "I ain't got nothin' to steal! I was just trying to help you guys!" he pleads with eyes that are wide with fear.

"We just need the car," Lorenzo says. "A Friend of ours will be here in a little while - I'll tell him to make it up to you."

The terrified man doesn't argue, keeping his hands in the air as he steps away from his car and moves to the guardrail. I look to Chozeq anxiously, shaking my head that we can't let them go. He doesn't answer but looks toward the janitor, beckoning for me to follow his gaze. My heart leaps in surprise to see two powerful angels standing beside the man, obviously guarding him.

"Get in the car, Mac!" Lorenzo shouts as he reaches into the back seat of their Mercedes and pulls out a sniper rifle. He tosses it quickly into the running car and jumps behind the wheel, shifting it into drive. Mac has barely pulled his door closed as he stomps on the gas.

Just as the tires begin to spin out, one of the angels raises a hand and simply motions for the car to stop. Instantly, the car's engine stalls, and its brakes lock, causing both men's foreheads to bounce off the windshield; they fall back into their seats, unconscious.

Immediately, a pair of state troopers come screaming up the highway with their lights flashing and sirens blaring. One of them blocks the path of the stolen car while the other blocks the right lane, closing it to traffic. Lorenzo and Mac, still dazed, are quickly cuffed and separated into the troopers' caged back seats while an inventory is made of their arsenal of loaded handguns and rifles. A quick search confirms that the Mercedes is stolen.

"You officers are an answer to prayer," the Janitor says gratefully. "How did you know?"

"A concerned citizen called 911. They saw you being held at gunpoint." The officer looks around, surveying the area, noting that there are no lights anywhere nearby. "Funny thing... they said the shoulder here was lit up like broad daylight — said they couldn't miss the sight."

Suddenly, I'm aware of Ardent's presence in the air above us, putting his flaming sword back into its sheath. He and Chozeq salute one another, each tapping a fist against their chest. Ardent nods to me with a smile and spreads his enormous wings, disappearing in a flash.

A MOMENT LATER, Chozeq and I are standing on my own front porch. Before I can discern whether I'm back in my own time, a pair of cars come racing up the street and screech to a stop in front of the house. Rap music is blasting loudly from both cars as a gang of men jump out. They're yelling to each other in a mix of gang slang and Spanish, and all of them carry M16 machine guns. Their faces are covered with tattoos. I figure they're gang symbols, but I don't know what they mean.

One of them points toward our house, and all of them raise their guns and begin walking forward. Halfway to the porch, the leader points again, signaling that he has seen a target standing in the living room. He raises his gun and takes aim — I watch his finger squeeze the trigger, and bullets begin to fly toward the house. All the others do the same, releasing a shower of gunfire.

I instinctively duck for cover before realizing that bullets are hitting the side of the house behind me — they're passing right through me! I've barely grasped that point when a massive flash lights up the front lawn — in fact, it lights up the entire neighborhood! A split second later, a gigantic crack of thunder shakes the air, rattling the whole house and blowing the windows out of the gang members' cars.

I run out onto the lawn, amazed that the brightness of the flash has not dimmed my sight. There are small craters on the lawn, one where each of the men stood. Turning quickly toward the house, I look up anxiously toward the bedroom windows where the O'Malleys are sleeping, expecting to see broken glass and splintered wood. The sight that I see instead makes me drop to my knees.

A troop of angels stands guarding that room like an impenetrable wall, and a thousand more hang in the air above and encircle the house, swords drawn and wings spread. As I'm staring, awestruck, a light comes on in the room, and Mr.'O carefully peers out through the unbroken window.

A SPLIT SECOND LATER, I found myself once again standing alone in the living room in my pajamas, exactly where I first stood to greet Chozeq. The mantle clock read 12:02 AM. The distant sound of squealing tires and Rap music could be heard getting closer, and it boomed loudly as the cars screeched to a stop in front of the house. I dove to the floor just as a hail of bullets tore through the downstairs, blowing out the windows and shattering the walls and furniture.

It only lasted for seconds — until the gigantic lightning flash made everything as bright as daylight. That was followed by a concussion of thunder that shook the house, making the floor where I was lying rise and fall like a ship on the sea. Outside, the cars' panic alarms were blaring — not just the gang members' cars — all the cars up and down the street.

THERE WAS SHATTERED GLASS EVERYWHERE — I could hear Mr. O' rushing down the stairs behind me and yelled for him to stop.

"I'm alright! Stop! Don't come down! There's broken glass; it's everywhere."

He stopped at the landing and switched on the light, then looked down at me with an astonished expression. The scene everywhere was nothing but splintered wood and shards of glass, except for a circle around the place where I was lying. The section of the carpet where I was lying was perfectly clean as if I'd been covered by a bullet-proof dome.

As I sat up and realized what he was looking at, I self-consciously ran a hand through my hair, hoping that he wasn't going to ask me to explain it. It turned out that he didn't have to ask — it seemed that everything he had already seen in the past few days had removed any sense of shock or surprise.

"Why am I not surprised?" he simply said.

"Um… could you throw me those sneakers?" I asked, pretending that there was nothing at all unusual about the scene.

⌘

2 4

REBUILDING

You will rebuild those houses left in ruins...
~ Isaiah 58:12

P olice sirens were racing closer as I hurried to pull on my sneakers. As I glanced around, I saw Amos' journal sitting on the floor beneath a splintered end table and stopped to stash it in an undamaged cubby beneath the stairs. The glass in the front door had been destroyed, and its wood frame was badly splintered. The living room's front windows were gone too. After switching on the porch light, I cautiously made my way down to the yard. Smoke was rising from a set of eight craters scattered haphazardly across the lawn.

Lights were coming on up and down the street, and people were slowly poking their heads out, checking whether the coast was clear. Mr. O rushed out behind me in his pajamas and a pair of dress shoes.

"Jimmy! Get back inside! It's dangerous!"

I waved to him to follow, signaling that it was okay, and then pointed to the smoldering craters. Two police cars came skidding to a stop at about the same moment, and the Sheriff's deputies ran toward me.

"Jimmy! Are you alright? What happened here?"

I just pointed to the gang members' cars and then to the craters without saying a word. One deputy looked back at me with a comprehending gaze and scanned the bullet-riddled house, his mouth dropping open.

"So it's true," he stammered. "Another bolt of lightning... it's like people have been reporting."

"People?" I asked.

"Neighbors — the whole neighborhood." He looked around at the people on their porches up and down the street. "We got at least a dozen 911 calls about gunfire and then... the lightning."

He brushed the edge of one of the smoking craters with his boot as he stared into it. Squinting into the darkness, he pulled out a flashlight and shined it into the hole. There was a boot inside — it still contained the charred remains of a foot and ankle bone. With a sour look on his face, he squeezed the mic on his lapel.

"We're gonna need forensics. Better call in the whole crew."

———

THIRTY MINUTES LATER, the street had been sealed off, and more investigators in white jump suites were combing the lawn and house. They pulled bullets from the woodwork with their special tweezers. Powerful lights illuminated the yard — the kind they use for highway construction at night. The lights revealed a few more boots and pieces of M16 machine guns, along with about five hundred shell casings. The gunmen's cars were being brushed for prints and meticulously searched.

It didn't take long for our phone to start ringing. PJ was the first to call.

"I heard what happened — is everyone alright?"

I looked at the kitchen clock; it was just 12:40 AM. "We're fine... how did you hear?"

"We heard the thunder. Mitch at the prison called right away, saying that it's all over the police radio; the whole State knows about it. I'm glad you're okay... this is so crazy!" He was quiet for a second, then lowered his voice as he spoke more closely into the phone: "Is it true about the lightning?"

"Uh-huh. There were eight of them this time — all eight men were hit in the same instant...."

I was tempted to also tell PJ about the army of angels but quickly realized that it would raise other questions... like how I managed to be in two places at once, for instance.

"...I think some of the neighbors saw it happen," I offered instead.

PJ whistled into the phone. "If that's not an act of God, I don't know what is!"

WHILE I WAS TALKING, Uncle Mike burst in through the busted front door — I heard him frantically calling for me. Sheriff Flanagan was right behind him.

"JIMMY!"

"Over here, Uncle Mike...

"PJ, I have to go now.."

"We're all praying for you, Jim."

"Thanks — that means a lot."

Uncle Mike didn't wait for me to hang up the phone — he grabbed me in a hug that felt like he was afraid I'd fly away. When he was done, Sheriff Flanagan gripped my shoulder and nodded. There was a regretful look in his eyes.

"I should have posted men... I should have known this would happen."

"If you had, they'd probably be dead," I tried to reassure him. "Those guys had machine guns — they did all this in five seconds."

We all surveyed the living room together, taking in the sight of complete destruction. Windows and walls were shattered, tables and chairs were in splinters, and the couch had been reduced to nothing but shredded stuffing.

The Sheriff glanced at Uncle Mike and looked to me.

"You're not safe here. We need to get you someplace where you can be protected."

The night's events with Chozeq flashed through my mind, along with his words: *Thou art safe in thy Father's care.*

"Look at this place and look at me," I insisted, pointing out that I was in pajamas and didn't have a scratch on me. "...I *am* protected."

The Sheriff looked at me and then at Uncle Mike, then back at me again. "I'll level with both of you. We've confirmed that Corvo *was* hired for a professional hit... on you, Jimmy." He distractedly scanned the wreckage around us, nodding toward it as he continued.... "This is different — this has all the earmarks of a bounty... a big one. We're talking about really dangerous people. It doesn't get any more dangerous than this."

He turned back to me again. "We have to figure out who wants to kill you and why."

"I told you, his name is Bahal Ebezej. All I know is that he's rich and powerful. He wants to stop what God is doing here. That's what he's trying to do. For some reason, he thinks that killing me will stop it."

My visit to Bahal's office with Chozeq flashed quickly through my mind, and I decided to share another detail... "He's been talking to someone else... a Senator named Devlon."

"Devlon Sheen?" Mike asked in surprise.

"Is he a senator?" I asked, realizing that I needed to start getting up to speed on current events.

The Sheriff nodded in answer to my question. "Isn't he the one who just introduced that bill to end religious exemptions?"

"One in the same," Mike confirmed.

As soon as he said this, I remembered Amos's journal, and Devlon's involvement became crystal clear. Mike recognized that I had made the connection and silently nodded in agreement.

Sheriff Flanagan looked at me seriously. "That's a very serious accusation and frightening if true. What are you basing it on?"

"If I told you, I'd be breaking a sacred promise. I can't explain to anyone how I know it, but it's true. My story about Corvo checked out, right?"

He studied my face for a moment.

"It's one thing to check with Stockslock about a visitors' log — checking out a sitting senator is another thing entirely." He thought about it for a minute... "But if someone with that much at stake knew you could implicate them, that could definitely explain the attempts on your life!"

He grabbed me by both shoulders... "We can't tell anyone about this — got that? Don't trust anyone else! I need to think about what to do."

Uncle Mike was standing with a sober look on his face. "I know what we have to do," he quietly offered.

The Sheriff stopped and looked at him expectantly.

"We have to pray!" Mike said, looking both of us in the eyes.

His suggestion resonated — under the circumstances, it seemed like the wisest thing I had ever heard Uncle Mike say. Putting our hands on each other's shoulders, we bowed our heads and began to seek the Lord — while white-suited analysts continued to comb the room around us.

It was after 2:00 AM by the time I'd given my statement for the second time to a pair of local detectives. My yawning was getting to be a giveaway that I was dead on my feet.

"Why don't you go get some sleep," Sheriff Flanagan suggested, waving the detectives away.

It sounded like a great idea, I thought to myself as I looked over at the shredded couch. Before I could answer him, I heard Mrs. O behind me...

"We moved our things into Maria's room — your bed has a fresh set of sheets," she explained with a friendly squeeze on my shoulder.

"What about Ryan?"

"He's in our room, sound asleep."

Too exhausted to argue, I mumbled my thanks with a hug and then stumbled up the stairs, kicking off my sneakers as I collapsed into bed. I was unconscious before I hit the pillow.

DAYBREAK BROUGHT AN EVEN LARGER crowd of reporters than the day before and twice as many helicopters. There wasn't going to be any press conference this time, though; the police had made it clear that the house was still an active crime scene, and the news vans were being kept at bay.

I had just finished dressing when the phone rang - It was Anna.

"Jimmy! I'm just seeing the news... Oh my Gosh! Are you alright! That was so horrible!"

My first reaction was to turn on the TV, but then I remembered that ours was full of bullet holes.

"We're kind of without a TV right now; what are they saying?"

"They showed your house. It's all smashed-up. And they keep showing those craters in the yard where lightning struck. Is it true that the people shooting were all struck by lightning, the same as Tuesday night?"

"Yeah, it is. It was pretty crazy."

"They're saying that the people who did it were members of a really bad gang. Why are all these people after you?!"

"They're trying to stop the thing God is doing here."

"But why you?"

"I don't really know, but it's not just people who are trying — it's a spiritual enemy. It's mostly that... spiritual."

"You're scaring me."

"There's no reason to be scared — there's really not. The One who is in us is greater than the one who's in the world. After everything I've seen, there's no doubt in my mind about that... God is way stronger."

"I know you're right... it's just harder for me to not feel scared. You're like, crazy-brave."

"Well, it probably is a little crazy, but think about it — I've been shot in the chest and had 500 rounds fired at me, and here I am. Not only that, these shooters have been taken out by bolts of lightning! That's pretty good evidence of God's protection."

"Yeah, okay, I get it. Just don't do anything stupid. Don't start kissing rattlesnakes or anything."

"Alright, point taken."

"So… What are you going to do about your house?"

"For now, I guess we're just gonna board it up. We'll have to get estimates for repairs. Not sure if the insurance covers showers of bullets — there's probably a clause against that."

Anna didn't laugh at my joke.

"I can help… I can come over to help you cleanup if you want," she offered.

"Wow, that'd be great if you want to. You don't know what you're getting yourself into, though. The place is pretty much a total disaster."

I had just said goodbye and hung up the phone when Uncle Mike poked his head in through the front door carrying a few big bags.

"Warm bagels and hot coffee," he announced in a loud voice. "Got plenty o' butter and cream cheese… whatever ya want."

Mrs. O poked her head out of the kitchen and smiled at him. "I'm just washing off the counters — Ward cleared and washed the kitchen floor. At least one room down here is livable."

We settled around the kitchen's small table. The room looked pretty good despite bullet holes in the walls and cabinets. All of us were starving. Uncle Mike looked like he didn't sleep at all last night. It's my guess that Mr. & Mrs. O didn't get much rest either.

"I have a friend with a truck," Mike said. "I was thinking of borrowing it to go get some plywood."

"Great idea," I agreed. "I'll help." An uncomfortable realization suddenly hit me… "But I don't really have any money, or credit cards or anything."

"Don't worry about it!" they all said at the same time.

"I can't think of a better cause for the *Kelly's Friends Foundation* to support," Mr. O said. "That reminds me, I need to run down to the bank this morning to make that deposit."

"You do that, and Jimmy and I will get the lumber," Mike suggested. "Meet you back here."

It took Uncle Mike and I longer than planned to pick up his friend's truck and settle on what supplies to get. Half-a-dozen sheets of plywood and a few pounds of deck screws later, we finally made it back home.

As we pulled up to the house, we were shocked to see a small army of kids from FCS and men in coveralls, some with carpenter belts, milling around in front. Others were measuring the windows and doors, while a few emerged from inside, pushing wheelbarrows full of debris. A truck was dropping off a huge dumpster in our driveway.

Mr. O met us at the curb. "Sheriff Flanagan has closed his investigation; he said they got everything they needed. That means we're free to start repairs."

As I hopped out of the pickup, Anna came running from the house.

"Isn't this great! We just let a few people at the church know that you needed help, and everybody started showing up!"

Pastor Wilkes walked over to say hello — I hadn't recognized him standing nearby wearing coveralls. He shook his head in disbelief as he extended his hand. "Thank God you're alright Jim, I've never seen anything like this. This is something… really something."

PJ and Pete emerged together from the house carrying pieces of broken furniture. They both nodded in greeting as they dropped them into a growing pile beside the porch.

"Hey Jim - really sorry about your mom," Mr. Fletcher said as he recognized me.

Mr. Steinbrink was beside him; "Saw you on TV last night. Could feel God's anointing right through the TV screen."

"This here was the devil's work," Mr. Harding declared from behind them as he looked around at the damage. "God's watchin' out for you; there's no doubt about it!"

By lunchtime, most of the shattered sheetrock walls had been stripped down to their studs, and the window and door frames had been removed. Pete was helping a separate crew who was removing the broken siding from the front of the house. Meanwhile, the downstairs had been cleared of debris. Anna was helping her mom and Mrs.

O as they organized salvaged items like family pictures and books for cleaning or repairs. Remarkably, the old mantel clock survived unscathed, although part of the mantel it sat on needed replacing.

Uncle Mike naturally took charge of lunch. He disappeared for a while and returned with boxes of fresh rolls and a sub-shop-sized order of cold cuts, lettuce, tomatoes, and onions. He appointed me to be order-taker, and I soon had a notebook full of orders. With practiced speed, he began churning them out as fast as I could deliver them.

The last of us were just finishing lunch when a truck from the local lumber yard pulled up. As the men started unloading it, I realized it was filled with sheetrock and trim materials, along with new windows, siding, and a brand new front door.

It was becoming obvious from watching the work that these were not all just a bunch of random church guys — many of them were pros. I finally noticed that their vans and trucks identified them as window and siding contractors, electricians, sheetrockers, and trim carpenters. Barely an hour later, the downstairs had been re-sheetrocked, the windows and door had been installed, and the front of the house had been half re-sided.

Realizing that I was pretty useless among all these professionals, I decided to go and tackle our unmowed lawn. Between our house and the O'Malleys', it turned out to be a bigger job than I thought — it was as tall as prairie grass. It was nearly 5:00 PM by the time I pushed the mower back into the garage.

THE CREWS WERE KNOCKING off work for the day. I was amazed to see that the siding was finished and the walls had all been taped and spackled.

"It'll be ready for a primer coat in the morning," the sheetrock crew-chief said as he shook my hand and headed out our new front door.

My head was spinning as I turned toward the others. The O'Malleys were busy cleaning the salvaged items — Mr. O took notes on the broken picture frame sizes. Anna was chasing Ryan, who was enjoying the adventure of it all. Uncle Mike and Anna's mom had begun working on dinner in the kitchen. She had been bubbling for hours over the news of his conversion.

A knock at the door drew my attention — it was PJ and Pastor Wilkes... they were carrying dining room chairs.

The pastor explained as I opened the door, "These were donated to the church. You're welcome to 'em. Figured you could use them until you get something better."

Pete followed close behind, carrying the top of a long oak table.

"Whoa, let me help with that!" I offered as I saw him, hardly able to believe that he carried it alone.

We quickly brought in the rest of the chairs and table legs and soon had a dining room set up, just in time for dinner. PJ and Pastor Wilkes agreed to stay for our first meal at the new table, and everyone helped to get the table set with plates and silverware. Moments later, Uncle Mike emerged from the kitchen with a huge platter of pasta covered in sauce.

"Couldn't wait to have more of Lena's marinara sauce," Uncle Mike said enthusiastically. "We added some clams and Italian sausage to spice things up."

Mrs. Mirabella followed close behind him, carrying a basket of oven-warmed rolls from lunch, which had been sliced and spread with melted garlic butter. In her other hand was a large bowl of salad made from the leftover lettuce, tomatoes, and onions.

PJ stood beside the table; "Let's give thanks for this wonderful meal."

There were echoes of amen as everyone gratefully bowed their heads.

> "Lord, we praise you for your gracious kindness to us and for
> protecting Jimmy and the O'Malleys from harm in the face
> of these terrible attacks. We know that all things have
> occurred in your providence and will be used for our good
> and your glory. We anxiously await the outcome of your
> plans in all these things. We don't yet understand your
> purpose but know in faith that it will be good and perfect.

"Thank you for all the workers who gave their talents and time today — please bless them as they have blessed us. Most of all, may the events of this week be used to draw many souls to your kingdom. We await your timing to continue your work here and throughout the world as the days draw nearer to your coming. In Jesus' precious name, amen."

⌘

25

INOCULATED

You shall not be afraid for the terror by night, nor for the arrow that flies by day...
~ *Psalm 91:5*

A long black limousine pulls to a stop on an abandoned pier along the waterfront. The scene is bathed in the warm golden light of a summer sunrise as the driver and two rugged-looking thugs climb out. They are dressed in expensive Italian suits that clash with the automatic weapons they are holding. One of them opens the rear passenger door, and a man steps out wearing sunglasses, impeccably dressed in a white suit, red tie, and matching red shoes. He tugs on the lapels of his suit jacket and confidently walks toward a shadowy broken-down building at the pier's edge.

Several groups of unsavory characters are waiting inside, keeping their distance from one another. They eye each other suspiciously as the white-suited stranger enters.

"The Crypts blew it," he begins with no introduction. "They failed. That's good for the rest of you — it means you all have a shot at the purse. My contact is upping the ante... an even $500,000 to whoever takes out the kid. No questions asked."

"Are you kiddin'! That kid is a death sentence!" one of them retorts from the shadows. "We'd be nuts ta risk it for a lousy 500 G's." The others echo the man's sentiments, shaking their heads in agreement.

"Besides," another pipes up, "...the cops'll be all over him now. If that lightning don't get us, then they will."

"You're gettin' soft," the man in white says disapprovingly as he removes his sunglasses. "Since when have a few flat-footed cops been a problem for you guys?"

"That's easy for you ta' say, Red. What about the lightning that killed all the others? That wasn't no coincidence!"

"Don't believe everything you hear," Red argues back. "They got careless — that lightning stuff is a cover, meant to scare you off."

"Cover! I saw the video o' when Corvo got it and those craters in the kid's yard. I suppose you're gonna tell us those were fakes."

"Don't be stupid!" Red dismisses. "The Crypts were taken out with artillery. They didn't watch their backs and went in too hot — they were chumps!"

"If you're so sure o' that, then why don't you take the kid out yourself!"

Red is silent for a minute, holding a hand to the earpiece in his ear. When he's finished, he looks around and opens his hands as he speaks. "Tell you what we'll do. I've been authorized to raise the bounty to One Million — and I'll go along myself. Except if I'm the one who kills him, then none o' you gets a dime. That's the deal."

"I still ain't interested," the first man declares. "A million ain't no good to a dead man."

The other teams echo his sentiments, waving their hands as they dismiss the offer.

"I'M IN!" a gruff voice yells out from further back in the shadows. Everyone grows silent as the man walks into the dim light. He is a mountain of a man, with a long scar down his face that runs halfway down his muscular neck. His head is bald and covered with tattoos that match the ones wrapping both his thick arms.

Red looks the man up and down -- he hasn't seen him around before. He looks back to the others.

"You know this guy?"

"Yeah — the gangs all know him as Ramrod. The dude is crazy," one of the team leaders answers. The others all mumble and shake their heads in agreement.

Red stares at him for a long minute with a cold stare. "You got a crew?"

"Don't need one," Ramrod answers bluntly.

"Confident, eh? ...Well, at least *that's* refreshing. What's your plan... guns or explosives?"

"My bare hands... I'll break the little runt in half. You jus' take care o' the cops an' leave the kid ta' me."

"Suite yourself," Red allows. "How much time do you need to prepare?"

Ramrod answers with a question: "You know where the kid is?"

"Yeah... he hasn't left home."

"...I'm prepared — let's go."

Red seems slightly taken aback, then he smiles at the hulk of a man with an evil grin. "Awright... no time like the present." He reaches out his hand, offering Ramrod a business card — on the back is scrawled an address: *32 Granite Drive, Center Springs.*

Ramrod takes the card then looks at the limo.

"I'm gonna need a lift... since you're goin' that way anyway."

Red contemplates the request for a moment. "Well, I'm probably gonna need to get the limo fumigated, but fine. You can ride up front with Sammy."

The driver rolls his eyes, biting his tongue, then raises an arm toward the car in invitation. Ramrod climbs into the front seat as Sammy opens the rear door for his boss, closing it after he gets in. He walks around to the driver's side, nodding to his partner at the opposite rear door, and then both of them climb in at the same time.

None of them give any notice to the thick storm clouds that have gathered suddenly overhead.

Red lowers his mirrored glass car window and dons his sunglasses despite the growing darkness that covers the pier. He grins with a cocky grin as he yells to his driver… "Let's go kill the little prick!"

Ramrod responds with a crazed battle cry and stretches his arm out his window, raising his fist in the air and shaking it at the black sky defiantly. Then, just as the car begins to roll forward, a blinding flash streaks from the sky, running right down Ramrod's arm and in through his open window. Its impact lights up the car's interior and instantaneously obliterates its occupants with a blast that blows the limousine's roof clear into the air. What's left of the stalled car rolls aimlessly for several yards across the old cracked pavement, engulfed in flames.

The explosive force shakes the pier and its rickety building so severely that its walls wobble violently, and parts of the roof collapse, sending the men inside running for their lives!

I SAT bolt-upright in my bed, shocked by the scene.

Chozeq was standing nearby with a somber expression etched in his wizened face.

"I wish you wouldn't surprise me with scenes like that when I'm sound asleep," I complained to him.

"I choose neither the time nor the place. I am merely thy safe-guard; thou art the Traveler," he reminded me.

Swinging my feet to the floor, I rubbed my head and eyes, noticing that dawn had broken outside the bedroom window. The clock read 5:53 AM. It occurred to me that the scene I'd just witnessed must have just happened… or is about to happen. The thought sickened my stomach, but not out of fear; it was more a sense of tragic loss. Those men will die by their own choice, even after being warned by the others.

From my upstairs window, I could see that a patrol car had been stationed in front of our house all night. While I was watching, Sheriff Flanagan pulled up behind it and got out of his car to talk to the officers on watch.

Quickly slipping on my sneakers, I rushed downstairs and out the front door, catching him as he was heading back to his car.

"Sheriff Flanagan!"

"Is everything alright, Jim?"

"Yes... we're all fine. ...I was just wondering, have there been any other unusual events this morning — like, you know, other lightning strikes, or anything?"

He looked at me with a sympathetic expression. "Look, I know it's been a rough week — the other night must have been a traumatic experience. But you don't have to worry; the Force is on full alert and on the lookout for any signs of another threat."

While he was talking, his radio received a call from dispatch. He looked at me for a second and switched the call to his earpiece, tucking the receiver into his ear. "Go ahead."

His expression grew serious, and he glanced back at me, then turned away as he spoke into his mic. "I see. Are you sure that's what it was? Alert all units to watch for anything unusual... anyone looking like they're out of place. Add another car to the watch on Granite Drive. Thanks for letting me know."

He turned back to me and studied my eyes as if wondering what had prompted my question moments earlier.

"There was an explosion at an old pier thirty miles from here — it happened about ten minutes ago. The responding officers found a burning car with charred remains inside, along with automatic weapons. Several witnesses at the scene said the car was struck by lightning."

He stopped to gauge my reaction. I got the sense that he could tell I was not surprised by the news. When he saw that I wasn't panicking, he continued...

"...A business card was found lying on the ground beside the car with an address scrawled on the back... your address. I'm doubling the number of officers on watch here, but we're going to need to move you somewhere else. Is there another place you can go — a relative or anyone?"

Mr. V's invitation came to mind. "Well, maybe Mr. Van Clief's farm... he offered. I'll call him."

"Good. We'll keep the location off the record; only share it with people you trust, don't tell anyone else. Keep me posted — use my personal number." He ripped a ticket stub from the pad in his pocket and wrote the number on the back.

"Thanks. Can you stay for breakfast?"

"Sorry, not today; too much going on." The radio in his car squawked again: <*Sheriff, what's your Twenty?*>

He looked back at the car and then to me again... "Gotta go — be sure to call me."

HEADING BACK INSIDE, I ran into Mrs. O, who was in the kitchen jostling Ryan on her hip while she poured him a bowl of his favorite cereal and then deposited him into a chair at the table. The kitchen clock read 6:12; I quickly concluded that Mr. V was definitely awake as I picked up the receiver and dialed his number.

"Yep..." I heard him answer.

"Uncle Jim? ...It's Jimmy."

"How are you, son? I saw what happened on the evenin' news."

"I'm fine... everyone here is fine," I quickly assured him.

"Well, it sure looked like your house was busted up pretty bad. My offer still stands if you need a place ta' stay."

"That's actually why I'm calling. If it's okay, I'd like to take you up on that. Is there room for the O'Malleys too?"

Mrs. O had a questioning expression as I caught her eye, obviously wondering what I was talking about.

"Well, sure, long as the three of 'em don't mind all sharin' one room."

"That's okay... they're doing that here already. I'll call you back in a little while... when I know what time. Thanks, uncle Jim."

Mr. O's voice surprised me. He was standing right behind me: "What was that about?"

I turned quickly to see him leaning casually in the kitchen doorway. Looking back and forth between both of them, I began to explain.

"Sheriff Flanagan was just here... I spoke with him outside a few minutes ago. There was another lightning strike at an old pier thirty miles from here." The two of them looked at each other with wary but confused expressions.

"It struck a car, and some men were killed. They had automatic weapons in the car... and there was a card found with this address on it. Anyway... The Sheriff thinks we shouldn't stay here — he wants us to go someplace else. That's what I was talking to uncle Jim... I mean, Mr. Van Clief, about. He says we can stay there at the farm."

Mr. O suddenly looked nervous. "Alright, I'll start packing our things."

"Where are you goin'?" Uncle Mike asked from the front door as he stepped inside, overhearing the tail end of the conversation.

He was carrying another bag of warm bagels and a gallon of milk, setting them down at one end of the table as I repeated what I had just told the O'Malleys. When I finished, he stood silently, thinking for a moment.

"Dude... that's a vaccine."

He looked around at all of our confused faces, realizing that he had better explain.

"Think about it... since Tuesday, everybody who has tried to get Jimmy has been struck by lightning. As if that weren't impossible enough, they haven't just been hit by it — they've been vaporized! Are you kiddin' me?

"Besides that, it's been all over the news, with pictures and everything! Now, these guys this morning have been hit for just *intending* to try it — while they were still 30 miles away! When this gets out, there won't be *anyone* nuts enough to try it again." He looks back at me; "If ya ask me, you've just been inoculated!"

He could tell from our expressions that we were skeptical, conceding it with a shrug of his shoulders.

"I suppose it's probably still a good idea to go stay at the farm, but I seriously doubt that anybody'll be comin' for ya'... just sayin'."

⌘

26

TIME

Prepare God's people for what's to come...
~ Amos

I was on my second bagel by the time repair crews began to show up.

"Want a bagel?" I said to Sam, the sheetrock crew chief, as I welcomed him at the door.

"Just had one," he declined with a smile, leading his three-man crew through the door. His men were carrying buckets of tools and odd-looking contraptions that looked like small stilts with boot stirrups on one end. They wasted no time strapping the strange gear onto their shoes and were soon ambulating around the room with their sanding blocks and wearing respirator masks, looking like a team of seven-foot-tall robots.

Another knock at the door drew my attention away from their orchestrated precision.

"Tate Beyer," he introduced himself. "I'm here for the kitchen. Just need to take some measurements, if that's alright?"

"Cabinets? I-I don't know if we can afford new...."

He interrupted me with his raised hand. "No need... it's already paid for. I've been sent by Lorenson's Kitchen & Bath Works — they're donating everything and covering the install costs. Appliances, cabinets, countertops... the works. Complements of Mr. Lorenson himself."

He handed me a letter on the store's letterhead, signed by Mr. Lorenson, confirming the promise of a total kitchen replacement. The part that caught my eye the most, however, was his explanation for why....

'Your interview stirred things within me that I hadn't felt in years. God has used you to bring me back to him — I can't thank you enough! God Bless!'

———

BEFORE LONG, a crew of painters arrived, and Uncle Mike and the O'Malleys helped pick out colors. I stood back, looking at the scene as repairs continued to happen around me with astonishing speed. It was almost as if the house was repairing itself.

The rooms around me looked strangely new yet were filled with memories... my entire life. Nearly forgotten scenes began to resurface, of dinners with Kelly and the O'Malleys, and games in the living room with Mom and Dad. The nostalgia made me think reluctantly about leaving here. It was inevitable, I realized honestly; there was no way to pay a mortgage, let alone the property taxes, insurance, and utilities.

Everyone else was busily focused on one thing or another. I found myself wandering toward the old staircase, suddenly feeling the need for a little quiet time in my room before it was time to leave for the farmhouse. As I approached the stairs, I remembered the built-in cubbyholes that dad made... recalling Amos' journal tucked safely inside one of them. Uncle Mike noticed me retrieving the old book and tucking it under my arm as I headed upstairs. He just nodded with a solemn look as if understanding what I was feeling. His glance at the journal let me know that he agreed with my choice to go and read it.

Dropping onto the bed, I settled back against the pillows and looked around the room in a conscious effort to memorize the sight. Amos's journal was tucked loosely in my hand; lifting it, I opened the old book to find the entry mom, and I were reading on Tuesday afternoon. The one from *April 19, 1870.*

I scanned forward until I got to the place where we left off.…

Amos' description of the scene around the tent brought a flood of memories from Tuesday. I braced myself against a growing tangle of unwelcome feelings and continued reading, coming soon to the place that Uncle Mike had shown me.…

…Without a word, he lifted it to his eye and aimed it at the kneeling boy, then fired.
His shot hit a woman...

Even though I already knew what to expect, Amos' words were sobering. They must have been jarring to Uncle Mike when he first read them.…

"It's the boy's mother.…"

As I read the words, I thought about how mom had read them too. Replaying our conversation over dinner that evening, I realized how clueless I had been. I was so preoccupied with my thoughts of Traveling and Amos that I barely heard what mom had been trying to tell me. Now, thinking back, I realized that she was thinking about *this* when she described what the journal said. I remembered the distant sound in her voice; her words sounded almost as if she was speaking to herself...

"I guess I just thought there would be more time. It seems like it's happening so fast."

A tear rolled down my cheek unexpectedly. The temptation to

blame myself was overwhelming. If I'd been more attuned to her and less focused on myself, then I might have saved her. Maybe I could have warned the Sheriff about Corvo. A few more tears began to flow.

"THIS GIFT IS both a blessing and burden...."

I recognized Amos' voice and looked toward the sound. He was old... older than I'd seen him before. He looked at me with understanding as he continued...

"Over the years, I've surely wished I could've foreseen more of the events for which I had the power of fixing. Funny thing about time, though... it can't be changed, even when you try.

"I've come to realize that God doesn't see time the way we do — in a series. He sees all of it at once. He doesn't see a timeline that's changing as it goes along — He sees everything happen the way it actually does. I suppose in that sense God doesn't *foresee* the future; He just sees it, the same as today."

"Then why show it to us at all? If we can't do anything about the future, then what's the point of us knowing?"

"The gift is not about doing. The sooner you come to terms with that, the better off you'll be. God has His reasons for revealing what He reveals and hiding what He hides. His reasons are bigger than you and me."

His words sank in — I couldn't deny the truth of them.

"I just can't help feeling like I could have saved her."

"Maybe you could have. Would your Uncle Mike or those other hundred-thousand souls have found redemption if you had?"

I didn't have any words for an answer. He didn't expect one.

"How far have you gotten in my journal?"

The change of subject jolted me. I flipped back a few pages to find the heading for the entry I was reading.

"I'm at the entry from April 19, 1870."

"Is that all? Well, you've had good reason for being distracted, I'll admit. You're going to have to get at it now, though... times are moving fast — the better prepared you are, the better chance of success you'll have."

"Success? I thought you said we couldn't change the future?"

"I'm not talking about changing it — just using it for God's glory. There are souls to be saved, boy — more than you dare to imagine. But to reach them, you'll need to keep one step ahead of the enemy.

"Chozeq tells me you've seen Bahal. That's good, then you know what he's capable of — don't underestimate him, there's more evil in him than in the Devil's consul. Bad as he is, though, his daughter Athaliah is a far-stretch worse. She's your real opponent."

"I remember that name — she'll be that new president's wife."

"That's right, and the worst enemy of God's church that the world has known, up till now. She hasn't taken her seat of power yet — that's your advantage. If you act wisely and use the time you have, you can prepare God's people for what's to come."

"Prepare them? How?"

"The journal will help some. For the rest, you'll need to trust God.

"You'll be moving soon to the farmhouse. When you get there, check the root cellar... at the east end. If it still works, there's a door there hidden in the stone. It hides a secret passageway; inside it, you'll find provisions — don't use them until you need to."

Amos looked tired as he turned to leave. I quickly called to him.....

"WAIT! What day is it? I mean... in your time?"

He looked back at me. "We've just finished the harvest. Tomorrow is the day of Thanksgiving... by President Wilson's proclamation. It's become a tradition ever since Lincoln did the same."

"The date, I mean... what's the date?"

"Thanksgiving is on the 27th... today is the 26th... November 26th, 1919."

There was something in his gaze as he looked me in the eye one last time — as though he knew that his journey was ending and mine had just begun.

"Godspeed, Lad. May the angels and God Himself protect and keep you."

⌘

27

SEASON

He thunders with the voice of his majesty; And he does not restrain the
lightnings...
~ Job 37:4

Turning into the entrance of Van Clief's farm, we could see the tent standing far off in the distance — it brought a sudden flood of memories from Tuesday night. A golden sunset was reluctantly giving way to night. I couldn't help feeling like it was symbolic of something profound that was happening in my life as well... maybe even in the whole world.

Mr. V was waiting for us as we pulled up the long gravel driveway toward the farmhouse. He came to the car and greeted me with a welcoming embrace as I climbed out. With his hand on my shoulder, he looked me in the eye...

"I'm awful glad ya came, Jimmy. Make yerself at home here — you're welcome for as long as you need."

His left hand patted my shoulder as he turned to the O'Malleys, extending his right hand.

"I reckon you must be Ward, Vince's friend. It's been a long time — good t'see ya again."

"Yes, that's right. I guess it's been about 20 years. Thanks for opening your home to us, Mr. Van Clief; it's really generous of you, we're truly grateful." He turned to Mrs. O standing beside him...

"This is my wife, Barbara."

Mr. V shook their hands in welcome, smiling as he saw Ryan being lifted from his car seat.

"Who's *this* young man?"

"This is Ryan," Mrs. O replied as Ryan squeezed against her neck bashfully.

"Well, hello, Ryan. It's been a fair number o' years since there's been a young 'un on the farm. I reckon it'll do the place some good."

He turned and waved toward the house; "Come on inside and get settled. I put clean sheets on the beds and gave the rooms a once-over. Hope yer not prone to dust allergies."

Mr. O and I unloaded the suitcases and carried them inside, as uncle Jim led us to our rooms. I hadn't been upstairs in the old house before; it was like a time capsule all on its own. From the upstairs hallway, we could see into each of the three small bedrooms decorated with nineteenth century Victorian furniture. It looked like the furnishings had not been updated in sixty years, but everything was neat and well-kept. The bedroom windows were open, letting the rooms air out, but their stuffiness suggested that they had been closed-off for a long time.

Each of the bedrooms was set in one of the corners of the old house, and a small bathroom occupied the remaining upstairs space. Its wood plank floor, four-legged cast iron tub, and antique fixtures hearkened back to its origins as a water closet — literally a large closet with indoor plumbing. Thick cast iron pipes ran through the floor, where they could be plainly seen in the kitchen below, running down in front of a wall. A summer breeze blew through the upstairs rooms, from one window to another. It was surprisingly comfortable for a house with no air conditioning.

After dropping the suitcases in our rooms, we all headed back downstairs. Mr. V waved toward an ice-cold pitcher of homemade lemonade.

"There's fresh ice cream there in the freezer — I jus' made it this afternoon. It goes pretty well with those fresh strawberries on the counter."

"Iced cream!" Ryan repeated enthusiastically, beating me to the comment.

Mr. And Mrs. O disappeared into the kitchen with Ryan while Uncle Jim settled into his favorite stuffed chair. It looked like he'd had a busy day; I got the sense that he would be in bed by now if we hadn't arrived.

"Switch on the TV an' let's see what foolishness the world is up-to fer today," he requested.

After looking around the room for a remote, I realized that he was asking me to get up and hit the actual power button on the TV set. I soon realized why he didn't need a remote — the old TV only got one channel. It was the local station, pulled in over its rabbit ear antenna.

The evening news happened to be reporting on the morning's lightning strike at the pier, complete with video of the burned-out limousine and mug shots of the deceased men. They didn't mention my name, apparently keeping that detail secret to aid in their investigation. In my mind, I could hear Uncle Mike making his point about being inoculated. It occurred to me that the other men on that pier were likely to do a better job of spreading the word than if it *had* been reported on the news.

"Even without 'em sayin' it, it's obvious that those thugs were after you," Mr. V observed. "I don't reckon there's anyone with half a brain who hasn't pieced that together. The lightning is a dead giveaway, sure as shootin'," he added, pointing out the futility of the Police plan.

Mrs. O called from the kitchen for me to come and get the Ice Cream she had served up for us.

"Add a few heaps o'those cut-up strawberries for me, and help yerself to 'em."

The ice cream was delicious — especially with his sliced strawberries! Another one of Mr. V's culinary surprises. Soon after he had emptied his bowl, Mr. V began to nod off. It was a signal to all of us that it was time to turn in for the night, and to be honest, after the excitement of the past few nights, we were as exhausted as he was. We announced that we were all heading to bed, giving him the excuse to do the same.

"There 're fresh towels on the shelf there in the bathroom; help yerself ta what ya need." Mr. V offered.

"Thanks, Uncle Jim… for everything," I said, catching him before he ducked into his room.

He gripped my shoulder supportively and looked me in the eye without a word. His eyes did all the talking, conveying a clear mix of sympathy and welcome. He turned to the O'Malleys with a quick nod… "G'night folks," then stepped into his room and closed the door.

They nodded to me as well with understanding smiles, saying their goodnights. I was the last to do the same, closing the bedroom door and turning to lean against it.

THE OLD BEDROOM felt comfortable and welcoming — kind of like an old robe or a favorite jacket. As comfortable as it was, though, I struggled to feel at home. In fact, the word 'home' had a strange and distant feeling to it — I wasn't sure I really had one… a home… right now.

Zipping open my suitcase, Amos' journal caught my eye. It was lying right on top, where I had quickly tucked it as we were leaving. Its thick leather cover felt warm in my hands as I held it before laying it down on top of the night table beside the bed. Amos' words from the previous night replayed in my head, reminding me of the way he had described my mission: *"There are souls to be saved… more than you dare to imagine. But to reach them, you'll need to keep one step ahead of the enemy."*

The charge felt sobering, spurring me to stop and breathe a prayer for help.

The contents of my suitcase filled just one drawer of the old dresser. After looking at the disorganized pile for a minute, I decided to spread things out. When I had finished, the drawers seemed mostly empty with just a few items in each, but at least they were organized. The last drawer was for my single pair of pajamas — my favorite pair. Mrs. O had washed them before we packed up... I was really going to miss all of her help when they headed back home.

After a quick change, my attention was drawn to the old bed. The empty suitcase slid easily underneath it as I shoved it under and climbed on top. Its old mattress felt a little lumpy, revealing the bed slats underneath, but the sheets were clean and fresh. All in all, I had to admit that it was better than sleeping on our old living room couch.

Finally, grabbing the journal from the nightstand, I cracked it open to the bookmark I'd placed inside.

~ April 26, 1870 ~

It was early in the morning when Chozeq's voice woke me from sleep. As I awoke, the visions in my head were troubling to me.
I had seen great armies with fearsome weapons in clashes of battle that left the land a barren waste. Their monstrous cannons shook the earth as they crushed and shattered trees and houses and caused the air to shudder as they thundered their mighty blasts. Clouds of yellow smoke blurred the skies, from which men fled wearing grotesque masks. Those who did not escape from it died gasping for breath — the terror of it etched in their faces. I saw men lying dead by the thousands in muddy fields and in long trenches and graveyards of crosses that stretched as far as my eyes could see.
As the scenes continued to shift from battle to battle, the weapons grew more terrible. Fire rained from the skies as airships flew overhead, buzzing like enormous wasps as they stung the earth with horrendous explosions. Cities were left burning in their wake. Great ships with iron hulls and guns as long as trains cast fire upon distant shores, rocking the earth with their thunder. On the seas, I saw mighty armadas in battle. Invisible enemies who hid beneath the waves pierced their huge ships with fearsome power, splitting them in two with explosions that reached into the skies, sending countless men to their doom.

In dismay, I watched as fighting and death were multiplied across the earth, with nation struggling fiercely against nation to consume one another. Finally, a weapon was revealed so terrible that it consumed even the nations' will to fight. It burned like the sun, swallowing whole cities like the yawning jaws of Hell itself! Coming out of the midst of this terrible cataclysm, I saw a fiery horse, all of red. Its rider bore a great sword, which he wielded above his head, swinging it triumphantly before sheathing it again and then vanishing from sight.

"Awake, my friend," Chozeq called, nudging my shoulder with his huge hand.
My sight cleared slowly, revealing that the sun had barely risen. My heart pounded in my chest as I looked upon my angelic friend, knowing by the look in his eyes that he understood what my vision had shown.
"Wars..." I stammered as I studied his face. "Terrible weapons... so much death...."
"The visions of thy head are indeed troubling; they are of terrible days yet to come."
"Was it the last war... Armageddon?"
"Nay. What thou hast seen are wars that are soon to come. Men will call the first of them: 'The war to end all wars,' yet it will barely have ended when another has begun, even more, terrible than the first. Their battles shall shape the world's last days."
"I saw a rider... a red horse...."
"He was a harbinger — a foreshadowing of the riders to come. When the seals are opened."
I knew what he was referring to; Revelation... The Great Tribulation. He simply looked at me and nodded in confirmation.

"Rise and make ready. There is much I must show thee."
I had no sooner fastened my boots than I found myself in the air, with Chozeq's hand at my back. As I watched, the scene beneath us grew wider and was soon stretching out for a thousand miles in every direction until nearly the whole of the continent was laid out below

us. I grew awestruck at the sight — not for its grandeur, but rather its devastation. All across the land, fires were burning, with whole forests turned to smoldering black ruins. Great storms of dust swept over the plains and consumed cities in their churning clouds. Rivers and lakes had run nearly dry, and the ground was cracked and hard as baked clay.

"What happened? What caused this?"

"Not what, but who."

I knew that he spoke of Athaliah. She was the cause of this great suffering. While I comprehended it, we suddenly stood amid a great multitude, starving and destitute. They carried jugs for water rations — men, women, and even children each carried their own.

Soldiers stood surrounding huge horseless wagons bearing tanks of water. They guarded them as though it was the most valuable resource on earth... and I suppose it was, from the look of things. We overheard some of them speak to one another.

"How long can this last? If we don't get some rain soon... we can't continue much longer."

The first soldier's partner shook his head disbelievingly; "No one believed it when he said it, but the Moretti kid was right when he said it wouldn't rain... he was right about everything."

The journal's words stopped me in place, making my heart race as I reread my name. How could *I* be mentioned... why *my* name?

My eyes roamed over the page of Amos' handwritten script, realizing that there was nothing random about the fact that I was the one to whom he revealed the journal's whereabouts. He, in fact, had me in mind when he hid it... all those years ago. The implications weighed on me like a great weight of responsibility as I carefully continued reading with increasing unease.

Overhearing their conversation, a third soldier leaned in toward her companions and spoke in a hushed voice, shaking her head. "Yeah, but he said it wouldn't rain until the country changed its ways... until America turned back to God. That ain't gonna happen, not with these people in charge — there's no way."

*Their sergeant suddenly barked at them, ordering them back in line.
"We're doomed..." she whispered to the others under her breath as they
all straightened to attention.*

*Her words were still ringing in my ears when the scene changed once
again. I recognized the new president seated at the head of a large
table with his sixteen cabinet members. Golden nameplates in front of
each member's seat identified their cabinet positions. The contrast was
striking between these well-dressed officials and the starving popu-
lace. They looked pampered and comfortable, with large pitchers of
water and filled glasses in front of each of them. Trays of unfinished
food filled a nearby serving area. Athaliah was seated to the president's right, behind a nameplate entitled 'Unity Enforcement Agency.'*
*"The time has come for the next phase of our emergency plan,"
Athaliah announced. "Through our seizures of retirement accounts
and corporate assets, and the prohibition against personal business
ownership, we have successfully transferred nearly all wealth assets to
the public treasury. In fact, the success of these policies has exceeded
our expectations."*
*"Success? There are bread lines in the streets!" the Treasury Secretary
argued in dissent. "People are losing their homes by the millions!"*
*"It is a regrettable consequence — all of us must sacrifice together," the
Welfare Secretary responded. "The government needs these resources,
and more, in order to provide for the destitute."*
*"Well, there are certain to be more who are destitute if we continue in
this direction," the dissenting secretary objected.*
*"Wall Street is not the solution to everything," the young Director of
Internal Revenue spoke up. "The country's resources belong to the
people, not to the rich Barrons!"*
*"You're talking about taking people's life savings! The people whose
investments have been seized were average families, not rich Barrons!
Their investments in businesses were what funded jobs and paid the
taxes in this country! Where will we get the money to fund these policies once everyone is bankrupt and unemployed?"*
*"It's very simple," the smug young Director answered him, "we'll give
them government jobs."*

"That makes no sense!" the flabbergasted older cabinet member responded. "Will we also tax them at 100% of their salary to have the money to pay them?"

Athaliah interrupts the escalating exchange. "Fighting among ourselves will not solve this! The fault lies with the cause of this ecological disaster — the Moretti boy is behind this... he must be found!"

"We have all our bureaus and law enforcement agencies seeking him," the Intelligence Director insisted. "We have even enlisted our foreign bureaus and cyber units in the search. If he's alive, we'll get him."

"Issue an edict," Athaliah said through her gritted teeth. "Anyone found aiding and abetting the boy will meet swift justice for harboring a fugitive — including imprisonment and confiscation of all personal property."

The Intelligence Director looked at her with an irritated expression. "Might I remind the Secretary that we are still in a democracy and not a monarchy! Americans are not ruled by edicts." He turned to the president; "I assure you we are doing all within our power."

"Then our power is insufficient," the president answered with considerable anger in his voice. He raised his gaze to look each cabinet member in the eye, settling finally on his Intelligence Director. "Must I remind you that we are in a national crisis? Find the boy — use whatever means necessary."

Athaliah looked pleased by the president's remarks. She looks to the others arrogantly as she continues... "We must move to the next phase. Use the President's emergency powers. As Secretary of Unity, I strongly urge that we must hold the country together in this time of crisis."

"Draft the Executive Order... I'll sign it," the President vowed. The cabinet officers looked at one another... some with surprise, while the expressions of others bore an air of delight. All remained quiet. No one around the table dared to challenge her any further.

"Tell me," I said to my guide, "what will become of the boy? Will he be safe?"

"Aye, his faith shall grow strong, even commanding the rain, as thou *hast seen. He will be greatly threatened, but God will shelter him beneath His wings. Yea, in those days, the enemy shall seek to destroy him and shall not be able. Angels shall be his guardians and lightning his deliverer."*

⌘

2 8

FARMHOUSE

A friend loves at all times...
~ Proverbs 17:17

Awakened by morning light, I quickly realized that a bright sunbeam was shining through a crack at the bottom of the window shade, directly onto my face. As my eyes adjusted, I could see the golden sun just peeking above the distant horizon. The house was filled with a delicious aroma that I'd recognize anywhere — the smell of French Toast and bacon.

After a quick wash, I rushed downstairs, propelled by the wonderful smell and the growling in my stomach.

"Thought I'd let ya' sleep a spell today... figured it's been a rough few days," Uncle Jim said without turning away from his griddle. He was busy flipping slices of his hand-cut French Toast creations as he said good morning. "How'd ya sleep in that old bed?"

"Thanks. I slept really well... great, in fact."

I was still talking as Mrs. O' entered the kitchen with Ryan on her hip.

"Mornin' to ya, Mrs. O'Malley," Mr. V said happily as he greeted her.

"Good morning... So formal. Call me Barbara, please."

"Fair 'nough. There's fresh milk in the ice box," he offered, glancing at Ryan's empty cup. "Help yerself."

"Thanks. That smells delicious."

"Wait until you taste them...." I promised her. "They're the best ever!"

"Be ready in a just bit," uncle Jim said as he flipped a few sizzling rows of bacon. "Jimmy, you can set the table if you please. The plates an' flatware are there in the cupboard.

"...And there's fresh coffee in the kettle Barbara if you're so inclined."

"We love this old house — there's so much character in it," she said as she poured herself a cup. Thanks again for your hospitality, Mr. Van Clief... this is all really generous of you."

"Now, who's bein' formal? It'd make me feel a mite less ancient if ya called me by my first name — Jim."

"Okay," she answered, looking back and forth at both of us with a sly grin. "Jim and Jimmy. That won't be confusing."

"You can call me 'Old Jim' if it helps," Mr. V cracked with his usual dry wit. "This-here hospitality, if that's what y'want ta' call it, is the least I can do. I owe Jimmy more than I can repay... in this life or the next."

His comment caught me off-guard; I stood looking at him for a minute speechlessly while Mrs. O' looked at me with a touched, pouting expression.

"Well, don't get so choked up over it," he said, looking over his shoulder. "Food's near ready — we'll be needin' those place settings."

"THAT SMELLS DELICIOUS..." we suddenly heard Mr. O' interrupt from the kitchen doorway. His hair was wet from a shower, and he looked dressed for the day.

"Mornin' Ward. We're near ready... ya got pretty good timin'."

"Yeah, Barb complains the same thing about me and housework," he responded with a smile as he kissed his wife good morning.

I had just finished setting the table in time for uncle Jim to deposit two huge platters in the middle, filled with French Toast and scrambled eggs.

"Grab that tray o' bacon for us, Jimmy," he requested with a nod over his shoulder.

Mr. O' beat me to it, stealing a strip in the process.

"Umm... this is amazing!"

"What's gotten into you?!" Mrs. O' scolded him with an appalled expression.

Uncle Jim just gave him a wink as he quietly took his seat. He looked around the table at all of us and smiled. "It's sure good havin' folk around fer a change. Hope you can stay awhile." He looked at me particularly as he said it.

"Careful what you ask for," I warned him. "You might be stuck with me for longer than you want."

"Wouldn't bother me one bit. I don't reckon I could live long enough fer you t' wear out your welcome."

Mrs. O' grabbed her heart in dismay.

"Don't worry..." he quickly assured her, "I ain't droppin' dead right away."

Once the laughter died down, he held out his hands. "My Pa always had us hold hands at grace... mostly here at this same table. I guess it's taken me too many years to follow in his example."

We smiled and nodded acceptingly, grabbing hands.

"Lord, you know I ain't been a good example in a lotta ways, but I'm grateful that you've loved me all these years in spite of it. Thank you for these fine folks who are here with me this mornin', especially young Jimmy. It's clear that you've got your hand on him. The path you've called him to walk sure ain't easy... we ask that you protect and keep him and be a comfort to him. Cause when all is said n'done, you're the only true comfort that lasts in this life." He paused for a moment and quietly cleared his throat before finishing.

"Bless this food that you have provided and give us strength for today. We're thankful for it. Amen."

There was a moment of quiet around the table. I was thinking about all the pain uncle Jim had experienced in his life, grateful that he had finally found the true source of comfort. It was also clear that the others were thinking about me and all that's happened lately. It occurred to me that no one had touched the French Toast yet.

"These are amazing!" I said with an enthusiastic smile as I poked my fork into a thick stack of them and pulled it onto my plate. A glob of uncle Jim's thick maple syrup was soon running down the sides, and I stuffed a fork-full into my mouth, closing my eyes in delight. They were even better than I remembered.

"Well, that's a ringing endorsement if ever I saw one," Mr. O' joked, stabbing a few slices of his own.

Mrs. O' cut up a slice into small bites for Ryan and then helped herself, quickly agreeing that they're the best she'd ever tasted.

"They have a secret ingredient," I said, smiling at uncle Jim, proud of myself for knowing about his trick of adding maple syrup to the recipe. He just held up a finger to his lips.

"That's a valuable family secret," he warned.

I placed one hand on my heart and raised the other in a promise not to tell, as everyone laughed.

"SPEAKING OF SECRETS," I added as the room grew momentarily quiet, "...no one else knows where we are - except Uncle Mike and Sheriff Flanagan. Maybe we should tell PJ and Pastor Wilkes?"

"I suppose so," Mr. O' conceded, stroking his chin thoughtfully. "We can't let the word get out too broadly... the fewer who know, the better."

Mrs. O' looked at my face for an instant and seemed to read my thoughts... "You probably want to tell Anna where you are. I think it'd be okay to let her and her mom know, don't you, Ward?"

He considered it for a moment and looked at my hopeful expression. "I guess that'd be alright... but no one else, they have to promise."

I agreed to his conditions with a nod. "Have you decided when you're going back?"

They looked at each other briefly. "Late next week, most likely,"

Mr. O' revealed. "I'm needed for a city council hearing on one of the company's proposals." He looked at me earnestly as he continued. "We'll need to settle on a day before then for the Memorial Service."

His comment brought the harsh reality of what was really happening rushing back to my mind. I looked down at my plate, playing with the fork for a moment. "I guess we should talk to Pastor Wilkes. Tomorrow is Sunday... would Monday work?"

"That's short notice," Mrs. O' noted. "Is there time to let everyone know?"

"I'm pretty sure everyone knows to expect it," Mr. O' carefully answered, glancing at me reassuringly. "Anna seems pretty good at getting the word out — do you think she could help with that?"

"Definitely," I agreed. Then a thought hit me... "Maybe we could invite Caden and Trudi or Vanessa to come... with a small news crew?"

"Well, I don't know about that...." Mrs. O' began. Mr. O' touched her arm to stop her.

"He may be right. After all that's happened... this is still big news."

"But do we want reporters at the memorial service?" Mrs. O' questioned.

Mr. O' looks to me... "That's up to Jimmy."

"I-I'm okay with it, I think. Maybe God can use it."

Mrs. O' looked worried. "What about... you know, the reason we're here? Is it a good idea to advertise where Jimmy will be?"

Her concern made sense, but it didn't worry me in the least. I got an idea that might help everyone feel more comfortable. "They can record it and show it after the service is over.

"Besides," I offered confidently, "I don't think we have to worry about that anymore." In my mind, I saw Chozeq's words from Amos' journal: *'Angels shall be his guardians and lightning his deliverer.'*

Mr. O' quickly agreed with his wife. "Now that you mention it, of course, you're right. It is dangerous to publicize the service; I'm sure Sheriff Flanagan would agree."

"You don't understand. Nothing bad will happen!"

"How do you know that, Jimmy? It's just too risky, after all that's happened."

I was silent for a moment as I thought about how to answer his question…. "Wait here, there's something I have to show you… I'll be right back!"

They looked up with startled expressions as I jumped up and ran for the stairs.

THE JOURNAL WAS TUCKED under a pile of shirts in the old dresser's center drawer. As I retrieved it, I couldn't help holding it in my hands uncertainly, wondering if I was doing the right thing. Mom's words of advice came to mind: *'You feel like God revealed it to you for a reason… If that's the case, then it'll all be fine. Doing the right thing is what's important.'*

I breathed a quick prayer and hugged the journal to my chest as I carried it downstairs. I could hear Mrs. O' talking to her husband from the kitchen…

"…Maybe you should go up and talk to him; all of this must be so hard on him."

Before Mr. O' could respond to her, I poked my head in through the door.

"It's okay… I'm fine, really," I assured them all as I reentered the room. "This is what I wanted to show you."

Carefully laying the journal down on the table between uncle Jim and me, I turned it toward him, holding my hand on the cover protectively. "This is a journal written by Amos Van Clief… your grandfather."

Uncle Jim looked back and forth between the journal and my face, unsure whether he had heard me right. "My grandad?"

"The way I came to have it is a long story… What's important is what it says." I looked back at the O'Malleys and then to uncle Jim again. "It contains visions that he had about the future… about us."

Everyone was sitting silently, trying to decide whether I was serious.

"Amos was a believer… a prophet. His visions were a secret — they were sealed, until now." I looked back at Uncle Jim; "Amos' son, Raymond… your father… was the pastor of the old Methodist church."

"That's right, he was." Uncle Jim lowered his gaze as if remembering a painful regret."

"Here, listen to this," I said, opening quickly to the entry that I was reading last night. Beginning by reading the date of his entry.

I READ ALOUD the journal's account of war scenes and naval battles, ending with Amos' description of an atomic bomb. They listened uncomfortably to the terrible account and looked at the book's pages as I read Chozeq's explanation:

'~ April 26, 1870 ~

What thou hast seen is soon to come. Men will call it 'The war to end all wars,' yet it shall barely have ended when another has begun, even more, terrible than the first. Their battles shall shape the world's last days.'

"He wrote this in 1870," I reminded them. "But wait — you have to hear what it says next...."

I read Amos' account of a devastating future drought, holding up my hand to be sure they heard the soldier's words as I read them aloud...

'No one believed it when he said it, but the Moretti kid was right when he said it wouldn't rain... he was right about everything.'

The O'Malleys and Mr. V all looked at one another in disbelief.

"Wait... what did he say?" Mrs. O' asks, shaking her head. "H-how could it say that? Why does he say your name?"

"There's more..." I continued, reading Amos' account of the President's Cabinet meeting.

Coming to Athaliah's name, I explained who she was: "She will be the president's wife — Amos wrote that in an earlier entry." I saw their astonished expressions as I read her threats against me. There was a growing look of fear in their eyes until I came to the end — reading Chozeq's assurance:

'...but God will shelter him beneath His wings. Yea, in those days, the enemy shall seek to destroy him and shall not be able. Angels shall be his guardians and lightning his deliverer.'

The three of them sat awestruck as they heard those words — unable to deny that they had been fulfilled - literally - on three separate occasions in just the past week.

"SO YOU SEE? There's nothing to be afraid of."

They all looked at me silently, trying to process the flood of questions in their minds. Mr. O' finally spoke; his voice was slow and unnaturally calm, as if he was trying too hard to sound open-minded while not entirely being convinced himself.

"It's an amazing coincidence that he used your name... along with that reference to lightning. But Moretti must have been a common name, even in those days, and the angel's comment, well, that sounds like a Bible reference.

"Besides, how do we know that the journal is as old as it says? Those things about the war could have been written in the '40s after it happened."

I half-expected his response, realizing that I'd be having a hard time believing it myself if not for Amos' visit and all that I've been through with Chozeq myself. I realized what would convince them, turning back the pages and bracing myself for the entry I hoped to avoid.

"Alright, it's hard to believe; I really get that. But, before you dismiss it, just listen to this entry... It was written on *April 19, 1870,* ~

I PAUSED to take a deep breath and let it out slowly before reading.

Chozeq turned toward the field behind us and pointed out a man who was walking toward the tent. He was not like the others in the crowd; his face was set with an angry scowl, and he walked purposefully, pushing others out of his way. I had seen men in war with that look... it was the cold, detached look of an experienced assassin.

Dark clouds suddenly appeared above the field, rolling and folding like smoke; the nearer the man drew, the darker they became.

As I watched, he stopped among the crowds seated in the grass and reached into the sack slung over his shoulder, drawing out a rifle. Without a word, he lifted it to his eye and aimed it at the kneeling boy, then fired.

His shot hit a woman who had quickly moved in front of the boy, striking her in the back, and I saw her thrown forward by the force of it.

Before the shooter could get off a second shot, the thick black clouds above us lit with a mighty flash, piercing the sky with the most terrific blast of lightning I ever saw... it struck the shooter square on the top of his head and blasted the rifle to pieces, sending parts of it spinning through the air. The sound of the thunderclap was so mighty that it shook the earth under our feet and sent crowds of people tumbling in all directions. When the frightful blast had cleared, there was little left of the shooter, except for his shoes and the empty sack from his back. No one else appeared to have been harmed except the poor woman he shot.

That's about the time that it dawned on me who she was.

My voice choked slightly, and I paused to clear my throat before continuing to read...

"...It's the boy's mother."

When I finished reading, Mr. O's mouth was hanging open in astonishment, and fresh tears were running down the sides of Mrs. O's face. They were both staring at the handwritten pages with eyebrows raised while they wrestled with a chaotic mix of fear and realization.

. . .

IT WAS uncle Jim's voice that broke the silence. It was barely above a whisper, almost as if he was talking to himself....

"That's pert near the exact way that it happened... I was standin' right there, an' I couldn't say it any better than that." He looked at the journal again; "My grandad wrote that?"

"Yeah, he did... Amos Van Clief."

He stared at the journal like the others, but his look also conveyed a different realization — as if pieces of a lifelong puzzle were suddenly falling into place.

Without a word, he got up from his chair and walked to a small china cabinet, pulling it open, then reached inside to carefully pick something up. I couldn't make out what it was that he was carrying until he set it on the table — the sight of it startled me. It was made of dark wood... with a beautiful marbleized wood grain and polished to a dull shine. Obviously hand-carved by a skilled artisan — it was an angel... a warrior, resting on one knee with wings partly spread. The angel's sword was unsheathed and planted in front of him as he rested his hands on its hilt. I recognized the angel's familiar face immediately.

"This-here angel belonged to our daughter, Abi." Uncle Jim paused as he used her name as if hearing it aloud had triggered a swell of memories. "She was sick... had the Polio — she was only eight at the time that she... when we lost her.

"Darnedest thing about this angel... she began to claim in her last few months that an imaginary friend visited her near every night. She said there was always an angel with him." He turned the angel to look at its face as he continued to recount the story.

"She kept tellin' me that her imaginary friend had given her a gift, and she insisted that I look for it. She told me where to look; under some loose floorboards in the attic. After a few days of askin', she wore me down, and I promised her that I'd go and look. I had a toy o' my own ready to bring to her, not expectin' t'find anything, an' not wantin' to disappoint the dear child. Sure enough, though, after I moved some old trunks and brushed away 30 or 40 years of dust, there were those loose floorboards, just where she said they'd be, and underneath them, I found this-here angel."

Uncle Jim looked up at all of us as he turned the angel over to show its base. "The man who carved it signed his name."

I heard Mrs. O' gasp aloud and felt a thrill as I looked at the name carved into the polished wood...

~AMOS~

⌘

MYSTERIOUS KEY

Now ya' jus' gotta figure out what it's for.
~ Jim Van Clief

Uncle Jim seemed quieter than usual as we finished breakfast and cleared the table.

"I can wash those," I offered as they were piled into the sink.

He agreed with a silent nod and grabbed a towel, drying the first one with it as I handed it to him.

Mr. O' cleared the table and laid down the last stack of dishes beside me.

"I think maybe I'll give Pastor Wilkes a call," he said quietly, interrupting the silence in the room. He pulled his phone from his pocket and headed out onto the side porch.

As I washed and then handed dishes to Uncle Jim, I could tell that he was going through the familiar motion of drying them with barely a notice, still obviously deep in thought. The longer we stood together in silence, the more nervous I became. I knew that I needed to explain how I 'found' Amos' journal. That was going to be hard enough, but I was more nervous about the fact that I'd had it for almost a week without telling him.

His voice startled me...

"Was it in a dream?"

"Wh-what... was what...?"

"The whereabouts of that old journal. Did y' see it in a dream?"

I wrestled with my answer — recalling how I let mom think I was shown it in a vision without actually saying it. When I turned to look him in the eye, however, the memory of *his* dream flashed through my mind — the one with Grampa Farro's prayer for him that we shared; I realized that that was the reason for his question.

"It was kinda like that."

He waited quietly, not probing, but clearly waiting.

"Uncle Jim... I'm sorry I didn't bring it to you sooner; I know it belongs to you... he was your grandfather, and it's yours. I meant to — I brought it here Tuesday night, the day I found it, but then...."

The tightening in my throat prevented me from finishing the sentence, and he didn't let me try. He placed his hand on my arm to stop me, then patted it a few times. When I looked at his face, it was filled with understanding; he shook his head and spoke softly.

"Don't be fearin' that. It ain't surprisin' that it came t' you and not me. It belongs to you, son — you're the one it was shown to. God likely has His reasons." I just looked back at him, feeling a great sense of relief but also discomfort over the weight of responsibility that was inferred in his words.

"How much of it have ya' read?"

His question caught me off-guard. "Just a little... a few entries so far. You can read it if you want."

He silently considered the offer.

"Maybe, someday. But I reckon it's more important that you get t'readin' it first. There's a reason it came to you."

I can't help thinking about Amos' own words to that same effect.

Uncle Jim put down the last dish and dried his hands on the towel before handing the towel to me to do the same. "There's somethin' I wanna show ya'. Go get dressed an' meet me out in the barn."

WHEN I ARRIVED at the barn, Uncle Jim was standing beside the long workbench. He waved me nearer as I entered and reached for a locker-sized cabinet — it looked as old as the barn itself, with a door made of darkened wood planks. Inside was an array of old hand tools, along with jars of screws and nails and an assortment of oil cans. However, my attention was drawn to the top shelf and its collection of old hand-carved animals — mostly dogs and horses. He handed me a few of them to examine... they all had Amos' name or initials carved in the bottom. While I was admiring the impressive figurines, uncle Jim reached into the back of the cabinet to pull out a wide wooden box, laying it down on the barn's old workbench. I immediately recognized the initials that were etched into its lid... *A.V.C.*

Inside the box was a pair of strange objects. Uncle Jim lifted out the first one and handed it to me — a large iron key, obviously hand-made. Its shaft was nearly six inches long, with a bit that was an inch tall. Inside the ring of its bow were a pair of letters, fashioned in iron: *VC.*

"Van Clief..." I said under my breath as their meaning dawned on me. "What's it to?"

"It's a mausoleum key," he explained matter-of-factly. "To the family crypt... up at the old church. I reckon if anything happens to me, somebody aught'a know where it is, so ya kin bury me proper." He winked at me and dropped the key back into the box.

"That ain't really the thing I wanted t'show ya'... it's this here." He lifted a strange-looking implement from the box and held it out for me to see. It resembled a tire iron, in the shape of a T, nearly a foot long and just as wide. At the bottom of the T — where a lug wrench would typically be — was a set of crisscrossing iron bars. They resembled a kind of large asterisk, about two inches across. Each of its spokes contained an arrangement of nubs that protruded above and below them like buds on a twisting branch. At the top of the T was mounted a ring, from which was hanging a thin chain attached to a small brass nameplate.

"What is it?"

"That's a fair enough question; never been able to figure what it's for, myself. Somebody went to a heap o'trouble makin' it. I figure it musta been my grandad, seein' as it's in this ol'box o' his. That ain't the whole mystery, though."

Uncle Jim held the oval-shaped brass tag that was attached to it between his fingers. "What's yer middle name?"

"Middle name? ...It's Matthew ...why?"

He turned the tag over, revealing a set of engraved initials in the tarnished brass: *J.M.M.*

I could feel my mouth drop open as I stared at my own initials.

"Never could guess whose initials those were... till this mornin' when you read what ya did from that journal. My grandad surely meant fer you t'have this. Now ya' jus' gotta figure out what it's for."

THERE WAS a sudden shadow in the barn's doorway...

"Thought I might find you guys out here."

Mr. O's voice surprised me more than it did uncle Jim, who calmly laid the strange item back into the box and closed the lid.

"...Barbara wanted me to remind you to call your Uncle Mike and Anna about the service tomorrow night. The pastor will be here around noon to finalize the arrangements."

"Yeah, okay, thanks," I agreed. I gave Uncle Jim a nod, thanking him for what he had shown me, and began walking toward the door.

"...Jimmy," Mr. O' said, stopping me. I looked at him curiously, sensing the hesitancy in his voice as he looked back and forth between uncle Jim and me.

"That journal, do you think it's really true... prophetic, I mean?"

I glanced back at Uncle Jim and the old box in his hands... "Yeah, I do."

The look in Mr. O's eye was anxious. "How far does it go... how far into the future?"

"I don't know... I mean, I've only read a little."

"That part that you read at the table — about the drought and that president... the way they referred to you as a kid. If I had to guess, I'd say that's not too far from now."

I just nodded as I understood his concern.

"Is there any way of knowing what's going to happen — to us, I mean? Will Barbara and Ryan be alright?"

His question reminded me of my own question to Chozeq about the same thing. I could practically feel his reassuring grip on my shoulder as I recalled his answer:

"Tho ye walk through Fire or flood, He is ever with thee.
Remember the safety of His hand — nothing shall
befall thee except for that which He allows."

"I honestly don't know. But I do know that we're in God's hands... nothing can change that."

Mr. O' looked down at the floor thoughtfully and then acknowledged what I was saying. His anxious expression softened a little as he gave me a pat on the back and nodded his head, admitting that he agreed.

"I'LL BE THERE, " Uncle Mike quickly promised over the phone as I told him about the planned meeting with Pastor Wilkes. He was quiet for a moment, then added softly...

"I picked up the ashes this morning."

I nodded into the phone, unable to answer. I knew which ashes he was talking about, admitting silently that it was easier to refer to them that way... saying 'her ashes' was still way too hard.

"I'll bring them when I come," he added quietly. The painters are almost done with the place. It looks good — the job came out real nice. Reminds me of when they first bought the place — I painted a lotta these rooms myself back then." His voice trailed off, sounding strained for a moment. He cleared his throat. "Guess they were due for a fresh coat anyways."

"Thanks for watching the house," I offered sincerely. As I was saying it, I was also breathing a prayer for God's protection of everyone there. He seemed to detect the concern in my voice.

"No sweat, kid. The Sheriff still has his guard detail parked outside. It's been quiet as a Sunday morning around here. I'm tellin' ya — you're inoculated!"

"It's not me I'm worried about," I confessed.

"Well, jus' keep yer whereabouts a secret then. Speakin' o' your whereabouts... Anna called. I told her you were indisposed... said you'd call her back. You gonna tell her where you are?"

"Do you think I should? Mr. O' said it'd be okay, as long as she knows not to tell anyone else."

"Sure, kid."

"Thanks. Well... I guess I'd better call her now."

"Knock yerself out. I'll be over there around noon."

ANNA ANSWERED the call so fast that I got the feeling she was waiting with the phone in her hand.

"Jimmy?"

"Yeah... Hi."

"Is everything okay? Your uncle sounded funny...."

"Everything's fine," I assured her.

"What's wrong? I can tell there's something you're not saying."

"You have to promise not to tell anyone... it's important."

"O-okay... I promise..."

"Sheriff Flanagan wanted us to find another place to stay. He made us promise not to tell anyone where we are... cause of, you know."

"Oh... yeah, I guess that's a good idea. I won't tell — I promise... Where are you?"

"We stayed at Mr. Van Clief's farm last night. We'll probably be here for a while, but we can't tell anybody — none of our friends. I promised the Sheriff."

"I won't tell, I promise!" She paused in thought for a moment... "How come you're telling me?"

"The O'Malleys and Uncle Mike said it would be alright... I guess they trust you."

"You *guess* they do? How about you?"

"Are you kidding? Of course... that goes without saying."

"I guess. Thanks."

"I need your help. We're having mom's Memorial service tomorrow night; can you help us get the word out? It'll be at the church, same as Kelly's."

"Do you think that'll be big enough? After everything that's happened, you and your mom are — like, famous now."

"That's why we just want to tell close friends... people who knew her — like kids from FCS and the church. Mrs. O'Malley and Uncle Mike are helping tell people too... they know all mom's friends."

"Okay, sure. I'd be glad to help." She paused quietly for a moment... "could my mom help with anything? I think she'd really like to."

"Yeah... that'd be great — mom would have liked that. Pastor is coming here around noon today to go over arrangements for the service; you can both join us if you want?"

"Is it okay? You're sure I can tell mom where you are?"

"Yes, definitely. You don't have to keep it secret from her."

"Okay, thanks..." her voice had grown quiet, then after a silent pause... "I can't stop thinking about all that's happened.... I'm so sorry, Jimmy. I don't know how you're handling all this so well. You're really strong."

The thought of seeing Mom and Dad with Daisy in that amazing vision of paradise flooded my mind; it brought a deep feeling of peace and calm.

"I'm not sure it's strength...it's more like reliance," I confessed. "To be honest, I'm leaning hard — harder than ever. It's amazing, though... sometimes I feel like I can't stand — like I'm just falling, you know? But those are the times when I can feel the most inspiration and comfort deep in my spirit. It's like Jesus is holding onto me, telling me I'm safe... that it'll all be alright. — it's like I can hear him sharing thoughts from his own heart."

"What kind of thoughts?" she asked quietly.

"Well, I guess the biggest has been about the way He comforts us. He hasn't promised us that we won't suffer, but Psalm 91 says that '*He will cover us with his pinions, and under His wings, we take our refuge.*' That has become so real to me lately. I've realized something amazing; it's really true that we're never alone, whether we're suffering or not. When everything is all blessings and trouble-free, He's always there, watching us fly. That's a beautiful thing for sure, but when our suffering makes us fall, that's when He's the closest, that's when we're under His wing — that's when He embraces us!"

She was quiet for a moment, then there was a sniffle, and her voice cracked slightly as she finally spoke. "That's beautiful... and so true. I never thought of it just like that before."

I could tell she was thinking about all she went through when her own dad died — she has had her share of suffering too.

"I know this is hard for you too," I offered. "I'm sure it brings back memories. If you want anything... to talk, I'm here, anytime."

Over the phone, I could hear her stifling tears. "You're amazing... Isn't there ever a time when you aren't thinking about everybody else more than yourself?"

"I wish that were true," I admitted, adding after a short pause, "... You're not exactly *everybody*."

"It's about time you noticed that," she joked through another sniffle, lightening the conversation. After a short pause of her own, she added...

"I'm here too... I'll be here for you anytime... always."

⌘

30

ASHES

A nna's words replayed in my mind for the rest of the morning, echoing as if I was in an invisible cave. I'd known all along that she was more than just a friend... the special connection between us was clear even on the first night we met. Back then, we pushed those thoughts away. Mom's words of advice at the time joined the others echoing in my head, '... just see what happens, just be friends.' It was the perfect advice at the time. 'Just see what happens...' those words seemed to float in the air like a premonition.

ALL THIS THINKING almost made me lose track of what I was doing — checking on the farm's irrigation system. A few of the gears had become entangled with tall grass. It was mindless work; the solitude was actually kind of nice for a change. I spotted Uncle Mike's van pulling up the driveway and watched as he began unloading. As usual, it looked like he had arrived with enough food for a small army. The boxes had all been carried inside by the time I made it back to the house.

"I brought over everything that was on ice at the house — figured it's more useful here. The subs are fresh — just made them at the shop; I forgot ta' cancel my Friday delivery orders — brought the rest of that over too."

We had just finished putting the cold stuff away when Uncle Mike tapped my shoulder and waved me aside, leading me into the dining room. He lifted an ornate wooden box from the table; it was a little smaller than a shoebox, with an engraved golden plate inlaid in the lid:

———

Maria Moretti

———

I WAS in a daze as I held out my hands to take it.

"I spoke to the cemetery," he said quietly, "they said we won't have to buy a plot; she can be placed in your dad's if we want. She could be added to his headstone."

Although I heard him clearly, the momentary numbness in my mind prevented me from answering or even nodding. The box was heavier than I expected. It was actually kind of beautiful with its polished wood and inlaid gold lettering — I couldn't take my eyes off of it. Uncle Mike put his arm around my shoulders, and we stood together silently. I tilted the box carefully, admiring it from different angles as I waited to reclaim my voice enough to whisper what was on my heart....

"I know it's not mom. It's just what's left of the earthly part — the temporary part." I looked back at him, catching his eye.

"We saw the real part — the part that matters... the eternal part. I saw your dad hug you. Did you see how happy they were?"

When I looked up at Uncle Mike, tears were running down his cheeks, and he was nodding yes, his own voice now missing. He wrapped both his arms around me, hiding his face against my shoulder. His shaking was a clue that he was letting a few sobs break loose, but I could tell that they were sobs of joy and not sorrow, triggered especially by the memory of his father's embrace.

THE SOUND of a knock on the wooden screen door drew my attention, and I looked up to see that it was PJ. Mr. O' greeted the pastors, making a request for quiet with a finger to his lips as he welcomed them. I noticed that Mrs. O' was standing at the stairs a short distance away, watching Uncle Mike and me — fresh tears were streaking her face. Uncle Jim was standing in the kitchen doorway; all their eyes were focused on the box in my hands.

Uncle Mike kept one arm around my shoulders as he straightened and wiped his eyes with his sleeve. He didn't look at all embarrassed about the wet streaks on his face. Uncle Jim was the first to move, holding out his arms to embrace us both. He then looked to the Pastors as he stepped away.

"Seems to me a prayer is fittin'…."

Reverend Wilkes agreed, inviting everyone to gather around. He glanced from face to face, especially uncle Jim's and mine, and then at the box before closing his eyes.

> "Lord, Your cross reminds us that true love involves suffering,
>   and each life that knows the joys of love and friendship
>   must one day also bear the pain of loss. It reminds us that
>   we are pilgrims in this life, passing on our way to a city
>   not made with hands, whose builder and maker is God. Yet
>   we know that in this life, You are touched with the feeling
>   of our pain. We understand that weeping may endure for
>   the night. Still, rejoicing will come in that eternal morning
>   when we see you face to face and are reunited with those
>   who have gone before.
> We're truly thankful for the time you gave us with Maria and
>   the beautiful way in which she enriched all of our lives.
>   While we look back on those blessed times, we also look
>   forward to a time to come when we will meet her again on
>   heavenly shores and rejoice together in eternal fellowship.

*We commit her to your care, just as we commit these who
loved her to the comfort of your Spirit and Your dear
embrace. In Jesus' name...."*

Everyone joined in an emotional "...Amen."

I carefully put the box on the table, thanking Pastor with a hug, then greeted PJ.

WHILE THE OTHERS were welcoming the Pastors, Uncle Mike nudged me on the arm and whispered.

"There's somethin' else you gotta see; it's out in the van."

We quietly made our way outside, as he explained.

"There was a card in your mailbox sayin' that you had somethin' for pickup at the post office. When I got there, they gave me all this."

He pulled open the rear doors of his van to reveal two large postal sacks. "These are all addressed to you — they started comin' yesterday."

He reached inside one of the sacks and pulled out a handful of letters, offering them to me. We scanned the return addresses — they were from all across the country!

"What are they?" I asked, honestly confused.

"As best I can tell..." he explained, "...it's fan mail."

THE SOUND of a car on gravel signaled that someone else was pulling up the long drive. I watched them approach, sensing my own enthusiasm as I recognized Anna and her mom inside. The car hadn't fully pulled to a stop when the passenger door swung open. Anna jumped out and ran towards me, surprising me by wrapping her arms around me in a hug. I caught sight of her mom smiling from the car as she watched, pulling her eyes away quickly as she saw me looking. She gave Uncle Mike a friendly smile as he made his way over to greet her.

Anna spoke quietly as she held both my hands in hers. "Thanks for what you said on the phone. I do miss my dad — I can imagine how you must feel." A sniffle revealed that she was holding back tears.

Her reaction surprised me but confirmed pretty clearly that we've both been struggling with the same truth about our feelings for each other. She stepped back, still holding my hands, and glanced over her shoulder to see if anyone was within earshot....

"I know Kelly was really special to you, and it's still really soon... I just want you to know that our friendship is the best thing that's ever happened to me."

Between the lines of her words, I could clearly hear her meaning. I couldn't help thinking about all the years that Kelly and I missed by not admitting our true feelings sooner. I didn't want that to happen with Anna. At the same time, however, I was struck by the seriousness of recent events and considered what was about to happen soon. Could it put her life at risk to be close to me?

Anna studied my eyes, examining my expression hopefully. She was about to speak when we were interrupted by the sound of the screen door. I gave her hand a reassuring squeeze as we turned to face PJ, who was stepping down from the porch.

He greeted Anna with a smile and gave me a slap on the shoulder. His expression turned serious as he stood back and stared at the empty tent in the distance. A lone police car could be seen parked beside it.

"We'll be back there soon," I assured him. He studied my eyes as if wondering what inside information I was revealing this time. "It's just a feeling," I admitted. "God started this — it can't end until He's finished."

"LUNCH IS ready if anyone would like it," Mrs. O' called from the porch. "Hi Lena," she said, welcoming Anna's mom with a broad smile as she was coming up the steps with Uncle Mike close beside her. They disappeared into the kitchen, engaged in a flurry of small talk.

PJ looked at us, detecting an awkward silence, then pointed over his shoulder at the door with his thumb, excusing himself.

"See you inside." With a kind-looking smile, he headed up the steps, leaving us alone.

"Do you really think we'll start having services again soon?" Anna asked me.

"Yeah, I'm sure we will."

"Does it say that in the journal?"

Her question struck me as a good one. "I don't know... I haven't read enough of it yet."

She looked surprised. "Don't you think you should? It's really important, right?"

I quickly surrendered, realizing that she was at least the third person in 24 hours to deliver that same message, including Amos himself!

"Things have just been busy... but, you're right. I'll start reading it soon... tonight."

She nodded, accepting my answer, then took my hand again as she looked up shyly.

"A lot is happening right now. I didn't mean to add any pressure with what I said earlier."

"No... it's fine — that was nice. I'm really happy we met too... you can't even imagine how much."

She gave my hand a squeeze, seeming satisfied with my answer. The flash in her eyes spoke volumes that my heart somehow comprehended, even though my mind was left searching.

"I'm starved... let's get some lunch," she said with a smile.

"EVERYTHING IS all set at the church," Pastor Wilkes said reassuringly as we gathered in the living room after lunch. "The cleaning team is giving the building a once-over today."

"I spoke to Caden and Trudi," PJ explained. "They promised to keep news of the service quiet until afterward. Their camera crew will tape it."

"Here's a draft of the program," Pastor Wilkes explained, handing out a few copies for people to share. "After the opening music, I'll give a welcome and open in prayer.

"Pastor Juan will lead the congregation in singing Maria's favorite hymn: 'God Will Take Care of You,' is that right?"

"Yeah, that was her favorite," I confirmed quietly. Anna clasped my hand supportively.

"Barbara, after the hymn, you'll give your comments, and then Ward will read Psalm 23.

"Following Ward, it will be Lena's time for comments."

Anna's mom nodded, and Mrs. O' gave her an encouraging hug.

"Mike, after Lena, it will be your time for comments." Uncle Mike nodded, swallowing noticeably.

"After our second hymn, there will be a time for open testimonies from anyone who would like to say a few words."

"The FCS kids have created a movie. They've been working on it all week," Anna revealed.

"That's wonderful," Pastor agreed. "We can show that at the end of testimonies." Everyone agreed enthusiastically.

"Following that, then, it will be time for Jimmy to say a few words."

My nod reassured him that I was ready to contribute. In fact, the memory of seeing Mom & Dad resonated so powerfully that I could hardly wait for the opportunity.

The pastor recognized my enthusiasm and joked as he continued: "Assuming there is an opportunity to do so, I'll follow Jimmy with the eulogy."

Everyone acknowledged the truth of Pastor's words, remembering how Kelly's service ended. It would certainly be welcomed if that happened again.

We spent the rest of the hour praying for exactly that.

I WAS FEELING INCREASINGLY restless as I sat in my bed later that evening. The house was quiet — the others had turned in for the night, exhausted from another busy day.

Together, we managed to open and read through all of the letters Uncle Mike retrieved from the post office. It took hours. The stories were incredible — telling of conversion experiences and healings that were connected in some way to the interview on Thursday night.

My spirit was deeply stirred. Thinking back to the interview, I felt thankful for the way God had provided the words to say and grateful for how He used them in so many lives. Yet, I had to admit an anxious feeling was building inside me... anxious for the next move. I was searching for what was supposed to happen next — haunted by the look on PJ's face today as he stared at the tent. We should be there, continuing the meetings! I couldn't help thinking that if God was protecting me, then maybe we should just defy the shutdown and meet anyway.

CHOZEQ'S VOICE broke the silence as he suddenly appeared.

"Always men are wont to move."

"Isn't that a good thing?" I asked quietly, being careful not to wake the others.

"Indeed, when He bids thee, it is surely good," Chozeq replied. "Perhaps the most difficult of God's commands is that which He gave to Moses before the Red Sea. *Stand still, and see the salvation of the Lord*[1]."

He looked at me with a gaze that seemed to emanate wisdom. "He has bidden thee to go from strength to strength, and so thou shalt, and neither death nor hell shall turn thee from thy course. What harm is it if for a while thou art called to stand still, to renew thy strength for a greater advance in due time?"

I couldn't stop myself from arguing the point. "But isn't time short? Shouldn't we be working? The night is coming soon!"

"Aye, Lad. Yet it is merely impatience that cries, '*do something.*' '*Stir yourself.*' Impatience warns that to stand still and wait is sheer idleness. This urge to be doing something at once is, in truth, a thought that *ye* must do it — instead of looking to thy Master. Forget not that it is He who will not only do *something* but will do *everything*!"

I got his point but couldn't seem to stop myself from wrestling with his words. "But isn't that what faith is? Shouldn't we believe in God's promise and press forward, even when we can't see?"

"Faith must not be confused with presumption. It is impudence that boasts that ye may march into the sea and expect a miracle. Faith listens not to presumption, nor to despair, nor to cowardice, nor impatience, but it hears God say, '*Stand still,*' and then stands, immovable as a rock.

"Yet, take heed to remain diligent. In thy standing ye must keep the posture of a soldier at attention, ready for action, expecting the orders that will surely come, cheerfully and patiently awaiting God's directing voice; and it will not be long ere He shall say to you, as He did to Moses: '*Go forward*[2]!'"

Chozeq's words calmed my anxious spirit and thrilled me with renewed anticipation.

"How long will it be? There must be something that I should be doing... to prepare."

"Aye, so there is..." he answered, nodding toward Amos' journal lying on the nightstand.

I acknowledged his point, feeling humbled at the number of reminders that God has had to give me. Without answering, I reached for the old book and then nodded to Chozeq, thankful for his encouragement. He nodded back approvingly with spreading wings and then vanished in a streak that passed straight through the ceiling and into the night sky.

⌘

31

MEMORIAL

*Even though I walk through the darkest valley, I will fear no evil, for you are
with me...*
~ Psalm 23:4

The church was packed for mom's memorial. Word spread
quickly among the churches and throughout town. Caden
and Trudi were sitting inconspicuously in the last pew, with
a pair of cameramen stationed in the far corners of the sanctuary and
one in the balcony. Derrick, the church's sound engineer, had
provided a connection to the PA system for their recording equipment. From the platform, I could see the standing-room-only crowd
that had filled the lobby, but mobs of news media had not descended
so far. Tremendous anticipation hung in the air like electricity.

I looked across the platform to where Uncle Mike was sitting and
noticed that he looked back at me. From the look in his eye, I could
tell that he had read the same entry in Amos' journal that I encoun-
tered last night. It was a description of a church service... a memorial.
It seemed as clear to him as it was to me that it was an account of

tonight. If we were right, Amos was just outside, watching the gathering crowd.

"The front lawn is full," PJ whispered as he sat down beside me. "Derrick set up loudspeakers outside for them."

"Thanks," I acknowledged, nodding discretely to Uncle Mike in confirmation.

At exactly 7:00, the musicians ended their opening prelude, and Pastor Wilkes walked to the podium, welcoming everyone. I barely heard a word he said; my attention was focused on the crowd of familiar faces, many of them etched with deep sadness. As he began to pray, their faces turned toward heaven — at first somber and sorrowful, then growing more and more impassioned.

PJ rose on cue to lead the first hymn, explaining that it was mom's favorite. Its words and melody brought a flood of memories. I couldn't help recalling the Sunday morning after Kelly and her parents left for California; it was the last time mom and I sang it together.

MRS. O'MALLEY STEPPED up to the podium with Mr. O' beside her, offering his support. She was drying tears as she unfolded her single page of notes.

"Maria was my best friend..." she began, wiping a stray tear from her cheek.

She struggled to make it through her notes, mentioning their college years, their marriages, and how their kids were raised together. "Maria was like a second mom to our daughter Kelly..." she began to say, stopping to quell a rush of tears. The congregation listened in rapt attention, many joining with her as she cried. The room was silent when she finally stepped aside to let Mr. O' take her place at the lectern.

Without introduction, he simply began to read from the 23rd Psalm. I felt a thrill running through me as he read verse 6: "...I will dwell in the house of the Lord forever." The memory of mom's eternal home flashed again before my eyes, leaving me breathless.

. . .

ANNA'S MOM was nervous as she stepped to the podium; her hands were shaking.

"I met Maria three months ago, but it feels like I knew her all my life...." Her account of those months described how close they had become, explaining how they related to each other on so many shared challenges. She spoke of the way they each struggled as single moms -- keeping a roof over their heads – praying together for their kids -- and the deep bond they shared over the fact that both of their husbands had been taken home on the same day. I glanced toward Anna, and I caught her eyes looking back at me, wet with tears, remembering our own shared bond.

WHEN SHE FINISHED and took her seat behind the pulpit, Pastor nodded to Uncle Mike. He acknowledged the signal and then sat for a long moment with his eyes closed as he sought the strength to stand. I whispered a prayer for him, and it was clear that nearly everyone in the church was doing the same. He stood with clenched fists — his knuckles were white as he fought his way through a hurricane of emotions to make his way to the pulpit. Looking out at the audience, he took a deep breath and blew it out noticeably.

"My kid sister was the strongest person I've ever known...."

He was forced to stop and place a hand over his eyes as tears quickly overtook him. He turned away from the crowd momentarily, and Anna's mom leaned forward with a handful of tissues, squeezing his hand as he gratefully took them. He mopped his face and cleared his runny nose before turning again to continue. His hands gripped the lectern tightly as he took another deep breath and slowly released it.

"...That strength that she had reminded me of our grandpa. She was too young to remember much of Pops, but she was a lot like him. He was a second-generation immigrant who grew up in Brooklyn and fought in WW2. He was usually a gentle man but was tough as nails when it came to the real important stuff. He valued family and friends, and mostly God, and wasn't afraid to stand up for all of 'em, no matter what it cost him personally.

"Maria had those same qualities. She fought hard for her family and friends and never hesitated to give all she had. I think now the whole world has seen that about her too."

There were heads nodding and whispers of 'Amen' throughout the audience. As moved as I felt, it was not sorrow but rather a gratitude that filled my heart. The words '...*you saved me first*' seemed to catch my ear, sending a thrill through my soul. I kept my eyes closed, blocking out the awkward stares of so many tear-filled eyes — focusing instead on the beauty of those words as she spoke them to me. Uncle Mike cleared his throat to ease the tightness and continued.

"When I was a little kid Pops explained to me what a hero is. He used a personal story that has stuck with me for forty years. It was about two of his buddies in World War Two. He said the three of them became close friends — *as close as brothers*. Pops always said that these two guys were the bravest men he had ever known, and he lived in awe of them both for the rest of his life. On a cold winter morning in 1944, their Rifle Regiment of twelve men was pinned down beneath a heavily-fortified ridge and running low on ammo. One of his two buddies volunteered for a daring mission to sneak out of the safety of their trench just before daylight and crawl close enough to take out the enemy's biggest gun with a hand grenade. He succeeded in taking out the gunner and also managed to destroy their entire cache of ammunition. The awakened enemy fought back like a roused swarm of angry wasps, critically wounding Pop's friend as he was trying to make it back. That's when Pop's second friend selflessly jumped into action, rescuing the fallen man and carrying him back to safety before being shot himself. That second man saved his fallen brother but gave his own life in the process. It wasn't long before the enemy was out of ammunition and surrendered their position.

"Pops asked me which of these brave friends was a bigger hero, the man who saved their entire Regiment or the man who saved his friend. I guessed that it was the first man, the one who saved every-one. Pops put his hand on my shoulder and said that I was right about him — but also wrong about the other. Both of them gave the same measure of devotion.

"A hero, he told me, is a man who thinks less of his own life than the lives of others. That's what makes a man a hero.

"I never forgot that lesson. Our dad proved it to me a few years later by givin' his own life to save mine...." Uncle Mike closed his eyes and fought back a swell of emotion. I could see him gripping the pulpit like he was hanging onto it for dear life. He took another deep breath to quiet his racing heart before slowly continuing.

"That's the same thing that makes a *woman* a hero too. By Pop's definition, his granddaughter... my kid sister... is a hero."

The audience broke into applause as Uncle Mike and I embraced emotionally, standing to their feet in a touching tribute to mom's memory. I could see uncle Jim standing in the front row with tears streaking his face.

Pastor Juan led another hymn and then invited anyone else who wanted to say a word to come forward.

Uncle Jim rose unsteadily to his feet, his face wet with tears. The church was silent as he made his way to the steps and onto the platform. I felt myself choke up as he stopped in front of Uncle Mike and laid his hand on his shoulder, knowing what my uncle's story had meant to the old man. He patted Mike's shoulder a time or two before moving on. I could feel the tears brim in my eyes when he looked over at me — the memory we shared of those events flashed through my mind, along with the intense emotional pain that I felt at the time... his pain. The memory of how God had shown me that traumatic experience in Uncle Jim's life washed over me all over again. I watched him grip the podium and clear his throat briefly, then he began to speak.

"I reckon God has His reasons for arrangin' things the way He does."

He looked again at Uncle Mike as he continued in a soft voice, "I don't reckon your grandpa told ya who those men were — those friends o' his in his story." Uncle Mike shook his head, no.

"Well, I can vouch fer the truth of it. I was there...." He looked over at me, seeing great grandpa's ring on my hand. "Jimmy is wearin' the ring o'the man who rescued and saved my life that day — it was his great-grandpa, Lou Moretti. So, ya see, it ain't surprisin' that Maria done what she done... bein' a hero is part of her heritage."

Uncle Mike looked stunned as it dawned on him who his grandfather's friends had been. He never would have guessed it in a dozen lifetimes, but the emotion in old Mr. V's face gave incontestable evidence.

Uncle Jim looked at the floor with a humbled expression and then looked out over the congregation as he continued. "Matt Farro, ... Mike's grandpa..., was a true friend ta me, even when I didn't deserve his faith in me. I'm alive because o' what Lou done... I ain't never forgot that. But the reason I'm standin' here at this pulpit tonight is as much because of your grandpa Matt as any other man. I owe my salvation to a prayer that he prayed — I only regret that it took me ninety years o' life to finally find my way.

"Maria was like him; Mike is right about that. There wasn't a judging or resentful sentiment anywhere inside her — she gave people the benefit of the doubt, even when they didn't deserve it. Leastways, that's what she done fer me.

"Anyways, I just wanted to own-up publicly to the fact that Lou Moretti saved my life, and he and Matt Farro were the best friends a man could ever have. Maria *is* a hero just like they were — I was blessed beyond any grace I deserved to have known all of 'em.

"It's taken me a lifetime to realize that God doesn't choose who to make a hero. He lets the heroes do the choosin'."

He turned toward me as he stepped away from the pulpit, and without a thought, I found myself standing and hugging him. The tears that were flooding my eyes were tears of joy and gratitude. I was vaguely aware of applause as the congregation showed their appreciation as well.

⌘

WINGS

He will cover you with his pinions, and under His wings, you will take refuge
~ Psalm 91:4

Uncle Jim had barely taken his seat when Pete Murphy began forward. His long strides carried him down the isle as fast as an average man running, and he rose to the platform with a quick pair of leaps, skipping several of the steps. He looked over at me with the sympathetic look of a close friend and then looked down at the pulpit in front of him, collecting his thoughts.

"I don't really remember my own mom." He stopped and cleared his throat — I saw him swallow with some difficulty as he gathered his courage. "God gave me another mom in Mrs. Moretti — the best mom ever. We called her 'M'…. It was short for her last name, but to be honest, I just thought of her as 'Mom.' She was like that for me.

"When I wanted to talk or needed advice, I went to 'M.' I guess I probably shocked her with some of the stuff I said, especially when I first met the Lord, but she never judged me. The truth is, I owe her my life for the advice she gave me.

"My dad is back there — it's the first time he's ever been to a church in my lifetime. It was M's prayers and advice that helped to get him here. What Mr. Van Clief said about her — about not judging anyone, that's true. Dad wouldn't talk to nobody about God, but he talked to her. She was the only one who really got through to him. She didn't care what he'd done; she just saw a man who needed Jesus. That's what she saw in me, too, I guess.

"I'm sure gonna miss her... we both will. I'm real glad, though, for the chance we had to know her and the difference she made in a lot of lives...."

Pete stopped to wipe a tear from his cheek and then looked over at me — I could see the deep feeling of loss in his eyes. My immediate reaction was to hug him, just managing to get one arm over his broad shoulder as his huge arms wrapped around my back. He could have broken me in half if he wanted to, but instead, I felt him shudder as tears flooded his eyes.

Pastor Juan shook Pete's hand with an arm around his shoulders and then waited for him to make his way back to his seat. Standing at the podium, he silently nodded to Derrick in the AV booth with a signal to start the video and then took his seat beside me while the large projection screen lowered behind him and the lights dimmed. He leaned toward me as he whispered:

"You can go ahead up after this is over... no need for an intro-duction."

I acknowledged with a nod, suddenly deep in thought, as the words I wanted to say began to run through my mind. I was leaning my elbows on my knees in prayer as the music ended and the lights came back up. PJ gave me an encouraging grip on my shoulder and nudged me forward.

THERE WAS complete silence in the auditorium as I stood behind the pulpit and looked over the faces in the crowd. A feeling of anxious anticipation hung in the air; it wasn't an anticipation of what I was about to say, but rather of what God was about to do. I wasn't surprised to see Amos suddenly appear, standing in the center aisle near the doors. The giant hand that I felt reassuringly on my shoulder revealed why Chozeq was not with him... he was with me.

I quietly cleared my throat and looked down at a few scribbled notes.

"THE PAST WEEK has changed my life."

I had to stop and take a gulp of air, quieting my racing heart before continuing.

"What can I say about mom..... Uncle Mike described her as strong — and she definitely was that. People have also talked about how accepting and nonjudgmental she was and how she cared about people and related to them — I saw that my whole life.

"I also saw her grit and determination when she fought through overwhelming grief after dad died. I watched her struggle to keep two jobs to keep a roof over our heads, and I remember how she always had time for me, despite all that. She was a great listener... and an even better advice-giver.

"I guess the thing I remember most, though, is how she prayed. She didn't say big, eloquent prayers; most times, she didn't even pray out loud. Her prayers were mostly silent and pretty much continuous, revealed only by a whisper or a shedding tear — or by the sheer impact they had on my life. It wasn't surprising to me that she was a hero — she was always a *warrior*."

I paused to take a deep breath, feeling the message burn inside me. I was aware of the cameras, doing my best to ignore them as I shared what was on my heart.

"This week, we've witnessed the stark reality of evil, but also of incredible goodness... we've seen both the darkness and light that are in the world. That light has been bright — not only reflected in mom's self-sacrifice but also in many other great acts of kindness and in the extraordinary move of God's Spirit within so many people's hearts.

"The truth is that both light and darkness have covered creation since the first day. That is one of the arrangements of Divine providence -- that day and night will not cease while creation remains. So I guess it's no great surprise that our earth-bound souls will also know both the sunshine of blessing and the midnight of suffering – both the joys of living and the pain of hardship.

"The lesson that God has shown me this week is that we are being taught to be content with both; to know the warm glow of our Heavenly Father's smile as well as the firm training of His hand. Sometimes that training can be so intense that it feels like a spiritual boot camp.

"In life, we learn to see the beauty in both the sunrise and in the sunset. We are meant to learn... not just to know in our heads, but to truly learn... in our hearts that whatever He ordains is wise and good. He makes both the evening and the morning rejoice when we praise Him for the night as much as for the day.

"Spurgeon wrote that, '*Warm daylight may be glorious, but the dews of grace fall heaviest in the night of sorrow and the beautiful stars of promise shine most brightly amid the darkness of grief*[1].'"

A few tears wet my eyes, surprising me, and I had to stop to wipe them away as I waited for the tightness in my throat to clear....

"I was sharing with a close friend yesterday that God is showing me what it means to be under His wings. Psalm 91 says that "He will cover you with his pinions, and under His wings, you will take refuge[2]."

"The truth is that we are never left alone in the day or in the night, but there's an amazing difference. In daylight, He watches over us while we fly, but in our night... in the times when we fall... that's when He embraces us!"

A SUDDEN THRILL filled my soul as the clear memory of all that had happened this week flowed over me. Looking over the crowd of faces, I could tell that many of them were remembering God's hand in their lives, too — some of them were nodding their heads while others sat with eyes closed and hands raised in silent praise. My eye caught Amos' face as he nodded at me, and the amazing reality of what God was doing hit me like a thunderbolt. I felt a surge of anointing bubbling up inside that exploded from within me in a near shout.

· · ·

"GOD'S STRENGTH is made perfect in *our* weakness, but there is nothing weak about His embrace! There is no failure in His saving rescue! I can testify tonight that His covering is steady and faithful! His covering continues both in the day and the night – in joy and in sorrow, as faithfully as the rising and setting sun, and will continue for as long as we dwell in these earthly houses!

"But I also know that a day is coming when only the *JOY* will remain: when we reach the land of which it is written: '***THERE IS NO NIGHT THERE!!***'

A cacophony of praises burst from people's lips, flooding through the room. Several people raised their hands in worship as the spiritual temperature rose rapidly. The louder it grew, the more it sounded like a blowing wind. I began to hear a rumbling sound, like the sound of a jet flying low overhead — except I knew it was not a jet, I'd heard the sound before. It was the same sound that I heard on the first night of tent meetings. It grew louder and louder until it was like the sound of a massive rocket engine. Far from being frightening, it was exhilarating — filled with earthshaking power; it was a move of the Spirit so mighty that the walls had begun to shake!

Looking down the aisle, I noticed that Amos had vanished from inside the sanctuary.

CHOZEQ'S HAND touched my back, and I immediately sensed that we were rising, quickly finding ourselves standing outside on the roof of the church. The sun was just setting in a red glow that hugged the horizon, but I barely noticed it; the sight directly above us was far too breathtaking! I was looking up into a massive column of fire — like a gigantic twister made of flaming light. It seemed to vibrate in a low rumble that shook everything around us — its glowing warmth pulsed through my soul! It was hovering in the air above the church, stretching upward into the clouds.

Looking down from our vantage point, I could see that the church was surrounded by a huge crowd of people who had gathered for mom's memorial. They were collapsing to their knees as they stared up at the sight in astonished wonder. Amos was standing amid the kneeling throng, clearly as amazed as I was. The Fire's power was frightening and awesome, but also so incredibly beautiful!

Yet, as amazing as it was, what happened next defied description....

⌘

33

FIRE STORM

I've come to set the earth on fire...
~ Jesus, Luke 12:49

As all of us stared wide-eyed at the fiery column, it suddenly *exploded* outward in a blinding flash — instantly bathing everything in an intense golden light! For as far as I could see, the air was suddenly filled with swirling light and warmth. The sight of it took my breath away... its beauty thrilled my soul — but it was the *feeling* of it that was truly breathtaking. It made me tremble and gasp, filling me instantly with overwhelming joy!

The amazing scene matched Amos' description of it perfectly, and yet its beauty far exceeded anything he could have written! In the twilight, a golden glow of small flames covered the vast multitude — hanging above each head like... well... *tongues of fire.* There were thousands of them!

The crowds were kneeling with eyes closed — some were bowed low while others held their hands in the air. I could see that some were being led to the Lord, bowed in wrenching remorse. Almost all of them were weeping. While I watched the incredible scene, I began to notice the appearance of brilliantly glowing angels mixed among the throngs, kneeling and ministering to people.

Amos looked up at us with an enthralled expression, clearly awestruck as he took in the sights all around him.

A familiar sound drew my attention upward, and I turned to see a news helicopter flying overhead. Then, I noticed the satellite dishes of news vans already scattered along the roads in the distance. Their cameras recorded the extraordinary event as it was beamed live throughout the country, to be quickly picked up by stations throughout the world.

Almost as soon as I noticed them, I was struck with a flurry of images flashing before my eyes. Scenes of strangers falling to their knees in awestruck wonder — in homes and offices, stores, airports, and public places. All bowing together with the throngs here, as the same tongues of fire appeared, hovering above their heads. There were even prison scenes with inmates dropping to their knees and war-torn battlefields, where people were experiencing the same fiery tongues.

Turning to Chozeq, I was nearly breathless as the realization swept over me...

"Mrs. M's vision... this is it! It's happening now!"

Chozeq gripped my shoulder reassuringly as he nodded.

"Aye. It has begun."

His eyes reflected a genuine joy over what God was doing at this moment. Yet, somewhere in his complex expression, there was also a solemn look. I had little time to ponder that — all at once, the scene dissolved in a flash.

IN AN INSTANT, I was standing once again inside the church, still behind the pulpit. From the looks on people's faces, I could see that I had returned to the point just moments before the amazing scene began.

People were worshiping, and I could hear the familiar rumbling sound beginning... growing louder and louder until the walls began to shake.

Looking down the aisle, I watched as Amos vanished from inside the sanctuary.

With an urgency that was surging inside me, I leaned close to the microphone and begin to shout.

"Everyone! There's something you all need to see... something amazing! Quick! Follow me!"

Turning, I saw Uncle Mike immediately rise to his feet. From the look on his face, I could tell that he remembered Amos' description of what happens next — there was a thrill in his eyes as he took Anna's mom by the arm and invited her to stand.

Jumping from the platform, I quickly grabbed Anna by the hand from the front row and began to run down the aisle toward the doors, pulling her along beside me. All the while, I was shouting to everyone as we went... "Hurry! Outside! Come outside! Come quick!"

Uncle Mike and Anna's mom were right behind us as we made it through the doors. Anna gasped in surprise when she saw the enormous crowd gathered. Then, she noticed how they were all looking upward with astonished expressions and followed their gaze, her eyes widening.

The crowds moved aside as we reached the lawn, continuing to make room as people filed out of the church. Pete and his dad were the next to emerge behind Uncle Mike and Anna's mom. Then it became a steady stream as everyone made their way out after them. Uncle Jim was the last one out, right behind Pastor Wilkes.

I was at the bottom of the steps waving people past as they moved onto the lawn, catching several of them as they stumbled while staring into the sky in shocked amazement.

The sight was no less thrilling for having seen it before. The fire's powerful rumble could be felt shaking the ground beneath our feet, and its glow warmed our faces. Moments later, I felt the blast wash over us as it suddenly exploded in a blinding flash — instantly bathing everyone in an intense golden light! It made me tremble and gasp, filling me instantly with overwhelming joy! For the second time, it took my breath away, thrilling my soul.

I couldn't help recalling the look in Chozeq's eyes as he acknowledged that this was the fulfillment of Mrs. M's prophetic vision.

I realized, though, that there was something else in his complex expression, too — as if he was stealing himself for a battle soon to come.

THE NEWS REPORTS show clear images of the amazing funnel cloud of fire as it hovers above the church. Bahal is watching the televised scene, seething with anger. He grimaces when it suddenly explodes outward, engulfing the throngs of people, and sending even the news crews to their knees in reaction to the overwhelming presence of God that has suddenly swept over them.

Bahal feels it, too, reacting with seething hatred. He lashes out at the scene with cursing and a sudden utterance in some ancient language that Devlon doesn't understand. The sound of it makes the Senator's skin crawl and raises the hairs on his neck.

Bahal's face is contorted in a hateful scowl as he looks at the images being broadcast by the news choppers, panning across a huge worshiping crowd with fiery tongues floating above their heads.

"You see now why this must be stopped," he angrily charges.

Devlon looks at the TV anxiously, clearly confused.

"Wh-what's happening… what is this?"

Without answering his son-in-law, Bahal turns to his daughter, whose eyes have grown dark with a hateful glare of their own. "You felt it?" he asks.

Athaliah nods her head slowly as if reeling from a heinous affront. She speaks through gritted teeth…

"I warned you about the boy."

Bahal sits back in his chair and raises his chin defiantly, the rage in his face resembling a bull prepared to charge.

"The boy is protected... our efforts failed to eliminate him."

Devlon's eyes grow large, and he looks back and forth between his wife and her father. "You said you had nothing to do with the attacks!" He pauses in thought as the rest of Bahal's comment registers. "What do you mean, *protected* — wh-who protected him?"

Bahal and Athaliah share a secretive glance that conveys more than Devlon can comprehend. Her angry expression changes like a curtain being drawn closed, and she turns her eyes to her husband with a provocative smile. Without a word, she slowly rises from her chair and climbs onto Devlon's lap, practically purring as she wraps her arms behind his neck and kisses him.

Bahal stands and excuses himself. "Thank you for a delightful dinner," he says with his back to the couple as he reaches for his jacket. "It's good to have you back from Beirut, my dear. I'll see myself out... good night."

As Bahal switches off the lights, a glow emerges in Devlon's eyes... turning them fiery red. They blink once and focus on Athaliah with a suddenly sinister expression. Her eyes respond, morphing into the eyes of a large predatory cat, bright yellow. Bahal listens approvingly from outside the door as the room begins to echo with peals of evil laughter.

THE WHOLE EPISODE with Bahal flashed past me in the blink of an eye, already a memory. I quickly looked up to see Chozeq standing nearby. From the look in his eyes, I sensed that he shared the same memory — I had the feeling that he knew it long before now. It was clear to me, in fact, that I only had an inkling of the whole story that was conveyed in his eyes.

⌘

34

PREPARE GOD'S PEOPLE

I have told you all things beforehand.
~ Jesus, Mark 13:23

S aturday morning ~ a week later...
It was surprising when people began arriving at the tent. There hadn't been any decision to reopen services, but they came anyway.

I FELT REMARKABLY WELL-RESTED when I woke up on that Tuesday, the morning after mom's service, despite getting to bed after 2:00 AM.

It was just after sunrise when I wandered from the farmhouse, feeling oddly compelled to pray at the tent's rugged altar. The prior evening's events filled my thoughts. The power of God's overwhelming presence still seemed to hang in the air over Center Springs, reverberating within my stirred soul. Nowhere did that sense of holy presence feel stronger than here at the tent grounds — it was as if it called to me, and I definitely wasn't alone in feeling it.

Not long after I knelt alone at the tent's rugged altar to pray, I felt PJ's hand on my shoulder; he knelt down beside me. Pete wasn't far behind. Yet, as unexpected as it was, none of us were *really* surprised to see each other there.

It wasn't long before more arrived... a dozen at first, then dozens more, then hundreds. Soon the tent had filled, and crowds began to overflow into the surrounding field. By evening the crowds were so large that people were standing among the parked cars. By the following day, extra loudspeakers were installed in the fields, and local pastors began to take turns delivering impassioned messages. No matter how many altar calls there have been each day, each one has been met with streams of people finding their way forward.

The crowds quickly drew reporters. Their news choppers have passed overhead regularly throughout the week. Part of the parking lot behind Carmine's Diner was quickly filled with satellite vans.

Sheriff Flanagan was pressured to shut the services down but refused. It's been clear that he feels the same pull of the Spirit in his own heart. Instead, he called in help from County and State Troopers for a security detail; little did he know that God had His own security detail already assigned. There have been angels standing shoulder to shoulder with his troopers throughout the week.

The whole experience has been surreal, to say the least. Those angel guardians haven't been the only remarkable things I've seen this week. Ever since the firestorm on Monday night, I've been able to see other things, too — spiritual forces practically everywhere. It wasn't like before when they just occasionally appeared in visions or confrontations; I had begun to see them all the time. It was like my eyes had been opened with a new kind of vision... it started soon after the column of fire.

I suppose I should have been terrified by some of the things I saw, but the sights had the opposite effect. In fact, it was the demons themselves that had fear in their eyes. Of course, I was sure that the ever-present army of angelic warriors had something to do with that.

In the meantime, I needed to seek every opportunity to sneak away and read Amos' journal. It was becoming clear that the coming days were about to get crazy. Amos said it best on the day I first met him: *"Things are about to get mighty interestin' in the world."*

I've come to realize a curious thing about Amos' journal entries — they were in no particular order. You can't really tell which ones happen first or how far apart the events are. Last night I read his account of tragedy here at the tent. I had to lay the book down after that entry — too many tears were clouding my eyes. There's no telling whether that might happen in a week or years from now, but I've decided that it's best to keep that particular entry secret for the time being.

ALL OF THESE thoughts were tumbling around in my head this morning as I made my way to the tent. Anna was waiting for me on the dirt drive — it was surprising to see her there so early. She had a backpack slung over one shoulder and a spark in her eye that signaled she'd had a sudden brainstorm.

"Hey," she said as she greeted me. "I was thinking... school will be starting again soon; we should think about preparing for FCS."

Wow, school, I thought to myself. I honestly hadn't thought about it in weeks. I stopped to take in the sight of the tent, remembering all that has happened here over the summer and motioned toward it with a nod of my head.

"You remember how all this started? It was because the FCS group didn't fit anywhere else. This technically *is* FCS... with some extra visitors."

She looked back at the tent with me and nodded in agreement, biting her lower lip as she scanned the field full of people.

"Yeah, I guess that's true," she agreed. "But I'm not talking about here... I mean, not *just* here. I'm talking about FCS everywhere."

She swung the backpack off her shoulder and pulled out a sports cam. "I think we should start a video podcast."

"What, like record the services?" I asked.

"Some... I guess." she accepted as if the suggestion hadn't occurred to her.

"But I'm thinking mostly interviews and man-on-the-street kind of stuff. You know, like 5 or 10-minute clips. Posts that can get shares... go viral!"

"Okay. Yeah, sure — do you think other FCS groups will use it?"

"I know they will!"

"Sounds like a great idea. Are you gonna be the host for it? Don't podcasts need a face... someone who talks and does the interviews and stuff?" I prodded.

She looked at me with an expectant expression, raising her eyebrows and waiting for me to catch her unspoken meaning.

"Me? Y-you, want *me* to host it?" I stammered my objection. "I don't know *anything* about hosting a podcast."

"All you have to do is talk. You're already pretty good at that. I'll help behind the scenes, and the kids from AV can produce the clips."

"Well, I don't know... what would I talk about? I wouldn't know what to say."

"You can start with *'yes.'*"

I could tell from the way she was looking at me that she didn't understand my hesitancy. I guess that my expression must have been baffling to her. My reaction was confusing even to me, to be honest.

"Okay, don't give an answer right now... just pray about it," she suggested, deciding to ease off.

What she didn't know was that all my focus these days was on trying to figure out what to do about the entries in Amos' journal. Amos' words from the last time I saw him have been haunting me for days: *"If you act wisely and use the time you have, you can prepare God's people for what's to come."*

How was I supposed to do that exactly?

In my silence, Anna turned again to look at the tent, which was already full at 7:00 in the morning. "It really is amazing, isn't it?"

Her comment drew my attention back to the incredible scene in front of us. "It definitely is... it's unbelievable. These people are so *hungry* for God! And it's not only happening here; all over the country, churches are bursting like this."

IT WAS NOONTIME when we arrived at Uncle Mike's shop. I was getting the hang of driving mom's old car, although I hadn't gone anywhere except back and forth between here and the farmhouse. Anna climbed from the passenger seat and followed me inside — she was working for Uncle Mike now. Since reopening the shop, he has needed extra help; the place has been packed with people in town for the tent services.

We both grabbed aprons from behind the counter and got right to work. Anna took her place at the register, and I grabbed a handful of orders, clipped them above the counter, and then started slicing rolls in half. Uncle Mike nodded at us over his shoulder in greeting as he finished taking an order from the phone.

The TV in the corner was showing local news, but I couldn't hear much of it above the din of conversation around the crowded tables. Most of the local talk was about the tent meetings — I was busy waving and nodding hello to folks I recognized and who had recognized me.

FROM THE CORNER of my eye, I happened to notice the scene on the TV and did a double-take. It was showing a man being interviewed on the Capitol steps; he was a man that I recognized immediately — it was Senator Sheen... Devlon Sheen.

Quickly grabbing the remote, I turned the sound up, waving for everyone to be quiet. Uncle Mike's hand on my shoulder let me know that he understood my sudden interest.

A reporter was asking a question...

"What do you have to say about the extraordinary events in Center Springs and other parts of the country in the past few weeks?"

Devlon shook his head in disdain for the question. "Given the difficult times in which we live, it is understandable that people can be swayed by mass hysteria. People are desperate for a feeling of hope — so much so that they even misinterpret unusual natural phenomena as supernatural signs.

"The failures of the current administration have brought us to this point. I intend to restore hope in our communities by strengthening our government institutions. I can assure you that a Sheen administration will conduct a thorough scientific inquiry. We will be governed by science and not religious dogma.

"We also must not forget that the movement at the heart of these events has been suspected of having ties with dangerous criminal gangs. My office has filed a request with the National Security Agency to open a full investigation into the matter."

The Senator declined further questions and was quickly ushered away.

There was a momentary silence in the sub shop as people stared at the TV with stunned expressions.

"What planet is that guy from?" one man was overheard asking his table-mate, drawing a response of nervous laughter from the room.

Uncle Mike and I shared a glance, and I could see from the look in his eye that he remembered Amos' journal. We both knew what was coming.

One of the customers was suddenly overheard talking to his friends nearby: "Someone needs to set him straight. We need to get the word out about what's really happening here before people start believing this guy."

His comment hit me squarely between the eyes as it was instantly bolstered by an echo of Amos' voice in my head: …*prepare God's people for what's to come.*

I TURNED TOWARD ANNA, catching her eye… "About that podcast… count me in!"

⌘

35

BLAZE

"What's happening here will be remembered for all eternity."
~ Jimmy

"Blaze! That's it! That will be the name of our podcast!"

Anna was suddenly energized as she described the idea that had just hit her. Until now, she'd been uncharacteristically quiet, hardly saying a word as we finished work at the Sub Shop. She'd remained silent since we got into the car.

"What?" I tried to clarify.

"We'll name it after the column of fire last Monday night. We can make the first few posts about the way people were affected by it!"

A thrill ran through me as I recalled my view of that scene from the church roof — I wished I could tell her about my version of the events, angels and all!

"*Blaze...*" I repeated. "That describes it pretty well. Are you thinking of making a movie of it from the news clips?"

She shook her head vigorously as she leaned forward. "No, not exactly. We should interview people who were there — get them to talk about what happened to them. Personal stories!"

"Yeah, that could be pretty cool," I agreed.

"I know! Right?" Anna's eyes were the size of saucers as her idea began to blossom into something tangible. "We can interview some of the reporters who were there, too... I'll bet their reactions will be priceless." She thought silently for a second and then added, "...maybe we can talk with some of the people who got saved!"

"We can start with Mr. Murphy — Pete's dad. His conversion at mom's memorial service was incredible," I suggested.

"Yes, that's perfect! And there were so many others too... I'll start asking around for names."

She immediately lifted her phone and hit speed dial.

"Who are you calling? It's after 10:00 PM."

"Everyone!" she answered with determined urgency.

She had managed to finish three calls by the time we made the short drive from the Sub Shop back to the tent. "Kyle and Hun have agreed to do editing and will help with the shoots," she informed me as she enthusiastically described her production plans. "Pete said he's going now to talk to his dad about doing an interview; they're at the tent tonight."

I nodded back to her speechlessly, duly impressed.

A BRILLIANT GLOW UP ahead illuminated the entrance to Carmine's Diner and the tent's parking area. Its brightness was only partly due to the troopers' security lights. To be honest, most of the glow I was seeing came from the radiant wings of angelic warriors who outnumbered the Troopers ten to one. I still couldn't get used to seeing them every time we arrived. I inadvertently pressed a fist to my chest and nodded in a silent salute, echoing the invisible angels' familiar greeting as we approached. The trooper standing beside our car nodded back in acknowledgment, apparently assuming the greeting was for him.

We were waved into a parking space behind the Diner, in the section reserved for the Press. One of the Deputies greeted us with a friendly smile. "Good to see you, Jimmy," he said as we climbed from the car. He nodded to his partner beside him, "We're here to escort both of you to the tent... Sheriff's orders."

As much as his offer of protection was reassuring, it honestly paled in comparison with the three angelic sentries who stood looking over the two deputies' shoulders.

"Thanks," I said with a grateful smile — only partly speaking to the Deputies.

It was a warm summer night, and a gentle breeze was blowing across the open fields, carrying the smell of cut grass.

Pete Murphy and his dad had seen us coming and met us at the edge of the parking lot.

"Hey Bro! dad's ready for that interview anytime — it's a great idea!"

"Thanks, it was Anna's."

Anna held her hand out to shake; "Thanks for agreeing, Mr. Murphy. It will make a big impact on a lot of people." She glanced back to me, "Jimmy will be the host — I know it will get a lot of views."

"Lord willing," I answered honestly as I shook his hand. I was uncomfortable with the newfound celebrity, still certain that it was only temporary.

"Well, I ain't sure why me, but I'm glad to help out," he replied. "When did you wanna do it?"

"Got your camera?" I asked Anna.

She pulled it from her backpack and held it up for us all to see.

"Where is good?" I asked next.

"How about there?" She answered, pointing to the spot right behind us. "Right here under this lamppost, with the tent behind you. That's perfect."

We stood together awkwardly, looking at each other for a moment, and I quickly realized that I didn't have a clue what to say. Only one thought came to mind... a need to pray.

"Let's have a word of prayer first," I invited the others as I bowed my head. Pete stretched an arm across my shoulders and did the same with his father.

"Lord, this is Your work. We're just Your grateful servants. As we seek to make a defense of our faith, we ask You to guide our actions and give us Your words to speak. Your word moves the heart. You don't need us to defend You, Lord, but You call us to stand in Your power so that others will know that You are a strong and wonderful God who never leaves us all alone. Give us the words to speak. Use us to prepare people for what's to come. Thank You for the help that is speeding to our aid at this very moment. In the beautiful name of Jesus... Amen."

"AMEN!" Pete yelled as we finished.

Anna nudged my arm and surprised me with a small microphone that she had pulled from her backpack. "Here, this is Bluetooth... it'll be better for the recording." She pulled a set of headphones over her ears and gave me a thumbs-up as she lifted the camera in front of her. Looking into the lens, I raised the Mic closer and began speaking into the camera.

"I'M JIMMY MORETTI. You've probably heard about some amazing things happening here in Center Springs. Some people in the media and in Washington say that it's all fake or connected with drugs and gangs. The truth is that there are thousands of people who can testify that it has nothing to do with those things... this is a genuine move of God. This video is being made to get the word out about what's really happening here.

"We'll start with the events here last Monday night. Unless you've been living under a rock, you've likely heard about them. You might be one of the millions of people who were touched by them — if so, then you already know how life-transforming they were."

Anna stopped the camera for a second: "We'll add a clip of the news footage right here. You can talk about what they just saw."

I nodded to her, stopping to regather my thoughts...

"...The significance of those events cannot be overstated. They were as earthshaking as the Day of Pentecost when the Church was born. Their impact is being felt everywhere. It truly has changed the world in ways that will be fully seen soon.

"We're here now with one of the people who saw it first-hand.

"Mr. Murphy..."

"Friends call me Big Jay," he revealed, inviting me to do the same.

Pete's dad was like an older and tougher version of Pete himself. The man was a huge mound of muscle. His clean, shaved head was offset by a thick full beard and tattoos covering his arms and shoulders from his wrists to his chin. It would be easy to mistake him for a member of a biker gang; he rides a Harley, in fact.

"You work as a longshoreman, right?"

"That's right. Dock Forman on Pier 111."

"You were at the church last weekend when the Fire Storm happened?"

"Yeah, I sure was. I'll never forget it for as long as I live!"

"Can you tell us about what happened?"

"Well, Pete — my son here — and me... we were sittin' at the back o' the church when we started to hear it. It started as a low rumble and then got louder and louder. Pretty soon, folks started movin' outside — we were one o' the first ones out. It sounded like a tornado... like a freight train, ya know what I'm sayin'?

"But it wasn't just the sound of it — there was a feeling that went through me, from the top o' my head to the bottoms of my feet. It shook me to the depth o' my soul. Then when I looked up and actually saw it, the sight blew me clear away. I only made it a few strides past the church steps when I felt my knees givin' way. Before I knew it, I was on my knees cryin' like a baby."

The look on his face conveyed more about the profound transformation in his life than his words ever could. Tears were welling up in his eyes as he recounted the experience. It was a dramatic contrast with the tattoos covering his neck and arms. I could see his hands shaking as he fought back the unfamiliar swell of emotion.

"You hadn't really been someone who went to church much, is that right?"

"That's fer sure…. It was Pete who got me to come for the memorial service. The only reason I came was outta respect for your mom; she was a real special lady, there's no doubt about that.

"To be honest, that was the first time I'd been in a church since my weddin' day, near thirty years ago. I wasn't religious — that's for sure. Anyhow, I sure didn't expect what happened."

"What do *you* think it was that was in the sky?"

"Not *what* — you mean *WHO*. I knew for sure who it was the moment I stepped outside. It was God himself! The power that came from that swirling fire cut through me like a hundred megawatts. In His presence, the guilt of everything I'd ever done came crashing over me. But the thing that surprised me most was that I didn't feel like He was judging me; instead, it was pure love. It was like a massive searchlight, showing me what my heart was like. I saw what I really was — deep inside. At the same time, I could feel Him accepting me just the way I was — He let me know that His love could forgive every last one of the wrongs that I'd done! It tore me up inside. I never knew there could ever be that much love!"

A tear escaped from his eye and ran down his cheek as he described the experience.

"Till that moment, I never coulda believed that God could ever forgive me. But here He was just puttin' His arms around me. Takin' me just like I was, just a broken man. I'll never be the same after that — not after I felt him hold me that way!"

There were a few more tears on his cheeks, and he rubbed them off with the back of his hand.

Glancing over at Pete, I could see that his eyes were closed in a prayer of grateful praise. His head was shaking slightly in complete amazement. I felt like I needed to give it a moment of quiet before interrupting the tender move of the Spirit in both men's hearts.

After the short pause, I moved the discussion as gently as I could to the question of whether all this is real or not….

"What would you say to the people who claim what's happening here is, somehow, criminal or gang-related?"

"I'd just dare 'em to come to see it for themselves. The folks who say those things don't know what they're talking about... or worse."

"Worse... you mean they're trying to mislead people?"

"I mean even worse than that. Look, I ain't no political genius, but I ain't a stranger to evil either — I wish I could say that I was. It's pretty clear to me that the ones makin' those claims are being motivated by somethin' truly dark. It don't take a genius investigator to know that it's the same darkness that has tried to kill this work by trying to kill you. The only power that wants to shut down what God is doing is an evil power."

A loud chorus of agreement echoed from just behind him, "...AMEN!"

Anna zoomed out to show a dozen guys who had gathered behind Big Jay, all as tough-looking as he was.

Pete's dad turned and introduced them. "These are guys from my crew on the docks. A few more have been comin' each night. Anwar, here is the latest one to find the Lord."

A giant of a man with rippling muscles and a tight-cropped afro stood near the front with tears streaking his face. The other guys all slapped him on the back with shouts of praise.

Looking at the men, my eyes were drawn to the wider scene around them. I was struck by the incredible wonder of it all as I took in an astounding spectacle. I wished the others could see the astonishing sight! Angelic hosts filled the skies and stood among the crowds ministering to souls everywhere. For a moment, I couldn't do anything except watch the scene in awe. I couldn't help being reminded of God's purpose in all of this. This is a harvest — the redemption of countless men and women before He comes to gather us all home!

Anna nudged me with her foot, trying to get my attention as she stood with the camera running. My eyes were drawn back to Anwar and then to Pete's dad, both with tears streaking their faces.

"This is what it's all about," I said as I turned to the camera. "God is doing something here that's profound and incredible. It's a miracle when *one* person is transformed by redemption, but what's happening here is truly massive. More than a thousand people have come to find salvation here in this week alone, and tens of thousands around the country."

Waving out over the crowds, Anna followed my lead and panned the camera over the vast throng of people that stretched from where we were standing. People overflowed the tent and filled the surrounding field with their hands raised — many in tears.

"What's happening here will be remembered for all eternity."

Sunday morning...

Anna's friends in the AV crew made quick work of editing her footage and had a polished video posted later last night. It started getting hits right away.

The views started in Asia and Europe, and by 7:00 AM Eastern US time, our blog had already been viewed over 100,000 times. Within a few more hours, it hit the one million mark. To our surprise, the words *'Center Springs'* and *'Fire'* had become the Internet's number one search phrase!

Anna was thrilled as she told me the news. The entire video crew was with her at the tent for Sunday morning's service, cameras in hand.

"We want to live-stream this morning's service!" she announced the moment she saw me.

She pointed back to a van in Carmine's parking lot that already had wires strung from it for network and electricity connections. It had a series of odd-looking antennas on the roof. Carmine waved to me from beside the van with a broad smile.

"Oh… okay," I reacted in surprise. "We should ask PJ and Pastor Wilkes if…."

"…Already did — they love the idea!" she interrupted.

"Al…right. In that case, I guess we're live-streaming this morning," I acknowledged nervously. "Will it be with this camera?"

"All of them!" Anna said. The crew around her smiled as they held up enough cameras to create a full-length documentary. "Josh will be doing a live edit." She pointed back to the van, where I saw Josh through the open side door sitting in front of a makeshift production studio. Anna explained the plan, sounding a little like Berith Gruner, the NNN Producer. "We'll take a team of cameras with us to do interviews in the crowd. The rest of the crew will fan out and film the service. It'll be awesome!"

"Interviews? You mean for me to interview random people?"

"Yeah — great idea, right?"

Before I knew it, the crew members began to spread out, ready to film everything in sight.

Anna and I started roaming through the crowds. There was no shortage of willing candidates to interview — dozens of families from every walk of life, along with doctors, off-duty cops, and people in every profession imaginable. They all had one thing in common — they had experienced a dramatic encounter with God in the past few weeks. Many of them spoke movingly of their experiences at the memorial service beneath the pillar of fire, echoing how Pete's dad had described it. Others shared incredible stories of how they were healed of terrible illnesses when the fire *exploded*.

AFTER HALF AN HOUR of moving testimonies, I stood beside the platform as the service continued behind me. I pointed to a huge pile of braces, wheelchairs, walkers, and crutches, explaining that they were the remnants of afflictions that had been healed within just the past two weeks.

Looking into Anna's camera, I felt moved to speak directly to whoever might be listening.

"The truth about what's happening here is not a secret; it's immediately apparent to anyone who comes within a mile of this place. This is truly God's work. What we are seeing here is an outpouring of God's grace and power... maybe the most tremendous outpouring in two thousand years. It's not mysterious or mystical — it's real and practical. God is rescuing and repairing broken souls and bodies — healing terrible illnesses as well as terrible addictions.

"The worst disease of all lives inside all of us — it's an affliction called sin, and it has hopelessly separated us from God and from each other. That is the *real* cause of terrible pain and suffering in the world. But it has an antidote: the shed blood of Christ — the blood of God's Son. There is power in His blood to forgive and transform everyone who comes to Him.

"Thousands have discovered that power in the past few weeks, finding mercy and forgiveness in His outstretched arms."

THE POINT I was making was suddenly punctuated by the sound of a man breaking down in tears as he fell to his knees at the altar directly behind me. Anna and I quietly moved further away, making room for PJ and others to pray with the man. Josh was using the interlude to blend in scenes from cameras all around the service, showing the powerful move of God that was evident throughout the crowds. In the meantime, we stationed ourselves a few yards from the tent.

From this vantage point, I was struck by the incredible scene of angelic interventions throughout the crowd. When PJ prayed and laid his hands on the repenting man, I noticed a dark swarm of evil forces hovering in the air above the man's head. They were becoming increasingly frantic and agitated the more PJ prayed. The dark beings proved to be no match for a troop of angels' fiery swords and were soon dispatched in a blinding flash of light. The moment they were gone, I watched the repenting man lift his hands in the air as a bright smile filled his face and praises flooded his lips. It was clear that he was sensing the newfound freedom of his soul's liberty!

The cameras hadn't captured any of that incredible pageant, of course. As I considered it, though, I was suddenly impressed with a truth that had gained instant clarity in my spirit. I signaled Anna and the others to cue the cameras — she pointed to me with a signal that Josh had cut back to us.

"WE'RE WITNESSING the grace of God. That's the real story of what's happening here.

"Unfortunately, there are also forces in the world that oppose what God is doing here — dark powers. Those powers don't want the world to see that truth. They thrive in darkness and gain strength from people's suffering. They seek to discredit and condemn what God is doing — even resorting to violence and murder to try to stop it.

"I'm asking every believer to pray for the people who are held under the sway of those powers. Pray that God will break their bondage and free them from the deception of those evil influences. Pray for those in power around the world who are bowing even now to those same influences. God can forgive their involvement in the plot to destroy this work.

"Pray for those leaders — especially the people who killed my mom."

Final words rushed from within me with an unction that I couldn't stop, barely giving me time to consider them before they crossed my lips....

"Pray for Devlon Sheen!"

⌘

THE END
OF BOOK TWO

THANK YOU FOR READING!

PLEASE TAKE A MOMENT TO LEAVE A REVIEW.

ALSO BY D. I. HENNESSEY

Books in the Within & Without Time Series:

Book 1: Within and Without Time

Book 2: The Traveler

Book 3: The Secret Door

Book 4: Evil Ascendant - Deliverance

For information on upcoming releases

Visit ArkHarbor Press

www.arkharbor.press

NOTES

9. UNSPEAKABLE GIFT

1. The words of Isaiah 57:15-19

30. ASHES

1. Exodus 14:13
2. Adapted from Spurgeon, C., Morning & Evening, July 24.

32. WINGS

1. Spurgeon, C., Morning & Evening, June 1st.
2. Psalm 91:4

Made in the USA
Las Vegas, NV
24 September 2022

55912293R00174